THE FIRST MOUNTAIN MAN
PREACHER'S
CARNAGE

THE FIRST MOUNTAIN MAN
PREACHER'S CARNAGE

WILLIAM W. JOHNSTONE
and J.A. JOHNSTONE

PINNACLE BOOKS
Kensington Publishing Corp.

www.kensingtonbooks.com

PINNACLE BOOKS are published by

Kensington Publishing Corp.
119 West 40th Street
New York, NY 10018

PUBLISHER'S NOTE
Following the death of William W. Johnstone, the Johnstone family is working with a carefully selected writer to organize and complete Mr. Johnstone's outlines and many unfinished manuscripts to create additional novels in all of his series like The Last Gunfighter, Mountain Man, and Eagles, among others. This novel was inspired by Mr. Johnstone's superb storytelling.

PINNACLE BOOKS, the Pinnacle logo, and the WWJ steer head logo are Reg. U.S. Pat. & TM Off.

ISBN-13: 978-0-7860-4721-5
ISBN-10: 0-7860-4721-6

First Pinnacle paperback printing: January 2021

10 9 8 7 6 5 4 3 2 1

Printed in the United States of America

Electronic edition:

ISBN-13: 978-0-7860-4722-2 (e-book)
ISBN-10: 0-7860-4722-4 (e-book)

CHAPTER 1

Preacher's arm drew back and then flashed forward. The heavy hunting knife in the mountain man's hand turned over once in midair as it flew straight and true through the shadows along the hard-packed dirt street, past the man in the beaver hat.

With Preacher's powerful muscles behind it, the foot of cold steel buried itself in the chest of a man about to fire a pistol into Beaver Hat's back.

The would-be killer grunted and reeled a step to the side. His gun arm sagged. In his death throes, he might have jerked the trigger anyway, but that was a chance Preacher had had to take. He couldn't prevent the callous murder any other way.

The man in the beaver hat might have seen the knife fly past him, or maybe he'd just heard it cutting through the air close to his head. But he heard the grunt of pain behind him and whirled around with surprising speed and grace for a man of his bulk. The cane he carried lifted and came down sharply on the wrist of his assailant's gun hand. The unfired pistol thudded to the street.

Beaver Hat drew the cane back to strike again, but it

wasn't necessary. After the assailant pawed for a second at the knife in his chest, his knees buckled. As he fell, Beaver Hat stepped back to give him room to pitch forward on his face.

Beaver Hat turned to face Preacher as the mountain man approached. He lifted his cane and said, "I warn you, sir, if that man is your partner and you intend to continue in the same vein, I shall deal with you harshly."

Preacher said, "Just who you reckon flung that pig-sticker into the varmint's chest, mister?"

"You?"

"Damn right."

Preacher stepped past the man in the beaver hat, hooked a booted toe under the corpse's shoulder, and rolled the dead man onto his back. He reached down, grasped the knife's handle, and pulled the weapon free.

After wiping blood from the blade on the dead man's rough, homespun shirt, Preacher straightened and slid the knife back into the sheath at his belt. He had a pair of flintlock pistols tucked behind that belt as well, but in the poor light, he had trusted his knife more than a gun when he spotted the man about to bushwhack Beaver Hat.

"Should we summon the authorities?" Beaver Hat asked as he looked down disdainfully at the corpse.

"Only if you want to stand around for an hour answerin' some constable's foolish questions. Did you know this fella?"

Beaver Hat leaned forward slightly to study the dead man's face in the faint light that came from a window in a nearby building.

"I don't believe I've ever seen him before."

"Then he didn't have any personal reason for wantin' to hurt you?"

"I can't imagine what it would be."

Preacher nodded, satisfied by that answer.

"The only explanation that makes any sense is that he planned to kill you, then rob you. A fancy-dressed gent like you, most folks in this part of town would figure you've got money in your pockets."

"So you're saying it's *my* fault this miscreant tried to attack me?" Beaver Hat asked rather testily.

"Take it however you want to," Preacher said. "It don't matter to me."

Beaver Hat stood there frowning for a moment, then said, "Well . . . at any rate . . . I owe you my thanks. I heard someone behind me, but I doubt if I would have been able to turn around and disarm that dolt before he shot me."

"Not hardly," Preacher agreed. "Usually, thieves like him would rather knife their victims or strangle 'em. But I reckon he figured a shot wouldn't draw enough attention around here to worry about. He'd have time to go through your pockets before anybody came to check on things. And shootin' a fella *is* a quicker, simpler way to kill him than those other ways."

"You sound as if you speak from experience."

"Mister," Preacher said, "if there's a way to kill a varmint who needs killin', chances are I've done it."

The man stared at him for a couple of seconds, then said, "Well, that's an audacious claim, anyway. I still owe you a debt of gratitude, and although a drink hardly has the same value as my life, at least to me, I'd very much like to buy one for you, sir."

"In that case," Preacher said, "I ain't gonna argue, and I know a good place."

* * *

Red Mike's Tavern was only a few blocks from the waterfront where the Mississippi River flowed majestically past the settlement of St. Louis.

Actually, calling it a settlement understated the situation. By this time, more than seventy-five years after its founding as a trading post by French fur traders Pierre Laclède and Auguste Chouteau, St. Louis had grown into a full-fledged town. So much so that Preacher, accustomed to the more-lonely reaches of the Rocky Mountains, always felt a mite uneasy among so many people and so many buildings. Not to mention, the air stunk of dead fish, smoke, and unwashed flesh.

However, he had spent some time in New Orleans recently, and that city at the mouth of the Mississippi was ten times worse in every way Preacher could think of.

Red Mike's catered to both rivermen and fur trappers, necessitating an uneasy truce between the two factions. The tavern was as close to a home away from home as Preacher had.

"Judging by all the greetings that were shouted as we came in, it appears that everyone here knows your name," Beaver Hat commented as he and Preacher sat down at a table. Each man had a big mug of beer.

"Maybe so," Preacher allowed, "but that don't mean they're all my friends. I could point out half a dozen fellas in here who wouldn't mind a bit seein' my carcass skinned and the hide hung up to dry."

Beaver Hat shuddered and said, "That's a rather grisly image. I suppose that in your travels you've actually witnessed such things, though."

Preacher shrugged and took a drink from his mug.

Beaver Hat drank, too, and continued, "It occurs to

me that we haven't been introduced. My name is Daniel Eckstrom."

"Folks call me Preacher."

Eckstrom was a heavyset man with jowls, side whiskers, and bushy eyebrows. Those eyebrows climbed up his forehead as his eyes widened in surprise.

"Preacher?" he repeated.

"That's right. Do we know each other?"

"No, but I've heard of you. In fact, I ventured into this part of town tonight specifically in search of you."

Preacher frowned and said, "You were lookin' for me?"

"That's right. I inquired among my acquaintances in the fur trading industry as to the identity of a dependable, knowledgeable man of the frontier, and your name came up repeatedly. Well, your *nom de guerre*, as it were. I assume your mother did not name you Preacher."

As a matter of fact, Preacher's mother had named him Arthur, and he had gone by Art during his childhood and adolescence, which had been cut short when he left his family's farm and headed west to see the elephant. After a few detours, including one to New Orleans, where he'd fought the bloody British with Andy Jackson's army, he had wound up in the mountains, where he had learned the fur-trapping business and earned the special enmity of the Blackfoot Indians. An encounter with the Blackfeet that almost cost him his life had resulted in the nickname Preacher, and it had stuck with him ever since, to the point that sometimes he felt like he barely remembered his real name.

He looked darkly across the table at Daniel Eckstrom, who went on, "I was also told that my best chances of locating you would be in this section of town. Several people whose opinions I sought knew that you had been in St. Louis in recent days but weren't sure if you were still here."

"I was fixin' to light a shuck for the mountains pretty soon. Too many people in these parts. I don't cotton much to bein' crowded."

"Then it's fortunate in more ways than one that I encountered you tonight. Not only did you save my life from that robber, but now I can tell you why I wanted to talk to you."

"Yeah, I was a mite curious about that," Preacher said dryly.

"I have a proposition for you," Eckstrom said. "I'd like to hire you."

Preacher nodded slowly as he pondered whether to hear Eckstrom out or grab the man by the collar of his expensive coat, drag him to the door, and boot his rump into the street. This wasn't the first time somebody had sat down with him in Red Mike's and tried to hire him for some chore. Every time he agreed—usually against his better judgment—he'd wound up in a heap of trouble. Every instinct in Preacher's body told him that this time probably wouldn't be any different.

But his curiosity got the better of him, and he said, "What kind of job are we talkin' about?"

"One that involves a considerable amount of gold coin," Eckstrom replied smoothly. "And the distinct possibility that you might encounter one or more of those . . . how did you phrase it? . . . varmints who need killin'."

CHAPTER 2

More intrigued than he wanted to be, Preacher took another healthy swallow of his beer and told Eckstrom, "Go on."

"I'm a businessman, as you probably surmised."

"In that outfit, I didn't take you for a keelboater."

"I have an interest in several enterprises here in St. Louis," Eckstrom continued as if he hadn't heard Preacher's comment, "but a partner and I also own a retail establishment . . . a general store, if you will . . . in Santa Fe, a town in the Mexican province of Nuevo Mexico."

Preacher nodded and said, "I know Santa Fe. Been there quite a few times."

"I'm aware of that fact. That was another question I asked of my acquaintances. I wanted a man who knew the ground, so to speak."

Eckstrom was the bush-beating sort, Preacher realized, and you couldn't hurry those fellas. He sat back and waited for Eckstrom to go on.

"My partner is a man named Armando Montez," Eckstrom went on. "A native of Santa Fe and a man of impeccable character. I supply the goods, sending wagon trains full of merchandise several times a year to Santa Fe, where Señor Montez sells them and we divide the profits equally. Twice a year, he sends me my share, in the form of gold coins, sending them back with the empty wagons since those wagon trains are always well guarded against the brigands who lurk along the Santa Fe Trail."

"Plenty of outlaws along the Santa Fe Trail, all right," Preacher said, "along with Kiowa and Comanch'. It's rugged country."

The mountain man recalled a journey he had made along the Santa Fe Trail a few years earlier, accompanying a wagon train full of immigrants. They had run into plenty of trouble along the way, including a huge grizzly bear that had seemed hell-bent on killing Preacher.

"In order to make the whole process safer," Eckstrom said, "no one knows exactly which trip will contain one of those money shipments except myself, Señor Montez, and his assistant, a young man named Toby Harper."

Preacher had told himself to be patient, but his restraint was starting to wear thin. He drained the rest of his beer, signaled to Red Mike behind the bar for another, and then said, "From the way you were talkin' a few minutes ago, I'm guessin' something happened to one of those shipments."

Eckstrom sighed heavily and nodded.

"Indeed it did. The last time Armando sent my share to me, the wagon train was ambushed and the gold was stolen. All the men traveling with the wagons were slain . . . with the exception of Toby Harper. He seems to have, ah, disappeared."

Preacher cocked an eyebrow and said, "Sounds to me

like this fella Harper set up the whole deal and was behind the ambush."

"Armando refuses to believe that. Harper was his assistant for several years, and Armando insists that he is absolutely trustworthy."

"You don't believe that, though," Preacher said.

"I've met the young man only twice. He seemed genuine enough, but no, in the face of the evidence, I have no reason to believe he's honest. However, Armando has another reason for feeling the way he does: Toby Harper was supposed to become his son-in-law. The young man is engaged to marry Armando's daughter Alita."

One of the serving girls brought Preacher's beer over and set the mug on the table in front of the mountain man. She bent forward as she did so, giving him an enticing view and a suggestive smile. Preacher was too rugged to ever be considered handsome, but the ladies seemed to like him anyway.

Normally he might have been happy to spend what he'd expected to be his last night in St. Louis with this gal, but he'd gotten interested in Daniel Eckstrom's story and wanted to hear more. So he returned the serving girl's smile but without any sort of commitment in the expression.

The girl recognized that and flounced away in mingled annoyance and disappointment. Preacher said to Eckstrom, "I can see why your partner don't want to believe the worst of Harper. It's possible there's some other reason his body wasn't with the others. If Injuns jumped that wagon train, they could've carried him off, plannin' to take him back to their camp and torture him to death."

"Would the savages do such a thing?"

Preacher shrugged and said, "Kiowa and Comanch'

ain't as bad about that as some of the other tribes, like the Blackfeet up north or the Apache farther west, but it's been known to happen."

"Isn't it just as likely he arranged the whole thing and is responsible not only for the loss of the gold but the deaths of all those other men, as well?"

"Based on what you've told me . . . yeah, I reckon it is. But what you *haven't* told me, Mr. Eckstrom, is what you want me to do about it."

"Naturally, quite a bit of time has passed since this occurred. Communication between here and Santa Fe is not swift, needless to say. But before the trail gets any . . . colder, isn't that how you'd say it? . . . Before the trail gets any colder, I need a good man to take it up, find Toby Harper, and discover the truth of his involvement, and recover that gold. And if Harper *is* to blame and the gold *can't* be recovered . . . then my representative can deliver some justice for those men who were murdered by killing Toby Harper."

For a long moment, Preacher didn't respond. He just sat there looking across the table at Eckstrom, his fresh mug of beer forgotten for now.

Finally he said, "That's putting it mighty plain."

"I'm a plainspoken man," Eckstrom said.

For the most part, that wasn't true, Preacher thought. Eckstrom was a man who loved the sound of his own voice. But clearly he knew when to be blunt, too.

The mountain man shook his head and said, "I'm not a hired killer, mister. If you'd said what you just did to any of the folks you asked about me, they'd have told you that. You'll have to find yourself somebody else."

"From what I've heard, there *isn't* anyone else with your

skills. Besides, I'm more interested in recovering those gold coins than in settling the score with Harper."

Preacher took a long swallow from the mug and thumped it back down on the table.

"Nope. My gut says this is something I don't want to get mixed up in, and I'm old enough to have learned to listen to it."

Eckstrom leaned forward and said, "There's actually more at stake than I've mentioned so far."

"I don't reckon there's anything you could say that would change—"

"What about a young woman's life being in danger?"

Preacher's eyebrows lowered. He said, "You must be talkin' about that gal who's your partner's daughter."

"Alita Montez," Eckstrom confirmed.

"I can see why she'd be mighty upset that the fella she figured on gettin' hitched with has disappeared and is mostly likely dead. And if he ain't dead, that means he's probably turned outlaw. But I don't see how that puts her life in danger."

"The last letter I received from Armando," Eckstrom said, "he told me that Alita was determined to prove Harper's innocence. He fears that she plans to launch a search of her own for him. A couple of the men who work for him are fiercely devoted to her, and she would have no trouble convincing them to accompany her." The business-man spread his hands. "Given the lag in communications, it's entirely possible that she's already set out from Santa Fe by now, even though her father assured me that he intends to keep a close eye on her. In my experience, it's quite difficult to keep a determined woman from doing what she wants to do."

Preacher grunted and said, "You're right about that. But you don't know for sure she's gone to look for Harper."

"Indeed, I don't. But the possibility certainly exists. She could be out there now, somewhere along the Santa Fe Trail—"

"All right, all right," Preacher interrupted him. "You done made your point."

"Sufficiently to persuade you to accept the proposition?"

"Well, you ain't exactly *made* a proposition yet, because you ain't said anything about what's in this for me."

Eckstrom placed both hands flat on the table and said, "Half of whatever money you recover."

"What if it's all gone?"

"Then you'll have the satisfaction of knowing that you did the right thing. And, as I said, perhaps will have dealt with the man responsible for committing such a foul act. So, you see, I'm not offering to pay you for killing Toby Harper. Not exactly."

Preacher made a little growling sound deep in his throat and said, "You talk around and around a thing, mister, until I ain't sure just what it is you're sayin'. But if there's a chance there's a gal out there gettin' herself into trouble—"

"A very good chance, I'd say."

"Then I can't hardly turn my back on the deal. Just out of curiosity, though . . . how much money are you talkin' about?"

"Armando sent me approximately two thousand dollars with the wagon train. So your share of the recovered funds could be as much as a thousand."

Preacher kept his face impassive, but he was impressed. One thousand dollars was a lot of money. More than he'd ever made in a season of trapping furs. After hearing about the girl, he'd already been leaning toward accepting the job from Eckstrom, but the chance of such a windfall clinched the deal.

Not that he would live his life any differently if he had that much money, he told himself. As long as he had enough for supplies to get him to the mountains, that was really all he needed. He could live off the land as well as the Indians.

Might be nice to spend some time in Santa Fe with plenty of *dinero*, though, he mused. There was a cantina there he liked almost as much as Red Mike's, as well as a few señoritas who had professed undying devotion to him. And then, when the money started to run low, he could get himself an outfit and head north through the Sangre de Cristos toward the big ranges of the Rockies. That was where he'd wanted to wind up all along.

Eckstrom was watching him with an eager expression on his beefy face. Preacher said, "All right. The way I see it, I'm goin' after three things: the money, the girl—if she's there—and the truth."

"If you find all three," Eckstrom said, "you'll have definitely earned your reward!"

CHAPTER 3

Since Daniel Eckstrom was a merchant with an interest in more than one store in St. Louis, he offered to furnish the supplies for Preacher's trip west. He also provided a pair of pack mules.

As much time as had already passed, Preacher didn't figure he ought to waste any more, so he told Eckstrom he wanted to be ready to depart by the middle of the next morning. He'd been spending the nights in the hayloft of the stable where he kept his rangy gray stallion, Horse, so that was where Eckstrom had the pack mules and supplies delivered.

Eckstrom himself showed up a short time later, even more sartorially resplendent today in a swallowtail coat, gray-striped trousers, and a different beaver hat. He clasped his hands behind his back, rocked slightly on the balls of his feet, and said, "I wanted to come by and make certain you have everything you need for the journey."

"Reckon I do," Preacher said, resting a hand on a leather pack draped over the back of one of the mules.

"Excellent. I—Good heavens! Is that a wolf?"

A huge, shaggy gray cur had just sauntered out of

the livery barn. The beast came to Preacher's side and sat down.

"This here's Dog," Preacher said as he dropped a hand to scratch the big cur's head between the pointed ears. "He may be part wolf, I couldn't say about that. But he's one of my trail partners, along with Horse here, and has been for quite a spell."

"I . . . see." Eckstrom swallowed. "Very well. Is there anything else I can do for you and, ah, Dog and Horse?"

"Nope." Preacher tapped the pocket of his buckskin shirt. "I've got the letter you wrote to Armando Montez in Santa Fe tellin' him who I am and what I'm doin' for you, in case I wind up out there and need his help. You've been more than generous when it comes to provisions, powder and shot, and such like. All I need to do now is go do the job I agreed to do."

"Then I'll wish you luck," Eckstrom said as he extended a pudgy hand.

"And I'll sure take it," Preacher told him as he clasped Eckstrom's hand.

Considering the wild country he was heading into, he'd probably wind up needing all the luck he could get.

Before starting out on the Santa Fe Trail itself, though, Preacher had to cross Missouri from one side to the other. The trail actually began over on the western side of the state, at the town of Independence.

He moved at a steady pace that ate up the ground without wearing out Horse or the two pack mules. There were some settlements on the road between St. Louis and Independence, but Preacher didn't stop at any of them, even when the afternoon waned and he needed a place to spend the night. Instead he pushed on, figuring he would find somewhere to camp.

He'd had a roof over his head too many nights of late. He preferred stars.

As the sun dipped toward the horizon, almost touching it, he left the road and found a good spot in some trees a hundred yards from the path. It was a grassy clearing, partially ringed by brush, with a few rocks scattered around and the thick trunk of a large fallen tree that served as a good seat. There was no spring or creek nearby, but Preacher had four full canteens. That would be enough water for him, Dog, Horse, and the mules until he could refill the canteens at the first stream they came to the next day.

He picketed Horse and the mules to graze, unsaddled the stallion, removed the packs from the mules, then gathered rocks for a fire ring and branches for fuel. When he had a small fire kindled, he fried some salt pork and ate it with biscuits he had brought from St. Louis, using one of them to mop up the last of the grease.

Dusk was closing in as he put out the fire. He poured water from one of the canteens into his broad-brimmed felt hat and let the animals drink from it, then took a long swallow from the canteen himself.

With that done, he spread his bedroll not too far from the glowing embers of the campfire, positioned his saddle to serve as a pillow, and stretched out, apparently to sleep peacefully until morning.

The two men approaching the camp in the dead of night were trying to be stealthy, but to Preacher they sounded almost like a parade coming down the street, complete with brass band.

Horse and Dog heard the skulkers, too. They lifted their heads, pricking their ears toward the small sounds, but they didn't show any other reaction. They wouldn't, unless Preacher ordered them to do so.

Men who spent their lives in town just weren't much good once they got away from all the crowded spaces and noise, Preacher thought as he stood with his back pressed against a tree trunk, holding a flintlock pistol in each hand with the barrels pointed up in front of his face.

The spot he had picked was in deep shadow, so he was confident the men wouldn't see him. He stood absolutely still, so they wouldn't hear him moving around, either. Their eyes and ears probably weren't very good to start with, even if he hadn't concealed himself so well.

He had noticed them earlier in the afternoon, hanging back on his trail, anywhere from a quarter to half a mile behind him. As the afternoon went on, they had closed the gap some, as if fearful of losing sight of him. He didn't know who they were, and it was always possible that they were just a couple of pilgrims who happened to be going the same way he was—but he didn't believe that for a second.

Maybe that fella who had planned to rob and murder Daniel Eckstrom the night before had had a couple of partners hanging back in case he needed help. Preacher had dealt with the situation so swiftly and lethally that the man had been dead before any partners could have done anything. Seeing that, they might have decided that the smartest thing to do was back off.

But they might want to avenge their friend, too, and Preacher was leading two fine pack mules loaded down with supplies. For all they would know, Eckstrom might have paid him some cash, as well. It added up to a tempting target, especially when they had him outnumbered two to one.

But when it came to Preacher, numbers didn't mean a dadblasted thing.

Breathing shallowly, he stood there as the two men crept nearer the camp. The route they chose to approach the spot where they believed he was sleeping took them within twenty feet of the mountain man. They were close enough his keen ears had no trouble hearing them whispering to each other.

"Is he still there?"

"Yeah, I see him silhouetted against the embers from the fire. He must be sound asleep. He ain't movin'."

Once it was good and dark, Preacher had arranged rocks under his bedroll to look like someone was still there, then slipped off into the shadows to await developments, taking Dog with him. The big cur sat beside him now, tensely eager for action, but Dog wouldn't budge unless Preacher gave the order.

"Well, he won't ever wake up," the first man said.

"I dunno," the other one objected. "Wouldn't it be good for him to know that he's dyin' because of what he done to Farnham?"

"He's dyin' because I want that horse and those mules and supplies. I don't really give a damn what happened to Farnham."

The other man sighed.

"All right. Got your pistols ready?"

"Yeah. Let's get this done."

The two of them stepped forward, pushing through the brush, no longer worrying about the crackling noises they were making because as soon as they moved into the clearing, they opened fire on what they believed to be their quarry, stretched out sleeping beside the campfire's remnants.

Each of the would-be killers carried a pair of pistols. The four shots boomed out, closely spaced, almost one on top of another. A cloud of powdersmoke rose around them, leaving the stink of brimstone in the air. The echoes rolled away in the night until they sounded like distant thunder.

As the noise died down, the one who had spoken of wanting Horse and the pack mules laughed and said, "Son of a gun never knew what hit him."

"Yeah, but you boys will," Preacher said as he stepped up behind them, staying out of arm's reach. He had closed in some already, knowing they wouldn't be able to hear him over the racket they were making with their guns.

At the sound of Preacher's voice, one of the men cried out in surprise and fear while the other cursed bitterly. Both tried to whirl around.

Preacher let them turn until they faced him. Their guns were empty, but the weapons could still be used as clubs, if they could get close enough.

Preacher didn't allow that. He stroked the triggers of both flintlock pistols. The hammers snapped down and the guns boomed as they spewed smoke and flame. He had double-shotted loads in both pistols, with heavier-than-normal charges of powder. It took a man with great strength in his wrist to handle such a discharge, but Preacher was used to it.

The lead balls slammed into the chests of the would-be killers and knocked them backward off their feet. One landed with his head and shoulders in the hot embers and started shrieking as he kicked and thrashed. The gruesome display didn't last long, though, before he died.

The other man lay on his back, gasping and pawing at the wounds in his chest. Preacher lowered the pistols and moved closer to him, saying, "It'll be over soon, you sorry son of a buck, and you ought to be glad. I could've just let Dog have you."

The man arched his back and then let out his last breath in a rattling sigh. Preacher tucked both pistols behind his belt, reached down, grabbed the ankles of the man who lay with his head in the embers, and pulled him clear. His hair was starting to smolder, and it stunk.

Some people might claim he had killed these two men in cold blood because their guns were empty and they were no longer a threat. Preacher didn't swallow that notion at all. Men such as these were always a threat. He had seen the way they emptied their pistols into what they believed was his sleeping body. That proved beyond a shadow of a doubt what sort of snake-blooded varmints they were. Sure, he could have let them go, tried to scare them into leaving him alone in the future.

But even if he had done that, the overwhelming odds were that they would have hurt somebody else in the future. Folks who didn't have Preacher's ability to protect themselves. It was for those innocents that Preacher had squeezed the triggers.

And he wasn't going to lose a minute's worth of sleep over it, either.

CHAPTER 4

After dealing with the two would-be thieves and murderers, Preacher saddled Horse, replaced the packs on the mules, and moved his camp another mile along the trail, annoyed that he had to leave what had been a perfectly good campsite.

He didn't want to spend the night with a couple of corpses lying around, though, and he sure as blazes wasn't going to the trouble of burying them.

The next morning, as he set out again, he saw buzzards circling lazily but intently in the sky a ways back and nodded in grim satisfaction as he nudged Horse into motion. Dog bounded out ahead, glad to be on the move again.

For the next week and a half, Preacher rode across Missouri, still avoiding the settlements for the most part although he didn't figure anybody else was on his trail. No reason for them to be. He just preferred being outdoors. He'd had enough of civilization for a while. By the time he made it to Santa Fe—if he did—he'd be ready to stay a spell in town, then it would be back to the mountains.

When he reached Independence, though, he knew he

needed to replenish some of his supplies before he started across the plains. He tied Horse and the mules in front of a general store, told Dog to stay, and went inside the building with LEONARD BROS. MERCANTILE painted on it.

He was heading toward the counter at the rear of the store when a voice rasped, "Hold it right there, you mangy, no-good rapscallion!"

Preacher tensed and his right hand moved toward one of the flintlock pistols tucked behind his belt, but then he saw the tall, lanky, gray-bearded man who stepped around a set of shelves to confront him. He stopped short and said, "I should've knowed you was in here as soon as I came in the door. There's no mistakin' that skunk smell!"

The two buckskin-clad men glared at each other for a second. Then the gray-bearded man whooped and stepped forward to throw his arms around Preacher.

They pounded each other on the back in greeting, then the gray-bearded man stepped back and said, "What are you doin' in this neck o' the woods? If you're headin' to the mountains, you missed the Big Muddy a good ways back!"

The Missouri River, or the Big Muddy as many called it, was the main "highway" between civilization, as represented by St. Louis, and the Rocky Mountains. Preacher had been up and down the river more times than he could count, and so had the man he was talking to now.

"I could say the same thing to you, Cloverleaf. Last time our trails crossed was at the Green River rendezvous, what, two years ago?"

"That's right, I believe," Cloverleaf Jenkins said, nodding.

Cloverleaf was an odd moniker for such a grizzled specimen, but it was the only one Preacher had ever known him by. He had no idea what the origin of the name might have been.

"Since then I've gotten out of the fur trappin' business and taken up a new line," Cloverleaf went on. "I been guidin' immigrant trains out to Santa Fe and some of 'em even all the way to Californy."

Preacher's eyebrows rose as he said, "Well, tarnation, you're just the fella I needed to run into. If you'll wait a few minutes while I get my business done, I'll buy you a drink and pick your brain."

"Make it a nice thick steak and I'll take you up on it."

Preacher clapped a hand on his shoulder and nodded. "Done."

Half an hour later, after Preacher had bought what he needed and loaded the bundles on the pack mules, the two men walked along the street to the Green Top Café, which according to Cloverleaf had the best food in town.

Over steaks and plates of greens and potatoes, with plenty of gravy and biscuits and hot, black coffee, Preacher filled Cloverleaf in on the job that had brought him to Independence, keeping back only a few things, such as the fact that the Eckstrom/Montez wagon train had been carrying a couple of thousand dollars in gold coins. He had no reason to distrust his fellow mountain man, but he was also in the habit of playing his cards pretty close to his chest.

When Preacher was finished, Cloverleaf let out a low whistle and said, "You're headin' out along the Santa Fe Trail by your lonesome? That's askin' for trouble these days. Even big, well-armed groups get jumped sometimes by bands of highwaymen or Kiowa and Comanch' war parties, like that one you just told me about. I expect there were a lot of outriders with that wagon train, and they'd all be fellas who still had the bark on."

"I know all that," Preacher said, nodding. "That's why I thought maybe the two of us runnin' into each other was a stroke of luck."

"Are you askin' me to come with you?" Cloverleaf grimaced. "I'm sorry, Preacher, but I can't. I just got back from a trip, and I've already agreed to scout for another wagon train leavin' for Santa Fe ten days from now. I gave those folks my word."

"And I wouldn't want you to break it. I'm a mite disappointed, but I understand. Just tell me everything you can about conditions along the trail these days. You say it's thick with outlaws and savages? It never was what you'd call safe."

"No, it sure wasn't. It's gotten worse, though, as more and more people are headin' west. That makes a lot more targets for thieves and redskins to go after."

"Have any of the wagon trains you've taken across had to fight their way through?"

Cloverleaf shook his head and said, "Not really. One time we had a little bunch of Injuns hit us and steal a few horses, but that seemed to be all they were after. They took off and we never saw 'em again. Couple of other times, we spotted some braves watchin' us from a distance, but they never tried nothin'. I reckon they figured there were too many of us. I never did see a redskin yet who liked to fight unless the odds were 'way on his side."

That wasn't strictly true, Preacher knew, but in general Cloverleaf was right. Indians were very strategic fighters and seldom attacked unless they believed there was a good chance they would emerge triumphant.

"You didn't see any white outlaws?"

"Nope. Never did. Of course, we're talkin' about immigrant trains. Those folks usually don't have much cash because they've done spent it outfittin' theirselves for the trip, and the wagons and the goods they're carryin' ain't all that easy to steal. Injuns'd be satisfied with killin' a bunch o' white folks and burnin' the wagons. Outlaws want to make a profit outta the deal."

That was true. They had made a profit out of the raid on the wagons being led by Toby Harper. One of the questions Preacher had to answer was whether Harper had shared in that profit.

While they ate, Preacher asked Cloverleaf about certain landmarks along the trail and whether the route had changed any since the last time Preacher had been over it several years earlier. Cloverleaf, like most frontiersmen, had a keen sense of direction and a good memory for details. By the time they finished the meal, Preacher could almost see the whole route in his head.

During their talks in St. Louis, Daniel Eckstrom had told Preacher that the attack on the wagon had occurred near a landmark called Devil Horn Buttes. Preacher thought he remembered where that was, but he double-checked with Cloverleaf.

"Yeah, 'bout ten miles west o' where the Cimarron route branches off southwest," Cloverleaf confirmed. "Hard to miss, since they're the only things stickin' up in those parts."

Even though Eckstrom hadn't known the details, just based on Preacher's knowledge of the area he would have guessed that the outlaws had hidden behind the buttes until they were ready to spring their attack. The trail ran fairly

close by. Some travelers even stopped at the Devil Horns
to enjoy the shade. The sun and heat out on the plains
could be fierce at times.

"I wish you luck," Cloverleaf said as they parted a short
time later. They shook hands, and he added, "Wish things
had worked out so's I could ride along with you for a spell,
Preacher. Wherever you are, things don't ever get too
borin' in those parts, that's for sure!"

Cloverleaf meant that as a compliment, Preacher knew.
To frontiersmen such as the two of them, nothing was
worse than boredom, so a tendency toward getting into
trouble wasn't really a bad thing.

As it turned out, however, the next two weeks were among
the most boring Preacher had ever experienced. The vast
prairie through which he rode wasn't known for its scenery.
Day after seemingly endless day, Horse plodded west
across the plains, a sea of constantly waving grass un-
broken by trees or hills, except for a very occasional rocky
ridge. Those were welcome breaks from the monotony.

At least water was in good supply most of the way, as
the trail roughly followed the wide, leisurely flowing
Arkansas River. By the time Preacher reached the spot
where the ruts of the Cimarron route angled off to the
southwest, the Arkansas had shrunk some but was still a
decent-sized river, at least for these parts. That was why
the trail followed it all the way into the mountains and on
to Bent's Fort before turning south for Santa Fe.

The first section of the Cimarron route was a long, dry
stretch absolutely without water. Travelers who started
across there were taking their lives in their hands if they
weren't carrying plenty of water with them. Eventually the

trail reached the Cimarron River—but some of those who took that route did not.

Preacher didn't have to worry about that, because he was moving straight ahead to Devil Horn Buttes, which were already visible up ahead, even though they were still miles away. The curved, reddish sandstone formations sticking up from the prairie didn't really look much like devil's horns, but at some time in the past they must have reminded somebody of such a thing. The Grand Tetons, a long way north of here, had been named by a Frenchman who must have been mighty lonely for some female company, Preacher mused as he and Horse and Dog and the pack mules continued on their way.

It was fairly late in the day, and Preacher figured on making camp at the buttes. As much time had passed since the attack on the wagon train, he knew he wouldn't be able to find any sort of a useful trail to follow. His only chance of finding out anything about the thieves and murderers who had raided the train would be to find somebody who had seen them going about their grim business.

In this part of the country, that meant finding some Indians. Or what was more likely, having some Indians find *him*.

In fact, as Preacher approached Devil Horn Buttes, the skin on the back of his neck prickled, and every instinct in his body told him that he was being watched right now.

CHAPTER 5

Preacher didn't ignore that warning sensation, but he continued to act as if he didn't have a care in the world as he rode up to the base of the closest butte. Some scrub brush grew along there, sustained by the water that collected in puddles every time it rained.

Without being too obvious about doing so, he scanned the countryside all around him. It didn't take long for his keen eyes to spot a couple of figures watching him from the top of a slight rise about a quarter of a mile to the north. He could see only their heads, which told him they were stretched out on their bellies. Probably they had left their ponies farther back where he couldn't see them.

He had no doubt that the watchers were Indians, probably Kiowa. Most of the Comanche ranged farther south, although from time to time they came far enough north to attack wagon trains on the Santa Fe Trail. The Kiowa had long considered this area one of their hunting grounds, though.

They had to be curious about a man who traveled through these parts alone. Preacher checked now and then to see if the watchers were still there while he unsaddled

Horse, removed the packs from the mules, and went about setting up camp for the night. For a long time, they didn't budge, but then suddenly, they were gone.

The question was, would they be back . . . and would they bring friends with them?

Since he couldn't do anything about that now, he enjoyed a leisurely supper, then rolled up in his blankets and slept. If anyone came skulking around, Horse and Dog would let him know.

The night passed quietly and peacefully, though. In the morning, Preacher had breakfast, then took a good look around in the light of a new day.

Word of the deadly attack on the wagon train had reached Armando Montez because some westbound freight wagons had passed along here several days after the massacre. The empty wagons were still there, along with the bodies of the slain guards and outriders. All the horses, mules, and oxen were gone.

The freighters had gone through the clothes of the dead men before burying the grisly remains and had found letters and other documents that identified them. They had taken those papers to Santa Fe with them and turned them over to the authorities. An investigation quickly determined that the dead men had worked for Montez.

Upon learning of this atrocity, Montez had led a party of men out to do his own investigation, taking with them enough mules to haul the wagons back to Santa Fe. From talking to the freighters, he knew how many men had been buried and had gotten good enough descriptions of them, along with the identification that had been found, to determine that Toby Harper's body hadn't been with the others.

All of this, Montez had written to his business partner

Daniel Eckstrom, and Eckstrom had passed it along to Preacher.

By now enough time had passed that Preacher found no signs of the attack around the Devil Horns, just as he expected. In his mind's eye, though, he could see what had happened. The attackers must have poured out from behind the rocks in overwhelming numbers and raced along the column of wagons, shooting down the guards and muleskinners. Riflemen might have been posted up on the rock formations to pick off the outriders. It would have taken a large, well-coordinated assault to defeat the men defending the wagons.

Obviously, that had happened, but Preacher had no way of knowing if the attackers had been white—or a mixture of white and Mexican, if they were outlaws—or red. According to the men who had found the bodies, the dead men hadn't been scalped, and the wagons hadn't been burned. That pointed more toward outlaws—but Indians were notional creatures, as Preacher knew very well. Often, they tortured and mutilated their victims, but not always.

While he was taking his look around, Preacher glanced at the rise where he had spotted the two watchers the day before. After a while, he grinned in satisfaction as he saw their heads pop up. Indians were curious, too. They hadn't been able to stay away because they wanted to know what he was going to do next.

He loaded up the pack mules, saddled Horse, and pulled out, leaving Devil Horn Buttes behind him. He continued following the Santa Fe Trail to the west. After he had gone a mile, he looked casually to the north.

Sure enough, two distant black specks were paralleling

his course. Most folks wouldn't have been able to spot them, but Preacher had eyes like an eagle.

He nodded to himself. His two watchers were still keeping an eye on him but not coming any closer.

A while later, he came to a dry wash snaking its way from north to south across the plains. Preacher rode down into it, but instead of crossing the sandy bottom and riding back out, he turned north and followed the wash. It wasn't deep, only ten or twelve feet in most places, but that was enough to make him invisible to anyone riding across the prairie.

He kept moving steadily, but not fast enough that the stallion and the mules would kick up any dust. He said quietly to the big cur, "Stay close, Dog."

It wasn't long before he heard horses not too far away. The watchers had noticed that he was gone and had come to look for him. He reined to a halt and hoped neither of the mules would decide it was a good time to let out a nice, loud bray.

Preacher swung down silently from the saddle and moved over to the wash's eastern bank. He listened intently as the soft thuds of the ponies' unshod hooves came closer. His hands wrapped around the butts of the two flintlock pistols at his waist.

Then the sounds stopped. A moment later, the two riders started talking to each other in low, puzzled voices. Preacher understood enough Kiowa to recognize the language as they conversed. He couldn't hear well enough to make out all the words, but he could tell they were wondering where he had disappeared to.

What made his forehead crease in a frown of surprise was that he could tell from the voices how young the two riders were. Boys, not grown warriors. And like all boys, they were curious and wanted to do things that would make them feel older—like trailing a lone white man across the plains. Maybe even thinking about trying to ambush and kill him.

Preacher sincerely hoped they wouldn't do that. He didn't want to kill any youngsters, but he wouldn't just allow them to kill him without fighting back, either.

He was relieved when they decided to go back to their village and tell their elders what they had seen. He could tell from the sound of the hoofbeats when they wheeled their ponies and rode away.

Preacher waited for a few moments, then pulled himself up the bank high enough to look over. He saw the two young braves several hundred yards away, riding northeast. He watched until they had gone completely out of sight, then slid back down the bank.

"Come on, fellas," he said to Dog and Horse. "We're gonna go pay a visit."

Preacher didn't get in any hurry. He had seen which direction the Kiowa youngsters had been going and believed they were headed straight back to their village, as he had hoped they would after the little maneuver he'd pulled. He rode in the same direction, taking his time so he wouldn't get close enough for them to notice him if they happened to look back.

The Kiowa and the Comanche were allies, generally banding together to battle against the Osage and Pawnee who roamed farther east. With the opening of the Santa Fe Trail, the Comanches had been more resentful of what they regarded as an intrusion of white settlers and traders through their territory. Although there had been instances where Kiowa war parties had attacked wagon trains, it was much more likely to have been a group of Comanche warriors that had jumped the Montez/Eckstrom wagons, if indeed Indians were responsible for the atrocity. For the most part, the Kiowa wanted to steer clear of a war with the white men. They had enough to worry about dealing with other hostile tribes.

Preacher knew that, and it was what he was basing his strategy on. If he was right, following those Kiowa boys back to their village might get him some useful information.

If he was wrong, they'd likely try to kill him. He would deal with *that* when the time came, if he needed to.

By the middle of the day, he smelled woodsmoke. That came from the cooking fires in the village, he thought. He let his nose guide him until he came in sight of several dozen tepees scattered along the banks of a creek with a grassy ridge on the other side to cut the cold north winds during the winter. A dark smudge on the prairie to the left of the village was the horse herd, Preacher decided.

As he came closer, a cloud of dust began to rise near the village. He reined in and watched as it moved toward him. After a moment he was able to make out the riders at the bottom of the column whose ponies were kicking up that dust. Somewhere around twenty warriors had left the village and were coming toward him.

"Looks like a welcomin' party, boys," he drawled to Dog and Horse.

Those two youngsters had told their elders about the strange disappearing white man, and now those warriors were on their way to check out the story for themselves. They wouldn't be expecting to run into him only a mile from their homes.

He sat waiting, not trying to hide or run. The Kiowa pounded toward him—then the warriors in the lead slowed suddenly as they saw him. The entire group gradually came to a halt.

One of the warriors rode out a short distance ahead of the others. He was about two hundred yards away from Preacher. He reined in and sat there on his pony for a long moment, staring straight toward the mountain man. That would be the chief, more than likely.

Then he turned his mount, and even though Preacher couldn't hear the words, he knew the chief had called out an order. Two of the other warriors burst out from the group, kicking their ponies into a run as they charged at Preacher, giving voice to shrill, yipping battle cries.

CHAPTER 6

Both warriors galloping toward Preacher wore buckskins and carried lances. Neither sported a feather in his black hair. They were young firebrands eager for glory. He hoped they wouldn't get too carried away, because he had a plan and he wanted to stick to it.

The lithe ponies swiftly closed the gap. A growl rumbled from deep in Dog's throat at the big cur sat beside Preacher, quivering a little from the desire to launch himself into action.

"Easy, Dog," the mountain man said quietly. He hadn't budged since the two Kiowa warriors charged him.

They were riding together, but when they were twenty yards away from him, they split up, veering apart to go on either side of him. One fell back slightly to let the other have the honor of striking first.

Preacher waited, well aware that he was betting his life right now.

Howling like a crazy wolf, the closest warrior drew back his lance and let it fly toward Preacher. The mountain man sat his saddle calmly, judging the lance's trajectory in a split second. It whipped past his right ear, no more than a foot away. The warrior who had thrown it peeled off from his charge.

The other Kiowa threw his lance a second later, but instead of sailing past Preacher, it stuck into the ground next to Horse on Preacher's left. The wooden shaft stuck up at an angle, swaying slightly.

The first warrior circled around and charged again. This time he plucked a tomahawk from a buckskin harness tied around his waist and waved the weapon over his head as he came at Preacher, shouting angrily.

Preacher reached over with his left hand, grabbed the lance the second warrior had thrown, and jerked it from the ground. The first Kiowa nearly rammed his pony into Horse as he came close enough to slash at Preacher's head with the tomahawk.

Preacher leaned away from the blow, even though he was fairly certain the warrior intended to miss. They were just testing his mettle, trying to see if he was courageous enough to let him live for a while.

The tomahawk cut through the air. Preacher lifted the lance and spun it in his hand. He lashed out with it and cracked the shaft across the warrior's back. He struck with enough force to drive the man forward over his pony's neck.

Preacher whipped the lance back the other way as the second warrior crowded in at him, also swinging a tomahawk. Anger and frustration twisted this man's face, and Preacher thought maybe he was mad enough to disregard the chief's order to test this strange white man but not hurt him. He might try to stove Preacher's head in and then claim it was an accident.

Preacher didn't let him get close enough for that. He swung the lance so that the butt end punched into the warrior's midsection and doubled him over, driving him backward off the pony. The man crashed to the ground and lay there writhing and moaning as the now riderless pony trotted off.

The first warrior was sitting on his horse a hundred feet away, looking dazed from the blow Preacher had landed. Keeping his face impassive, the mountain man nudged Horse into motion and rode slowly toward the chief and the rest of the party that had come out from the Kiowa village.

The Indians watched him closely as he approached, but he didn't make any threatening moves and neither did they. When he was about ten feet from the chief, he stopped, held out the lance, and tossed it gently on the ground.

"One of your warriors dropped this," he said in Kiowa.

The chief's expression remained as stolid as Preacher's, but the mountain man thought he saw a flicker of amusement and admiration in the Kiowa's dark eyes. The chief half-turned on his pony's back and gestured. A warrior rode forward and leaned far down to pick up the lance, then rejoined the others.

"I'm called Preacher," the mountain man went on. He could tell that the chief recognized the name.

"Preacher," the man repeated. "It is said you are a friend to many Indians . . . and a deadly enemy to many more."

"I've never harmed a man, red or white, who wasn't trying to harm me or someone else."

"But you have counted coup, as with my warriors."

Preacher looked over his shoulder. The man he had knocked off his pony was back on his feet but still bent over as he stumbled around trying to catch his mount's reins. The other warrior shook his head groggily and rode over to help his friend.

Preacher looked back at the chief and said, "I didn't believe you would want me to hurt them. They seem like good men."

"They are." The chief lifted his pony's reins slightly. "I am called Buffalo Bull. Come with me. You are welcome in our village."

Preacher knew that he was relatively safe now that Buffalo Bull had extended the village's hospitality to him. He heeled Horse into motion and rode forward with Dog stalking alongside. Buffalo Bull turned his pony. The group of warriors split into two bunches so that Preacher and the chief could ride between them toward the tepees.

The warriors closed ranks behind them, but Preacher didn't worry. His gamble had paid off—for now.

Time would tell what the results of the wager were, and whether or not he would survive it.

The warriors who hadn't accompanied Buffalo Bull to confront Preacher, as well as all the women and children in the village, turned out to gawk at the mountain man as he rode in at the chief's side. A few of the village's dogs ventured toward Dog, but a quiet growl from the big cur had them retreating.

The group of warriors dispersed. Nobody expected Preacher to try anything funny here in the middle of the village, and in fact, such a possibility was the farthest thing from his mind. He rode with Buffalo Bull to one of the larger tepees, where they dismounted and Buffalo Bull signaled to some of the boys who had followed them.

"They will care for your horse and mules," he said.

"Thank you," Preacher replied, equally gravely.

Buffalo Bull waved a hand toward two women who stood in front of the tepee.

"My wives, Spring Flower and Laughing Water."

Spring Flower was the older of the two, probably Buffalo Bull's first wife. Laughing Water was young and pretty and kept her eyes turned shyly toward the ground.

The women went back into the tepee. Buffalo Bull motioned for Preacher to follow them. He did so without hesitation. No chief, not even a Blackfoot, would dishonor himself by attacking a guest in his own lodge.

Preacher and Buffalo Bull sat cross-legged on buffalo robes next to the firepit in the center of the tepee. The chief said, "Why does a white man come alone into the land of the Kiowa and the Comanche?"

"I seek knowledge," Preacher replied. "You know the road used by the white men to journey to the land of the Mexicans?"

"The Santa Fe Trail," Buffalo Bull said in English, a little awkwardly. He switched back to Kiowa as he went on, "I have seen it many times." He grimaced. "The white men's wagons leave scars on the land."

He didn't say whether he had ever attacked any of those wagon trains, and Preacher certainly wasn't going to press him on that point. Right now, he wanted information, that was all.

"I need to find out what happened to some wagons headed back to St. Louis from Santa Fe. This was some weeks ago. The men with the wagons were killed but not scalped, and the wagons were not burned."

Buffalo Bull considered this, then nodded and said, "It seems you already know what happened."

"Yes, but not who was responsible."

Buffalo Bull drew in a breath and regarded Preacher

with a somewhat cooler gaze as he asked, "Do you believe the Kiowa did this thing?"

"No," Preacher answered without hesitation. "It was either the Comanche or white and Mexican thieves. I need to know so I can find them."

Buffalo Bull frowned. "After all this time? What can you do now?"

Preacher didn't want to say anything about the missing gold coins. Indians generally had no use for money, but some of them had figured out that it could be traded for things that they *did* want.

Instead, he said, "One of the men who was with the wagons is missing. I believe whoever attacked the wagon train may have taken him prisoner. I'd like to find him and free him if I can."

"A white man?"

"That's right."

Buffalo Bull shook his head and said, "I know of no white man being held captive by any of the bands in this area. And I know nothing of the attack on the wagons you speak of. I regret that I cannot help you, Preacher. From what I have heard about you, it would be good to have you as a friend of my people."

"I plan to be your friend whether you know anything that helps me or not, Buffalo Bull. Your most welcome hospitality and your honor assure that."

Preacher could tell that the flattery pleased the chief. In general, Indians were vain folks and loved being praised. Of course, that pretty much held true for all other sorts of people, as well.

"I can tell you that none of my warriors have reported seeing any roving bands of white or Mexican thieves in this area in many moons," Buffalo Bull said.

"Are you saying it's likely a Comanche war party attacked that wagon train?"

Buffalo Bull shrugged. The Comanches were nominal allies. He probably didn't want to cast too much blame in their direction, even though he might believe that to be the case.

"I have told you what I know. Now we will eat."

Laughing Water, the younger of Buffalo Bull's wives, brought Preacher a bowl of stew. He dug in with his fingers and enjoyed the meal.

Buffalo Bull appeared to be thinking about something as he ate. Whatever it was, Preacher was content to let the chief mull it over. He knew he couldn't drag information out of the man. He had to let Buffalo Bull decide to volunteer it.

When they were done, Buffalo Bull packed tobacco into a pipe, and he and Preacher passed it back and forth for a while. After blowing smoke to the four winds, the chief said, "I have not seen it with my own eyes, but I have heard it told that the band led by Black Horn has taken prisoners in the past moon."

"Black Horn is a Comanche chief?"

Buffalo Bull nodded and said, "His village is three days' ride south of here."

"But the prisoner isn't a white man?"

"No. A young Mexican woman and two old Mexican men."

Preacher made an effort to keep a look of surprised recognition off his face. He remembered what Daniel Eckstrom had told him about Armando Montez's daughter insisting Toby Harper was innocent. Alita, that was the girl's name, he recalled. Montez had worried that Alita would leave Santa Fe and go to search for Harper, the man she had promised to marry. Eckstrom had even mentioned that two of Montez's servants were devoted to the girl and might go with her to help her and try to keep her safe.

If all three of them had landed in a Comanche village as captives, they were far from safe. In fact, it was entirely possible the two old-timers were dead by now and the girl was either a slave or some warrior's new wife.

Either way, though, Preacher couldn't turn his back on this knowledge. Would rescuing those prisoners—if, indeed, they were still alive—bring him any closer to recovering the stolen gold? He didn't know, but it was possible the Comanches led by Black Horn were the ones who had attacked the wagon train. If they weren't, at least he could eliminate that as a possibility.

"Will you seek out Black Horn and his people?" Buffalo Bull asked.

The chief hadn't just let that information slip accidentally, Preacher thought. Buffalo Bull had had a reason for telling him. Maybe there was no love lost between the two bands. The Kiowa and the Comanche might be allies, but that didn't mean they always liked each other.

"I seek a white captive," Preacher said casually, "but perhaps I will ride in that direction."

"If you do, take care. The Comanche are not as hospitable as the Kiowa."

Preacher nodded and couldn't resist drawling, "If there's one thing I've never heard the Comanche accused of . . . it's being hospitable."

CHAPTER 7

Preacher kept a close eye out behind him as he rode away from the Kiowa village. Once he left, he was no longer under Buffalo Bull's protection. He didn't think any of them would come after him, intending on lifting his hair, but he couldn't rule it out completely, either.

He pushed Horse and the mules to as fast a pace as they could stand easily and put distance between himself and the Indians. His backtrail remained empty all afternoon, and when he stopped to make camp that evening, he hadn't seen any signs of pursuit. Clearly, Buffalo Bull had kept any young hotheads in his band from going after the mountain man. The chief never would have said anything about Black Horn's people having those Mexican captives if he hadn't wanted Preacher to go after them.

Maybe Preacher would cause trouble for Black Horn. Maybe the Comanches would kill him. Either way, Buffalo Bull had stirred things up, yet his hands were clean.

Preacher had crossed the Arkansas River a couple of hours before he stopped for the night. He was well south of the Santa Fe Trail by now and into the dry stretch through which the Cimarron route ran. Unless it rained and left some puddles, he wouldn't come across any more water until he reached the Cimarron River. Knowing that, he had refilled all his canteens when he crossed the Arkansas.

He made a cold camp at the edge of a bluff where a few hardy clumps of grass sprouted from the reddish, rocky ground. Horse and the mules cropped at it for a sparse supper. Dog went off in search of a rabbit or prairie hen. Preacher sat on a rock and watched the light fade from the sky as he gnawed on a strip of jerky.

The next day he pushed on and came to the Cimarron when the sun was directly overhead at midday. The river looked brassy as it flowed between rugged sandstone banks. Despite being red and silty, it was still water, and Preacher fashioned a filter out of a clean, homespun shirt and filled his canteens.

Then he continued south, not making camp until the sun was down. He knew that the next day, he ought to be in the area of Black Horn's village—*if* Buffalo Bull had been telling him the truth. Preacher had no reason to believe the Kiowa chief had lied to him, but he had a habit of not accepting the truth of anything until he'd seen it with his own eyes. That habit had helped keep him alive this long, so he didn't see any reason to change it.

Preacher didn't know where Black Horn's village was located, so as he continued south the next day, he kept a close watch on the countryside all around him. The terrain had been more rugged around the Cimarron River, but now it had flattened out again. As he estimated how far he had come, he decided there was a good chance he had left the United States and was now in the Republic of Texas.

A few years earlier, he had spent some time in Texas when that land was winning its independence from Mexico, but he hadn't been back since. This part was called the Panhandle, he remembered, not only because of its shape but also because it was flat as a pan—and most of the time as hot as one sitting on the fire. That was the case today as the heat built up the farther south he rode. He began taking more frequent rests so Horse and the mules wouldn't get too worn out.

In the early afternoon, he noticed dust in the air ahead of him, a thin but widespread cloud. As he came closer, he made out a large, sprawling dark mass at the base of the dust.

That was a buffalo herd, Preacher realized after a few minutes. Not one of the huge herds numbering in the millions that could take several days to stream past a place like an ocean of muscle, bone, and hair. This was a tiny bunch in comparison to those, probably only a few hundred.

The sound of yipping cries drifted faintly to the mountain man's ears. Those came from the riders who dashed around the outskirts of the herd on nimble ponies, firing arrows into the great, shaggy beasts.

That was a Comanche hunting party, Preacher realized, and based on what Buffalo Bull had told him, he strongly suspected that they came from Black Horn's band.

That was exactly what he had hoped to find, somebody to lead him back to the Comanche village where those three prisoners supposedly were being held.

Preacher reined in and waited where he was as the buffalo hunt continued. The herd milled around as more and more of them died, vaguely aware that something was wrong but not smart enough to figure out what it was. Eventually the smell of blood must have spooked them, because they stampeded off to the west. The Comanches let them go and got busy at the gory task of skinning and butchering the slain animals.

Preacher stayed close enough to keep an eye on what was going on but not so close that the Indians were likely to notice him. Those hunters probably didn't figure there were any white men closer than the Cimarron route, or beyond that on the main Santa Fe Trail.

By late afternoon, the warriors were on their way, dragging hides loaded down with cuts of meat behind their ponies. Often the village was nearby and when the hunting was done, the women would come out to deal with the skinning and butchering, but the fact that these men were hauling the spoils of the hunt back with them told Preacher the village was farther away.

People liked to talk about how the Indians used every bit of the buffalo in their day-to-day lives, as well as for food and shelter, but that wasn't strictly true. They used whatever they needed at that moment and what they could handle, and sometimes that meant leaving parts of the carcasses behind.

They hadn't left much today, Preacher mused, as he rode past the bloody remains.

He stayed back and followed the hunting party south across the plains. Late in the afternoon, the Comanches rode down a long, gentle slope into a broad valley. Preacher saw a twisting line of brush and scrubby trees in the distance that he knew must mark the course of a small stream. That was where the Comanche lodges were set up. On the far side of the valley was a line of shallow red cliffs.

Preacher would have to get a lot closer to find out if there were any prisoners in the village, but he couldn't do that while it was still light. He pulled back far enough to be well out of sight, unsaddled Horse but left the packs on the mules for now, and settled down to wait for dark.

In years past, during his periodic wars against the Blackfeet, he had acquired the reputation of being able to slip into one of their villages at night, slit the throats of half a dozen warriors, and get back out of the camp without anyone knowing he had been there until the bodies were discovered the next morning. This made his enemies fear him on a supernatural level and prompted them to dub him the Ghost Killer, to go along with his earlier nickname the White Wolf.

He wasn't out to kill any of Black Horn's Comanche tonight, but he did want to know if Alita Montez and the two servants were there. And if not, were there other captives in the village?

Once the sun slipped below the western horizon, night fell quickly. Preacher waited while the sky turned a deep blue and then black, with stars popping out across the heavens. The moon hadn't risen yet, so shadows lay thickly across the landscape. When Preacher checked, fires still burned in the Comanche village, but they appeared to be dying down for the night.

He traded his boots for high-topped moccasins and saddled Horse, just in case he needed to light a shuck in a hurry. The big stallion would gallop to him like a streak of lightning if he whistled.

"Stay with Horse," he told Dog. The big cur whined. "I know, you want to come with me and help with whatever I'm doin'. But you can help me more by stayin' here."

He lashed his hat to Horse's saddle and then trotted silently down the slope into the valley, toward the Comanche village.

As he approached, he saw a few people still moving

around, dark shapes passing between him and the fires. He dropped to a knee near one of the tepees and listened intently. He heard a few people talking quietly, and snores already came from some of the lodges. The village was settling down for a peaceful night.

Preacher didn't want to do anything to disrupt that. Not just yet, anyway.

He took the flintlock pistols from behind his belt and tucked them away at the small of his back, then stretched out on his belly and crawled between two of the tepees. He stopped when he was in position to have a good view of most of the lodges and lay there in the almost impenetrable darkness, watching and listening.

A few warriors walked back into the village, probably returning from checking on the horse herd. From time to time one of the women left her lodge, bound on some errand or other, and came back a few minutes later. An elderly woman with an armful of broken branches moved around the village, pausing by each of the fires to lay a stack of wood nearby so it would be there in the morning to use as fuel when the flames were rekindled to ward off the early chill.

When she had laid out all the branches she carried, she turned and motioned to someone following her. Preacher's jaw tightened as he watched a slender figure shuffle forward into the faint glow cast by the almost-dead fires.

The newcomer was a young woman who also carried an armful of branches. She wore a black split riding skirt and a dark red shirt, both of them ragged, dirty, and much the worse for wear. Her black hair was twisted in ratty braids that fell over her shoulders. At first glance, she might have been mistaken for a Comanche, but the shape of her face told Preacher that she wasn't an Indian. It was much more likely she was Mexican.

Preacher had no way of knowing if the girl was Alita Montez. She might be, but it was possible the Comanches had stolen her away from some family across the border in Nuevo Mexico, or from some travelers who had strayed foolishly into Comancheria, as they called the region where they ruled supreme.

But the mountain man's instinct told him there was a good chance he was looking at Alita. He was going to find out.

The old woman roughly took some of the branches from the girl. As she did, the rest of the branches slipped out of the girl's arms and tumbled to the ground. The old woman hissed a reprimand at the girl for being clumsy and started slashing at her with one of the branches. The girl hunched her shoulders, lowered her head, and took the punishment as the old woman continued hitting her on the back and shoulders. She must have been through a lot in her captivity to be cowed like that.

When the old woman stopped hitting her after a few moments, the girl hastily gathered up the branches she had dropped. She followed the old woman as they finished their circuit of the camp, getting the fires ready for the next morning. Then the two of them went into one of the lodges.

Preacher made a mental note of that lodge's location. He was pretty sure Black Horn had given the prisoner to the old woman as a slave, so that was where the mountain man would find her later. And although judging by what Preacher had just witnessed, her existence had to be a very unpleasant one, it was probably the best the girl could have hoped for when she was captured. At least she hadn't been given to one of the warriors as a wife.

Preacher spied on the village for another hour, until no one was moving around anymore. He backed out, still on his belly. When he was far enough away, he stood up and headed back to the place where he had left Horse, Dog, and the mules.

He wasn't ready to make his move yet, so he unsaddled Horse again and removed the packs from the mules. He took a coil of rope from one of the packs, cut off some pieces, and fashioned a couple of crude hackamores. Then he stretched out in his bedroll to get some sleep. He had always possessed the knack of waking up whenever he wanted to, and he knew that ability wouldn't fail him now.

It didn't. He awoke several hours later, when a faint gray tinge of false dawn hung in the eastern sky. This was the time of night when people were at their lowest ebb and slept the deepest. There was a good reason military commanders often launched their attacks at this time. That was when they were mostly likely to take the enemy by surprise.

He saddled Horse, put the packs on the mules, and led the animals down the slope, closer to the village. He left the mules cropping at some grass, knowing that they wouldn't stray far from the spot. Taking Horse with him, he stealthily approached the village and circled it, taking the gentle night breeze into account as he came closer to the pony herd. He didn't want them scenting Horse and causing a commotion. The stallion smelled the ponies and made a little snuffling sound, but all Preacher had to do was say, "Shhh," and he quieted down.

As he came up to the ponies, he took out the hack-amores he had made and catfooted closer. He began talking in a low, calm voice. Several of the ponies pricked up their ears and moved away a few steps, but as Preacher continued soothing them, he was able to approach until he could slip one of the hackamores over a pony's nose.

This was the sort of headgear they were used to, so the pony didn't spook. He allowed Preacher to lead him over to one of the other ponies, and in a matter of seconds, the mountain man had a hackamore on that one, too. He took them back to where he had left Horse, tied the ponies together with a short length of rope, then tied a lead rope from that to Horse's saddle.

Preacher swung up onto the stallion and rode around to the far side of the Comanche pony herd, leading the two he had bridled. As he started to crowd in on the ponies, he took off his hat, slapped it sharply on the rump of one of the animals, and let out a high-pitched whoop. He drove Horse forward into them, striking left and right with the hat as he continued to caterwaul.

The ponies panicked, just as Preacher expected, and with shrill whinnies ripping through the early morning stillness, they stampeded straight for the village.

CHAPTER 8

Preacher charged after the ponies as they bolted. His yelling and the drumming rumble of hoofbeats roused some of the sleeping Comanches. Several warriors rushed out of their tepees to see what was going on, shouting questions at each other as they ran around aimlessly.

Then Preacher heard yells of alarm as the men had to dive for cover to avoid being trampled by the out-of-control ponies. Some of the panic-stricken animals rammed into tepees and toppled them.

Preacher headed for the lodge he had seen the captive enter with the old woman the previous night. When he reached it, he swung down from the saddle before Horse had stopped completely. He knew the stallion would stay right where he dropped the reins, and since the two ponies were attached by the lead rope, they couldn't run off. Calling "Guard!" to Dog, he ran to the canvas flap over the tepee's entrance and thrust it aside.

He took a chance and called, "Señorita Montez! Alita Montez! I'm a friend!"

Since she lived in Santa Fe, where there were a lot of American inhabitants, her father was in business with an

American, and she was engaged to marry an American, he figured there was a pretty good chance the girl spoke English. If she actually *was* Alita Montez, that is.

"Oh!" The gasped exclamation came from his left and made him think he had guessed correctly.

From his right came a shriek of fury. It was almost pitch dark in here, but Preacher heard footsteps rushing at him and knew the old woman was attacking. Something swished in the air.

He ducked under the club or knife or whatever it was and stepped forward. The old woman blundered into him. He wrapped his arms around her scrawny waist and picked her up.

"Alita! My horse is outside! Mount up!"

He heard the girl hurry past him. Turning as the old woman squirmed and fought in his grip, he kicked around until he felt a pile of buffalo robes and dropped her on it so the robes would cushion her fall. Then he ran after the prisoner.

She hadn't gotten on Horse like he had told her, but she stood beside the stallion with a hand on the saddle.

"Get on, señor, and I will ride behind you!"

That was probably best. Preacher got his foot in the stirrup and pulled himself up, then extended his left hand to the girl. She grasped his wrist with both hands, and he clamped his fingers around one of her wrists. It was no strain for his powerful muscles to haul her up behind him. She was on the petite side.

The pony stampede had moved on past the village, but things were still pretty chaotic around them with men running and yelling. It was dark enough that Preacher hoped nobody would notice him and the girl right away.

"Are there any other prisoners?" he asked as he turned his head toward her.

She slipped her arms around his waist and hung on, then replied, "Sí! Pablo and Laurenco! They are there!" She pointed at one of the other lodges. "You must save them!"

Preacher reined Horse around. As he did so, one of the tepees that had been knocked over by the stampeding ponies caught on fire from landing in still-hot embers. Flames shot up, casting a garish, flickering light over the camp.

At that moment, the old woman burst out of her lodge, shrieking at the top of her leathery lungs. Even with all the commotion going on, that drew attention. A warrior spotted Preacher and rushed toward him, yelling and brandishing a tomahawk.

Preacher let the Comanche get close enough to kick him in the chest. That sent the warrior flying backward. Preacher kneed Horse into motion. The stallion leaped forward.

Another warrior stopped twenty feet away and tried to nock an arrow onto the bow he held. He fumbled with it, as if he had been jolted out of a sound sleep and wasn't fully awake yet, and that cost him his life as Preacher pulled one of the pistols from behind his belt, eared back the hammer, and squeezed the trigger.

The pistol roared and bucked in Preacher's hand. The lead balls struck the Comanche just as he got the bow pulled back. The impact knocked him to the ground, and when he released the bowstring the arrow flew almost straight up, vanishing into the darkness.

Preacher never knew where it landed, because he was

already racing past the fallen warrior as the man thrashed in his death throes.

"Pablo!" the girl shouted as they approached the lodge she had pointed out. "Laurenco!"

Two men ran out of the tepee, moving with surprising spryness considering that one had white hair and the other was bald, but right behind them came another warrior. Snarling, he raised a tomahawk and was about to bring it smashing down on the head of one of the old-timers trying to escape.

Preacher had already tucked away the empty pistol and drawn the other gun. In this bad, shifting light, firing a shot in the general direction of the two elderly Mexicans was a risk, but he didn't have a choice if he wanted to save them. He hauled back on Horse's reins with one hand and thrust out the pistol with the other.

The gun roared and the tomahawk never fell as the man wielding it staggered. Preacher's shot had blown away a fist-sized chunk of his head. Momentum kept him staggering onward for a few steps before his nerves and muscles realized he was dead and pitched him forward on his face.

"Jump on those ponies!" Preacher called to the two old men, then repeated the order in Spanish.

As they hurried to do so, another warrior rushed at them from the side. Dog met that charge, bounding high to crash into the Comanche and drive him off his feet. The big cur's teeth flashed in the firelight as he ripped the man's throat out.

The two old-timers scrambled onto the ponies. Preacher hoped they could ride bareback, because there was no other choice right now. He whirled Horse toward the nearest opening between tepees and charged through it, calling for Dog to follow them.

Angry shouts rose behind them. Some of the Comanche were starting to figure out that the prisoners were being rescued. But they couldn't really give chase until they rounded up some of the ponies Preacher had stampeded. He hoped that would slow them down enough to give him and his new companions a reasonable chance to escape.

He headed north, back in the direction he had come from. As he rode, he turned his head again and said to the girl who was clinging to him, "You are Alita Montez?"

"Sí, señor! My servants are Pablo and Laurenco."

So she had defied her father's orders and come out here on the plains to look for the man she loved and intended to marry, refusing to believe that he might have turned outlaw. That was exactly what Armando Montez had worried about and Daniel Eckstrom had warned Preacher might happen.

"How do you know my name?" she asked. "Did my father send you to find me?"

"Never mind about that right now. Did you find Toby Harper?"

He felt a shudder run through her. She pressed her face against his back.

"No," she said, "but I . . . I have an idea—"

That was all she said, because at that moment one of the old-timers trailing them on the Indian ponies called, "Señor! Señor! They come after us!"

Preacher had been expecting that. He looked back and was relieved to see only a few mounted warriors galloping out of the village. The tepee that had caught on fire was blazing brightly now, and he thought maybe the flames had spread to at least one more of the lodges. The hellish light from the fires washed over the plains and silhouetted the men who were giving chase to the fugitives.

Preacher headed for the spot where he had left the pack mules. Getting the animals would delay their flight momentarily, and they couldn't move as fast with the mules, but he wasn't prepared to abandon all those supplies, either, not when they still had to cross miles of desolate plains to get back to the Santa Fe Trail.

The eastern sky was growing lighter now. True dawn was approaching. Enough of the grayness filtered across the landscape for Preacher to spot two dark shapes he recognized as the mules. He veered Horse toward them.

As he hauled back on the reins and brought the stallion to a stop, he turned to the two old-timers and asked, "Can you boys ride all right like that?"

"Sí, señor," the bald man replied. "Pablo and I have been riding since we were boys and never knew a saddle until we were grown."

The man spoke good English, although with a slightly different accent than Preacher expected. He shoved that thought aside for the moment and pulled his knife. He leaned over and cut the lead rope, then tossed the knife to the bald man and said, "Cut that rope between you and then each of you grab the reins of one of those mules."

Alita kept casting nervous glances over her shoulder. She said, "We must go. They're coming!"

"Just a minute."

Preacher threw his leg over the saddle and dropped to the ground next to Horse. He pulled his long-barreled flintlock rifle from the sling attached to the saddle. The sky was light enough now for a man with a good eye to aim. He turned Horse so he could rest the rifle on the saddle, pressed his cheek against the smooth wood of the stock, and drew a bead on the warrior who had pulled out a little ahead of the other pursuers.

Once he had his aim, Preacher didn't waste any time. He squeezed the trigger and the rifle kicked against his shoulder as it boomed. A cloud of grayish-white smoke gushed from the muzzle. Through that smoke, Preacher saw the warrior fling his arms out to the side and fall off the racing pony.

That sight made the other pursuers slow momentarily. It had been a long shot, and Preacher had made it perfectly. If he could kill one of them at long range like that, he could do it again, and all of them knew it.

At the moment, however, Preacher didn't take the time to reload. He put the rifle back in its sling, mounted up, and as Alita tightened her arms around his waist again, he said to the old-timers, "You boys ready to ride hard?"

"Sí, señor," responded the bald one, who seemed to be the spokesman for the pair.

"Then let's go!" Preacher said, and he kneed Horse into a run again.

CHAPTER 9

The Comanches were nothing if not stubborn. As the eastern sky turned rose and then gold with the rising of the sun, the warriors from Black Horn's village continued their pursuit. When Preacher looked back, he saw that the number of riders chasing them had grown. There were at least two dozen back there, he estimated, and their ponies were kicking up quite a cloud of dust.

That cloud was coming slowly but steadily closer, too. In their fury at having their captives stolen from them in such an audacious raid, the Comanches were pushing their ponies hard.

Preacher didn't ask that much of Horse, the two Indian ponies, and the mules. Right now, he was hoping to stay ahead of the pursuit long enough that the warriors' mounts would wear out and start to falter. Then he and his companions might be able to pull away.

As the morning wore on, he didn't see any signs of that happening. When they stopped briefly to let the animals rest and drink a little, Preacher watched the pursuit with narrowed eyes. His plan wasn't working. The Comanches were going to overhaul them.

Like it or not, that meant he needed to start looking for someplace they could fort up. If he could kill enough of the pursuers, they might abandon the chase. The Comanches, like other Indians, would weigh the price of recapturing the prisoners and punishing the man who had dared to invade their village. If they could see it was going to cost too many lives, they might turn around and ride away.

Unfortunately, there wasn't much in the way of places to take shelter here in the upper reaches of the Texas Panhandle. The terrain was flat and semi-arid, cut by an occasional dry wash twisting its way across the landscape.

The next time they came to one of those washes, Preacher called another halt. The dust cloud wasn't more than a mile behind them now. He sat in the saddle and looked both ways along the wash, which ran east and west.

Then, following his gut, he nodded toward the west and said, "This way." He nudged Horse into motion and rode down into the arroyo.

"What are you doing?" Alita asked. "We should keep going."

"They'll catch up to us a long time before we get to the Cimarron," Preacher said. "The country's rough enough around there we might find a good place to put up a fight, but we'd never make it that far."

"You believe we will have to fight, señor?" the bald old-timer asked. Preacher knew by now that he was called Laurenco. The one with wispy white hair was Pablo.

"I don't see any way of gettin' around it," Preacher replied. "I don't want to get caught out in the open, though."

"You think they will not see our tracks and follow us in this arroyo?"

"I know they will. I'm just hopin' we'll find someplace where there's a little cover."

Pablo said, "It is not likely."

"Maybe not, but as long as I'm drawin' breath, I'll keep lookin' for a way we can battle outta this predicament."

Dog walked ahead of the riders. Preacher and Alita came next on Horse, then Laurenco and Pablo leading the pack mules. Laurenco suggested, "We could shoot the mules and use them for cover."

"If it comes down to it, we'll do that," Preacher said.

If things got that bad, though, none of them would have much of a chance.

"We might have been better off you had never taken us away from the Comanche village," Alita said with a petulant note in her voice. "Our lives there were miserable, but at least we were alive. Now Black Horn will kill us all."

Pablo said, "You do not know that, señorita. Perhaps he will spare us and kill only this man who calls himself Preacher."

"You're welcome 'most to death for me tryin' to help you," the mountain man said dryly.

"We do not care so much for ourselves, señor," Laurenco said. "We are old and have lived our lives. But Señorita Alita has so many of her days still in front of her. Such misfortune never should have befallen her."

Since they still had some time before the Comanches caught up to them, Preacher said, "You came out here to look for your fianceé, didn't you, señorita?"

"Toby never would have done the things my father accused him of," she replied, angry now. "He is an honest man, a good man. If he was not, I . . . I never would have fallen in love with him . . . never would have agreed to become his wife."

"Did you really think you could find him after so much time had passed since the attack?"

Alita didn't answer that because Laurenco said, "Pablo and me, we are trackers, señor. No one in the rain forest was ever better at following a pathless trail."

Preacher turned his head to frown back at the bald man. "Rain forest?" he repeated. "What are you talkin' about?"

"We are from Brazil, señor," Pablo said. "We grew up in the jungles along the Amazon."

Preacher looked around at the sandy-bottomed arroyo and said, "This country's about as far from a rain forest as anybody could ever find. How in blazes did you wind up in Santa Fe?"

"We had the, how do you say it, the wanderlust," Laurenco replied with a shrug. "After seeing everything there was to see in Brazil, Pablo and I went to sea. We sailed around the world and wound up in Mexico. From there a series of circumstances—some comic, some tragic—led us to Santa Fe, where we have worked for Señor Armando Montez for the past twenty-five years."

"Longer than the señorita has been alive," Pablo added.

"We consider ourselves more Mexican now than Brazilian," Laurenco went on, "but the rain forests and the mighty Amazon will always be part of us, as well."

"I can understand bein' fiddlefooted," Preacher said. "Restless, I mean. I've been all over this country, and not that long ago, I was on an island over in the Caribbean. Never been to Brazil or anywhere *that* far south of the border, though."

Pablo said, "Perhaps you will go sometime, señor."

"Yeah, maybe I will."

"If you live through this day," Laurenco said. "Which is not guaranteed for any of us."

"The odds, they are against it," Pablo added.

Preacher couldn't argue with that. But he had faced bad odds before and was still alive and kicking.

As they rounded a bend in the arroyo, he spotted something up ahead that might make those odds just a little bit better.

The arroyo had deepened until the walls were close to twenty feet tall. The flash floods that struck this region from time to time had washed out an area along the base on one side, causing large chunks of dirt and rock higher on the bank to break off and fall. They had piled up to create a wall of sorts. There was space behind those chunks where the water had eaten away at the bank. The place was where the arroyo curved, so that had increased the flooding's effect.

This wasn't much in the way of shelter, but it was the most Preacher had seen so far since they'd fled from the Comanche village. He and his companions could crowd behind those fallen rocks. The arroyo was narrow enough that not all of the warriors could come at them at once, and the overhanging bank would protect them from above. The location on a bend gave them a field of fire in both directions.

Of course, once they took cover there, they would be pinned down. The Comanches could sit back and wait, starving them out. Preacher had enough food and water on the mules, though, to last for several days. Just how patient would Black Horn and his men be?

By now the Comanches couldn't be far behind. Preacher and his companions didn't have any time to waste. He heeled Horse forward.

"We'll have to turn the mules loose," he told the others. "There's not room for them back there. But we'll unload the supplies first and put them behind those rocks where we're going to take cover."

Horse would have to fend for himself, too, but Preacher wasn't too worried about the stallion. Horse wouldn't stray too far. He wouldn't allow the Comanches to capture him, either. Once he was free to run, even those speedy Indian ponies would be no match for him.

Preacher reined in. He would have helped Alita down, but she slid off Horse's back before he could do so. He dismounted and started unsaddling while Laurenco and Pablo began loosening the straps that held the packs on the mules.

"Can any of you shoot?" Preacher asked.

"We are crack shots, señor," Laurenco said.

"I'll give you each a pistol, then." The mountain man asked Alita, "Can you reload?"

"Yes, of course."

"She can shoot, too," Pablo said. "We taught her."

Preacher had extra pistols in his gear. He would give one to Alita and hope she wouldn't need to use it.

He put Horse's saddle behind the rocks and then helped the two old-timers with the supplies. They might be advanced in years, but both men were spry, wiry, and strong. They showed no sign of fear, either, and Preacher understood that. They had lived long, adventurous lives, evidently on their own terms from what Laurenco had said, and if those lives were to end today, they would know they were going out the way they would have wanted, battling to the end.

That was the way Preacher lived his own life.

While they were getting ready to defend the little nest in the rocks, Preacher listened with one ear for sounds of the Comanches approaching. He didn't know anything about Black Horn. The chief might have a cautious temperament and so would follow the arroyo slowly and carefully, wary of an ambush. Or he might be a firebrand, consumed by pride and anger and charging ahead to strike back at someone who had dared to defy him.

When the animals were unloaded, Preacher rubbed Horse's nose and said, "Get on outta here now, fella. You go on, and take Dog and those mules with you."

Dog whined from where he had sat next to Preacher's leg. Preacher reached down and scratched the big cur's head.

"I know you'd rather stay and fight. You and Horse can make it out here on your own if you have to, though. If we get through this, I'll find the two of you. You can count on that."

A while back, Preacher had traveled with an elderly Crow warrior named White Buffalo, who had claimed that he could speak to any animal and have them understand him. He knew what they were saying to him, too, or so he insisted. Preacher had seen some evidence that the old-timer wasn't lying, and he knew from his own experience that his trail partners seemed to know what he was saying and what he wanted from them. Now, Dog licked Preacher's hand and Horse bumped his head against the mountain man's shoulder.

"Head on out now," he said quietly. "Those Comanch' are bound to be here pretty soon."

With obvious reluctance, Dog and Horse moved slowly on down the arroyo, both looking back several times before they vanished around the next bend. The two mules and the Comanche ponies followed.

Preacher, Alita, Pablo, and Laurenco settled down in the rocks to wait. Preacher had his rifle and one of the pistols. The other three were each armed with a pistol. All the weapons were loaded.

Because almost anything was better than sitting there and brooding about the fate that might be closing on them, Preacher said, "When the three of you went lookin' for Toby Harper, did you have any luck?"

"I regret to say that we did not," Laurenco replied. "Even great trackers such as Pablo and myself have limitations."

"Too much time had passed," Preacher said.

Laurenco shrugged eloquently.

"But that does not mean we failed," Alita said.

Preacher looked at her, puzzled.

"If you weren't able to pick up his trail—"

"While we were prisoners in Black Horn's village," the girl said, "we heard talk about another band of Comanche."

"Not really another band," Laurenco interrupted. "A war party."

"A *big* war party," Pablo put in. "More than a hundred warriors."

Alita went on, "They stopped at Black Horn's village, and they had a prisoner with them. A white man, according to the gossip we heard."

Laurenco nodded and said, "More than one of Black Horn's people mentioned him. A white man with fair hair . . . like Señor Toby."

Preacher knew how Indians liked to gossip. His pulse quickened a little. This might be an actual lead to Toby Harper that would bring him one step closer to answering the questions that had brought him here.

If he wasn't about to be wiped out by Comanches, that is.

He shoved that thought aside and asked, "Where did this war party go?"

"Farther south," Alita said. "They took the prisoner with them. He had to be Toby. I just know it. And it was Twisted Foot and his warriors who attacked the wagon train and wiped out everyone else."

"Twisted Foot," Preacher repeated. "He's the war chief leadin' that other bunch?"

"So we were told," Laurenco said.

"And Black Horn's people had no reason to lie about it," Pablo said.

No, as far as Preacher could see, they wouldn't have. Twisted Foot might have all the answers he needed . . .

At the moment, though, it looked like he'd never get to look for Twisted Foot and that war party, because with shrill whoops, a dozen mounted Comanche warriors burst around the nearest bend and charged toward the rocks with bloodlust in their eyes.

CHAPTER 10

"Pick your targets!" Preacher told his companions. "Everybody aim for a different warrior. I've got the fella in front. Alita, hold your fire for now."

Smoothly, he brought his rifle to his shoulder and centered the sights on the warrior leading the charge. He didn't know if that was Black Horn, and there wasn't time to ask the others. And it didn't really matter, Preacher knew.

Whoever the varmint was, he was about to die.

The rifle boomed as Preacher stroked the trigger. The warrior rocked back as the heavy lead ball slammed into his chest. He twisted in agony on his mount's back, and that caused the pony to veer sharply to the side, into the path of one of the other charging warriors. The ponies collided, and both went down in a welter of dust and flailing legs.

Laurenco and Pablo fired, the shots coming so close together they almost sounded like one. A warrior toppled off his lunging pony, and another sagged forward and then slowly slid off to fall under the slashing hooves of several other ponies. More of the animals went down, whinnying shrilly.

That volley broke the back of the charge. Yipping and shouting, the other Comanche reversed course and pulled back around the bend.

"Are they gone?" Alita asked.

"For now," Preacher said.

He knew the retreat wouldn't last. He and the two old-timers had done enough damage to discourage the warriors for the moment but not enough to make them give up. The only real hope right now was that Black Horn was one of the men they had killed. Without the chief, the other Comanche might be more reluctant to continue the attack.

As Preacher reloaded the rifle, he said to Laurenco and Pablo, "Did either of you recognize any of those fellas we shot?"

"If you are hoping that one of them was Black Horn, I regret to say that is not the case," Laurenco replied. "He must have stayed farther back. This attack was just to test our defenses."

Preacher nodded and said, "I figured that much. Well, we'll get the son of a gun next time."

The ponies that had fallen had struggled back to their feet. They trotted off, around the bend, rejoining the others.

That left the bodies of four warriors sprawled in the arroyo. None of them were moving. Three had been shot, and Preacher supposed the fourth man had been injured in the fall from his mount. The man was either dead or unconscious, but either way, he was out of the fight, at least for now.

The tension was obvious in Alita's voice as she asked, "How long will they wait before they attack again?"

"I reckon Black Horn's lettin' us stew in our own juices for a while," Preacher said. "Try not to let it get to you."

To get the girl's mind off their predicament, he went on, "Tell me more about Toby Harper."

"He is a good man, as I said. Very smart and a hard worker. My father could not have picked a better man to help him run his business."

"How long has Harper been workin' for your pa?"

"Three . . . no, four years now. He began as a clerk in the store."

"Worked his way up, eh? That means you were pretty young when he started there."

Alita tossed her head a little as she said, "Old enough to know that I liked him. And he liked me, as well. But he was always a gentleman. Always."

Laurenco put in, "To be fair, Pablo and I saw to that."

Alita sniffed and said, "Annoyingly so, at times."

"What can I say, señorita? Your father charged us with ensuring your well-being. We would never neglect the duties with which he entrusted us."

Preacher said, "In spite of these two old pelicans, you and the boy must've spent enough time together that you decided to get hitched."

"Toby was a proper but persistent suitor," Alita said. "I chose him over others in Santa Fe who courted me."

"I imagine you had plenty of beaus, bein' as pretty as you are and havin' a pa with a successful business."

That actually brought a smile to Alita's face. "You believe me to be pretty?"

"I ain't blind. Some folks've been known to say that my eyesight's pretty good, in fact."

Laurenco cleared his throat and said, "You should not speak of such things, señor. The señorita is young enough to be your daughter."

"Oh, shoot, I know that," Preacher assured him. "I was just talkin'—"

With no warning, he snapped the rifle to his shoulder and fired.

"Everybody down!" he called.

On the other side of the arroyo, the Comanche warrior he had just spotted doubled over, dropped the bow and arrow he'd been about to fire, and pitched head-first off the bank. The man turned over in the air and crashed down on his back. He spasmed a couple of times from Preacher's rifle ball in his guts.

Several more warriors had climbed up there with him, though, and they were able to launch their arrows. The shafts whipped through the air, too close for comfort above the heads of Preacher and his companions as they ducked for cover. Some of the arrows struck the hollowed-out bank behind them and embedded there; others landed among the supplies they had stacked behind them.

"Watch out!" Preacher said as the warriors crouched back down out of sight. "Those varmints might be just a distraction!"

His guess turned out to be right. More mounted warriors tore around the bend and pounded toward them, yelling and firing arrows. The feathers on one of the shafts brushed against Preacher's cheek as it barely missed him.

He snatched up the pistol he had placed in front of him and aimed quickly. The gun boomed and one of the Comanche fell off his pony. Laurenco and Pablo had reloaded their pistols, and they fired again, as well. Pablo grunted and fell back a little, blood appearing on his sleeve where an arrowhead had ripped the cloth and grazed him.

"Pablo!" Alita cried in alarm.

"I am all right, señorita. Stay down. Protect yourself!"

The Comanches on the opposite rim sent another flight of arrows toward them. The missiles were buzzing all around like hornets now, and the riders were coming closer. They weren't going to have time to reload, Preacher knew, before the Comanches were on them. It was about to become a hand-to-hand fight with knives and tomahawks, and they were so outnumbered there was no chance . . .

A wave of gunfire roared from the rim above them. The Comanche bowmen on the other side fell, riddled by rifle and pistol balls. Some of the shots slashed through the mounted warriors, as well, driving men and ponies to the ground. Blood splattered across the sand. Dying screams, human and animal, filled the air.

It was a slaughter, but against all odds, Preacher and his companions were not the victims, as had appeared inevitable only seconds earlier.

Laurenco and Pablo hovered over Alita, who huddled between them. Preacher knelt nearby, watching the warriors fall under the unexpected onslaught. Several of the Comanches turned their ponies as sharply as possible and galloped off down the wash, yelling in a mixture of anger and fear. They would come back later to retrieve their dead, Preacher supposed, but he didn't expect their flight to stop any time soon.

The firing gradually died away. As the echoes rolled across the plains, a man called, "Hello, in the arroyo! Anybody alive down there?"

Alita opened her mouth to reply, but Preacher stopped her with an outstretched hand. He motioned for Laurenco and Pablo to be quiet, as well, and to stay where they were.

He stepped out into the open and looked up at the rim above the hollowed-out area. Three men stood there, and there had to be more where Preacher couldn't see them. At least a dozen guns had been firing only moments earlier.

"Howdy," Preacher said. "I'm mighty obliged to you fellas for steppin' into this little dustup like that. Seems you got here just in time."

"Better than too late," one of the men said. He stepped closer to the edge and leaned down to peer closely at Preacher. He was a tall, lean, lantern-jawed man with a tuft of brown beard on his chin. His buckskins resembled Preacher's but were greasier. Surprise was evident in his voice as he went on, "By the great horned spoon! Is that you, Preacher?"

Preacher had known there was something familiar about the man as soon as he laid eyes on him. He squinted and said, "Mallory? Styles Mallory?"

The man whooped with laughter, bent over, and beat both hands against his thighs in amusement.

"Who'd have believed it?" he said. "Out here in the dad-blamed middle of nowhere, hundreds of miles from any place, with nothin' around but rattlesnakes, tarantulas, and red Injuns, and who do I run into but good old Preacher!" Styles Mallory straightened and turned to his companions. "Boys, meet Preacher. Him and me have shared a jug at many a rendezvous!"

Mallory was exaggerating. He and Preacher had met three or four times, and while they might have passed a jug of who-hit-John back and forth—such things tended to happen a lot at the annual rendezvous when fur trappers got together—they weren't close friends. It would have been stretching things even to say that they were friends. They were acquainted, that's all.

But right now, if Mallory wanted to think they were friends, Preacher wasn't going to argue with the man. It was thanks to Mallory that he and the others weren't dead or prisoners of the Comanches.

Mallory leaned his head toward the man on his right and went on, "This here is Lupe Garza. And this other fella is Goose Guidry."

Garza was a bear of a man, tall and burly for a Mexican, with a bushy black beard. He wore a steeple-crowned sombrero with little silver balls dangling from the outer edge of the huge brim.

Guidry was even scrawnier than Mallory, a stick figure of a man, hollow-cheeked, with deep-set eyes that burned like he had a fever even though his face was sallow, not flushed.

Preacher didn't like the looks of either of them. As he recalled, Styles Mallory didn't have the best reputation in the world, either. Preacher had never had any trouble with him, but he'd heard other fur trappers speculate that maybe Mallory wasn't quite as careful as he should have been about taking furs from another man's traps. He had a hot temper and had gotten into a number of fights at various rendezvouses, as well.

But most men on the frontier had some rough edges about them. Many hadn't been good at following all the strictures of civilization. That was why they took off for the tall and uncut, the wild and lonesome places where they could live as they saw fit and not have to answer to anyone for it. Preacher couldn't begrudge anybody doing that, since he had lived his life the same way.

Besides, Mallory and the men with him had saved the lives of Preacher and his companions. There was no getting around that.

"What in the world are you doin' out here, Preacher?"

Mallory asked. "This is a hell of a long way from your usual stompin' grounds."

"I could say the same for you," Preacher responded.

From the corner of his eye, he saw Alita start to move and gave her a quick glance that he hoped would freeze her in place until he determined how many men Mallory had with him and why they were out here.

She was a headstrong girl, though, and before he could stop her, she stepped out into the open and looked up at the men in the rim, lifting her right arm to shade her eyes with her hand.

Doing so made her breasts lift as well, and push out more against the silk shirt.

"Preacher was trying to help me and my friends," she said. "He rescued us from the village of the Comanche chief Black Horn."

Lupe Garza's dark eyes bored in on Alita. Goose Guidry let out a low whistle of admiration. But Mallory's reaction was the one that surprised Preacher.

"Señorita Montez, is that you?" he asked. "We've been lookin' all over these blasted plains for you!"

CHAPTER 11

Alita took a step back as if she had been pushed. Mallory's words came as that much of a shock to her.

"How . . . how do you know who I am?" she asked.

Mallory grinned and said, "Your pa hired me to come out here, find you, and bring you back home to Santa Fe safe and sound."

Alita looked over at Preacher and said, "Just as Señor Eckstrom hired you."

"What was that?" Mallory asked sharply. "You signed on to look for this little gal, too, Preacher?"

Alita had spilled the important details already, so there was no point in holding back now. Preacher nodded and said, "That's right, only it was her pa's business partner who hired me, back in St. Louis."

Mallory nodded. "I reckon that makes sense. And you found her!" He frowned. "But where's the rest of your bunch? The Comanch' wipe 'em out?"

"There ain't nobody else. Just me."

Guidry laughed and said, "You came out here in the middle of Comancheria by yourself? Are you crazy, or were you wantin' to get your hair lifted?"

"Those sound like the same thing to me, amigo," Garza rumbled.

"I've got her, don't I?" Preacher answered curtly.

Guidry stroked his pointed chin and said, "She's standin' down there next to you right now, but that don't mean she's yours."

"I am no man's," Alita said coldly. Preacher kept his face impassive, but he wished she'd be quiet. Talking like that wasn't going to help matters.

Smiling, Mallory said, "Of course you're not, señorita. No point in worryin' about who found you, the important thing is that you've been found and you're safe. Preacher, why don't you and the señorita come on up here and join us? No point in you stayin' down there in that wash."

That had to be dealt with sooner or later, so it might as well be now, Preacher decided. He said, "We'll gather up our livestock and find a place where the bank's gentle enough to climb out."

"Sounds good," Mallory responded with a nod.

Preacher motioned for the two old-timers to come out from under the overhang. Then the four of them walked along the arroyo in the same direction Horse, Dog, and the other animals had gone. Preacher noticed that Goose Guidry sauntered along the rim in the same direction, obviously keeping an eye on them.

A whistle brought Dog bounding to join them, and Horse trotted into sight a moment later. The mules and the two Indian ponies followed.

As Dog ran toward the mountain man, Guidry exclaimed, "Good Lord, a wolf!" He started to lift his rifle.

Preacher still had a loaded pistol behind his belt. He drew it with blinding speed and eared back the hammer as he aimed at Guidry.

"Pull that trigger and it's the last thing you'll ever do," he said.

Guidry stiffened. Some color came into his narrow, pale face as anger bubbled up inside him. Clearly, he didn't like having a gun pointed at him.

But Preacher didn't like having anybody threaten Dog, either, especially not an obvious sidewinder like Guidry.

Lips pulling back from his teeth in a grimace, Guidry rasped, "Are you sayin' that ain't a wolf, mister?"

"That's Dog," Preacher said. "One of my trail partners. And you'd do well to remember it."

Guidry lowered his rifle and shrugged bony shoulders.

"If you say so. But *you'd* best remember I don't cotton to anybody pullin' a gun on me."

Styles Mallory came striding along the rim and said, "Here now, what's this all about?"

"Just a misunderstandin'," Guidry replied. His voice held a challenging note as he added to Preacher, "Ain't that right?"

"Yeah," Preacher said heavily. "A misunderstanding."

He lowered the hammer on the pistol and slid it behind his belt again. Dog came up to him and got a good head-scratching. Horse joined in, nuzzling against Preacher's shoulder.

With that reunion out of the way, the party moved on along the arroyo. Behind them, several men lined up on the rim and fired down into the wash with rifles, reloading and firing again a number of times. Preacher knew what they were doing.

They were making sure none of those fallen Comanche warriors would ever be a threat again.

As the gunfire died away after a few minutes, Preacher

and his companions came to another place where the bank had crumbled, but this one formed a sloping exit. They led the animals back out onto the plains.

This allowed Preacher to get his first good look at the group of men with Mallory. Even though he was grateful for the last-minute rescue from the Comanches, what he saw gave him distinct feelings of unease.

A quick count told him there were fourteen men in the bunch, counting his old acquaintance from the mountains. They were about evenly split: eight gringos and six Mexicans.

And all of them were hard-faced, dangerous-looking men. Just the sort someone would expect to venture into a wild land on a perilous mission.

They had half a dozen extra horses with them, as well as several pack animals. It was a large, well-armed, well-provisioned group.

Too many of them were looking at Alita with ill-concealed lust in their eyes, too. Laurenco and Pablo saw that just as well as Preacher did and bristled with offense.

"Take it easy, fellas," Preacher told them quietly as Mallory strode toward them. "They hired on to take the señorita back to Santa Fe safe and sound. Mallory will keep them in line."

He hoped that was true. He hoped Mallory would be *able* to keep the others in line.

"If you folks have been on the run from the Comanch' for a while, you must be worn plumb to a frazzle by now," Mallory said as he came up to them. "I figured we'd make camp and let all of you rest for a spell, especially the señorita."

"Muchas gracias, Señor Mallory," Alita said. "You are right, it has been a terrible ordeal."

Mallory turned to Laurenco and Pablo and asked, "Who are these two hombres?"

Laurenco drew himself up straighter and replied, "We are the señorita's chaperones and protectors."

Pablo looked equally stern as he nodded in agreement with that statement.

"Well, you two old fellas can rest and relax now, too," Mallory said. "We'll be lookin' after the señorita from here on out."

"We are very grateful for your assistance, señor," Laurenco said, "but our obligation to Señor Armando Montez will not be discharged until we have returned his precious daughter to him safely. We must perform this task *personally.*"

Mallory's smile didn't budge, but Preacher saw a flicker of annoyance in his eyes. Mallory said, "I reckon the important thing is that she gets back to Santa Fe safe and sound. That's all I care about. Come on. Let's find a place to camp." He jerked his head toward the arroyo and added, "The buzzards are gonna be gettin' mighty thick around here in a while, and I don't figure they'll want our company."

When they went to mount up, Preacher swung onto Horse's back and then extended his hand to Alita.

Before she could grasp it and let him pull her up behind him, as they had ridden earlier, Guidry came up on his horse and said, "The señorita can ride with me if she wants. I don't weigh a lot, so my horse can carry double without any problem."

"That's all right," Preacher said flatly. "She's used to ridin' with me, and Horse won't have any trouble carryin' us."

"You could let her decide," Guidry drawled. Preacher could tell that he was still angry about the earlier confrontation and was just spoiling for trouble.

"I will ride with Señor Preacher," Alita said.

"You sure about that? I'm a whole heap younger and better-lookin'," Guidry said with a grin.

Laurenco was mounted on one of the Indian ponies again. He moved the animal between Guidry's horse and Alita and said, "The señorita has told you what she will do."

Guidry's grin disappeared as he said, "Don't crowd me, old man. No dried-up lizard of a greaser's gonna talk down to me."

Lupe Garza had ridden up behind Guidry while he was talking. The big Mexican said, "You should have more respect for your elders, Goose."

Guidry's mouth twisted in a snarl as he turned his head toward Garza, but he controlled his angry reaction with a visible effort. Maybe that was because he was afraid of Garza, Preacher mused, or maybe it was because Mallory was riding up, too.

Either way, Guidry looked at Alita again and jerked his head in a semblance of a polite nod.

"I meant no offense by the offer, señorita. You're free to ride with whoever you please."

Alita barely acknowledged that with a nod of her own, then reached up to Preacher, who clasped her wrist and helped her onto Horse's back behind him.

"Looks like everybody's ready to go," Mallory commented.

"Yeah," Preacher said. "Lead the way."

For now, he added to himself. For now . . .

Instead of heading farther west or north, as they would have if they'd intended to proceed straight back to Santa Fe, Mallory led the group east, back the way Preacher and the others had fled along the dry wash. That move didn't take Preacher completely by surprise. He didn't like it much, either, but with circumstances the way they were, there wasn't much he could do about it.

They traveled several miles, putting some distance between themselves and the site of the battle with the Comanches, before Mallory called a halt again. By now the physical and emotional ordeal through which they had gone was really catching up to Alita. Preacher felt her slumping against his back and knew she was exhausted.

The place Mallory picked for a temporary camp wasn't much different than anywhere else on these trackless plains, with the exception of a small clump of mesquite trees. Bushes, actually, that didn't come up much higher than Preacher's waist. But they would furnish a little shade and some respite from the sun if Alita stretched out underneath them to rest.

The first thing she did after Preacher helped her down from Horse's back was sink to the ground next to one of the mesquites, but Preacher stopped her by saying, "Hold on a minute, señorita. Better take a good look under those bushes first. You wouldn't want to be sharing that shade with a rattlesnake."

"Oh!" she exclaimed as she leaned back from the

mesquites. "I . . . I should have thought of that. I've lived in the Southwest long enough to know better."

Pablo said, "You are too tired to think, señorita. No one can find fault with you for that."

Preacher dismounted, poked around under the bushes with his long-barreled rifle, then said, "I don't see or hear any of the scaly varmints. Go ahead and cool off and rest, señorita."

Gratefully, Alita moved farther into the shade, pulled her knees up, and rested her arms and head on them. Laurenco came over, knelt beside her, and held out a canteen to her.

"Drink, señorita. You must have water."

"What I must have is sleep," she said. "But water first, I suppose."

She took the canteen and tilted it to her mouth.

"Not too much," Preacher warned. "Water can be scarce out here. It's always a good idea to make it last as long as possible."

Reluctantly, Alita lowered the canteen and handed it back to Laurenco. With a sigh, she lay down on her side. Her shoulder brushed the branches and made the dried seedpods hanging from them rattle.

Mallory's men began to dismount, but they didn't unsaddle, which told Preacher that they didn't intend to spend the night here. Mallory was just letting everyone, human and animal alike, rest for a while before moving on.

And it was evident from what Preacher had seen so far that their destination wasn't Santa Fe.

After giving Horse and Dog a drink from his hat and taking a swig from the canteen himself, he walked over to where Styles Mallory stood with his arms crossed, gazing toward the mesquites where Alita Montez lay.

"You look like you got something on your mind, Preacher," Mallory said.

"I thought you said earlier that Armando Montez hired you to come out here and find his daughter."

"That's right." Mallory grinned. "It sure was a stroke of luck that we heard all that shootin' and went to see what it was about."

"Was it luck," Preacher asked, "or had you already located her and were tryin' to figure out a way to get her away from Black Horn's bunch when I came along to do the job for you?"

Mallory could have gotten offended at that question, Preacher supposed, but instead it drew a chuckle from the man.

"Well . . . I'm not sayin' one way or the other, you understand. Not sayin' we might've run across a lone Comanche buck out huntin' and, uh, *persuaded* him to tell us some things about prisoners Black Horn might have and that other war party that passed through these parts . . . but if it had been that way, it wouldn't have hurt anything to sit back and let you try gettin' away with the señorita and her amigos, would it?"

"Señorita Montez could have been killed while I was tryin' to get her out of that village."

"Everything in life's a gamble, ain't it, if you boil it down fine enough? Anyway, it all worked out, and the girl's safe." Mallory got a canny look on his face. "And if you're worried about the ree-ward for bringin' her back, why, shoot, I don't see any objection to lettin' you have a share of it. You did a good chunk of the work, after all."

"That's not what I'm worried about. Money's never meant that awful much to me."

Mallory shrugged and said, "Not everybody feels that way."

"One more thing," Preacher said. "I'm curious, Styles. If you're bein' paid to find the girl and bring her back, then why are you goin' in the wrong direction?"

Mallory finally looked sharply at the mountain man.

"Now, Preacher, you know the answer to that one just as well as I do. Señor Montez loves his daughter, I reckon, but that ain't the only thing out here that he's interested in. He wants to know what happened to all the gold that got stole, too, and he wants it back."

Mallory's lips quirked in what was either a grin or a snarl. Preacher wasn't sure which one, and he didn't figure it mattered.

"And I plan on me and my boys bein' the ones who find it."

CHAPTER 12

Preacher didn't see any point in arguing with Mallory just now, so he nodded and didn't say anything else. When they broke camp after an hour or so, he made sure that Alita was mounted behind him on Horse again.

He was going to keep her as close to him as possible while they were traveling with Mallory's bunch. Laurenco and Pablo must have had the same thought, because they rode right behind Preacher, protecting both rear flanks.

Preacher turned his head to Alita and asked quietly, "Are you feelin' any better now?"

"Perhaps a little. I could have stayed there for hours. And it was so nice to be able to rest without that witch Little Duck screeching at me and beating me."

"That's the old Comanche woman?"

"Yes. Black Horn gave me to her as a slave. Some of the warriors wanted me as a . . . a wife . . . but Black Horn refused. I think he hoped to trade me back someday and wanted to . . . preserve my value." Alita sighed. "Sooner or later, though, one of the warriors would have worn him down and gotten him to agree, or else he would have taken me as a wife himself. You saved me from that, Señor Preacher."

"Just make it Preacher," the mountain man said. "No need for the 'señor.'"

Alita rode in silence for a moment, then asked, "Why are we going in this direction? Is not Santa Fe the other way?"

"It is," Preacher said. "I reckon Mallory's got somethin' else in mind."

There was no reason not to discuss it with her. She was smart enough to figure out pretty quickly what was going on.

"He is going after Toby and the gold coins."

"Your pa wants that money recovered, and he wants to know what happened. At least, that's what his partner Eckstrom wants, and I expect they feel the same way, only your pa has you to worry about on top of the other things."

"I am sorry for the pain and upset I have caused him. But I could not just abandon the man I love, or have him blamed for a crime of which I am certain he is innocent."

"Did you really believe you could come out here into this big ol' heap of nowhere, just you and the two old-timers, and find Toby Harper?"

"I found out that he is probably the prisoner of the war chief Twisted Foot, did I not?"

Preacher frowned. She was right about that; there was no disputing it. But the odds had been so high against her . . .

Determination and good luck could go a long way toward improving those odds, though, and Preacher knew it.

Besides, right now they didn't know for sure that Toby

Harper was the prisoner Twisted Foot had had with him when his war party passed through Black Horn's village.

They rode on in silence as the afternoon waned. The dry wash petered out, and Mallory swung south with the others trailing behind him. Their course would take them well east of Black Horn's village, but Preacher kept a close eye out for signs of trouble, anyway. Being careful was the best way to stay alive out here.

They came to a small creek with barely a trickle of water in it, but any water was better than none, so Mallory called a halt.

"We'll make camp for the night here," he announced without saying anything about what his plans might be beyond that. Preacher intended to bring that up with him later, though.

He helped Alita down. Laurenco and Pablo had already dismounted and moved in quickly to stand on either side of her, keeping any of Mallory's men from approaching her. Goose Guidry saw that and scowled.

"Come, señorita," Pablo said. "We will find you a good place to sit down."

Preacher took charge of watering their horses and mules, then when that was done, he picketed the animals apart from the other horses. He didn't want Mallory getting the idea that their horses now belonged to the group in general. If it were up to him, they wouldn't even be traveling with Mallory's bunch.

If he had objected, though, there was a good chance Mallory and the others would have just killed him and the two servants. Then Alita would have been at their mercy. Maybe Mallory would have tried to keep her safe until they got back to Santa Fe, but he was just one man and there was a limit to what he could do.

While it was still light, a couple of the men got a small fire going so they could boil a pot of coffee and fry some salt pork. Despite the lingering heat of the day, the weary travelers welcomed the hot food and coffee.

After they had eaten, the fire was put out completely, covered with earth so that not even any embers glowed. The sun had set, and darkness would close quickly over the landscape. After the bloody defeat the Comanches had suffered that morning, it was unlikely any of them would be out and about tonight, but again, caution didn't hurt anything.

Leaving Alita sitting with the two old-timers, Preacher went over to Mallory and said quietly, "I reckon we'd best have a talk, Styles."

"I've been expectin' that," Mallory said with a nod. "Sure, come on, Preacher. We'll palaver."

They strolled out a short distance away from the camp, toward the arch of red and gold along the western horizon. When they stopped, they weren't far enough away to be completely out of earshot, but if they kept their voices low enough, they weren't likely to be overheard.

Mallory faced Preacher in the fading light and said, "All right, what is it you want to talk about, Preacher? Although I reckon I can make a pretty good guess."

"I'll speak plain. I know you want to find Toby Harper and recover that gold, Styles, but there's no good reason the girl has to go along. You could split your group and send some of them back to Santa Fe with her right now. Well, first thing in the morning, anyway."

Mallory grinned as he shook his head. He said, "You figure I didn't think about that? I want to keep that little gal safe just as much as you do. I'll speak plain, too. She's worth good money to me." He nodded toward the men.

"You think I'd trust any of that bunch to go that far with her? They're good boys for what I need 'em for, but they're only as civilized as they have to be. And even if those two old-timers went along, they wouldn't be able to protect her if things got out of hand. You know that as well as I do."

That was the bad part about it, Preacher thought. He *did* know what Mallory was saying, and like it or not, the fella wasn't wrong.

"Unless," Mallory went on, "you wanted to go back to Santa Fe with 'em. That would make things different."

Preacher had considered that. He figured he, Laurenco, and Pablo could keep Alita safe. But that wouldn't recover Daniel Eckstrom's money, and that was what he had agreed to do. Alita's life was more important than gold coins, of course, but there was Toby Harper's life to consider, too. If Twisted Foot's war party had attacked that wagon train, then in all likelihood Harper was innocent of any wrongdoing. There was a good chance he was dead, but he might still be a prisoner.

Taking Alita back to her father, rescuing Harper, and recovering the money all added up to one hell of a job— but Preacher had tackled plenty of big, difficult, dangerous jobs in the past.

They might have talked more, but at that moment, an angry shout came from the camp. Preacher and Mallory turned around in time to see a scuffle going on. A scarecrow-thin figure who could only be Goose Guidry lashed out at a smaller man and connected with a solid punch, knocking him off his feet. Preacher and Mallory started in that direction in a hurry.

Quite a few of the men had been sitting or lying down, resting, but they were on their feet now as Preacher and Mallory hurried up. Most held rifles or pistols pointed at

Laurenco, who had the pistol Preacher had given him aimed at Guidry. Pablo was the one who'd been knocked down. He appeared to be stunned. Alita knelt beside him, trying to help him sit up.

"Laurenco, hold your fire," Preacher said sharply. He knew that if the old man pulled the trigger, he might kill Guidry, but the others in the party would riddle him with lead.

"He attacked Pablo," Laurenco said, his voice shaking a little with rage.

"Only because the old buzzard yelled in my face and shoved me," Guidry flared back. "You expect me to just ignore that?"

"You insulted the señorita!"

"I said that Bardwell's got a fiddle in his saddlebags and I reckoned I could talk him into playin' a few tunes if she wanted to dance!"

"Señorita Montez will never dance with the likes of you," Laurenco said with a curled lip.

Mallory said, "All of you settle down, blast it! Put your guns away."

One of the men said, "Not as long as that *viejo* is pointin' his gun at Guidry, boss."

Calmly, Preacher said, "It's all right, Laurenco. No need to fuss over this."

"He knocked Pablo down," Laurenco said. "It is an insult to our honor."

Guidry sneered and said, "Well, ain't that just too bad."

"Come on, Laurenco," Preacher said as he put his hand on the old man's arm. "If guns start goin' off around here, the señorita's gonna be in danger, and you know it."

"Well . . ." Preacher could tell that his words had gotten through to Laurenco. "I would never do anything to endanger the señorita." He lowered the pistol. "But there still must be a reckoning."

Guidry spread his hands and laughed.

"Fine, old man. We can settle this without weapons, I reckon. Just you and me. Shoot, I'll take on both of you at the same time. I ain't worried."

Preacher turned toward him and said, "How about me, mister? I don't mind standin' in for these amigos of mine."

Guidry's jaw jutted out defiantly as he all but spat, "Fine by me. I'll fight anybody, any way they want. Fists, knives, guns—"

"Goose, shut up," Mallory interrupted him. "You don't know what you're doin'. This here is Preacher."

"So?" Guidry sneered. "You reckon I'm scared of him? He may not be as old as those two greasers, but he ain't no spring chicken, neither!"

Impatiently, Mallory grabbed Guidry's shoulder and shoved him back. He pointed a finger at the man and said, "I told you to shut up. You've pushed this far enough. It's over! And the smartest thing you can do right now is apologize for startin' a ruckus before it gets out of hand."

"Apologize?" Guidry repeated. "To those old trouble-makers?"

Preacher said, "How about this? Apologize to the señorita instead."

"For suggestin' that maybe we could dance a mite?" Guidry shook his head. "There was nothin' wrong with that. I don't have a blamed thing to apologize for."

Pablo had made it back to his feet. He stepped forward with Alita still holding his arm and said stiffly, "I was the one who was struck. It is up to me to demand satisfaction."

Guidry laughed harshly. "A duel?" he said. "You're talkin' about a duel?"

"When we return to Santa Fe. Then you and I shall settle this debt of honor, señor."

"You've got a deal, old man. I'll be glad to kill you . . . when we get back to Santa Fe."

"All right," Mallory said, "the rest of you go on about your business. The trouble's over. Right, Guidry?"

"Sure, boss," Guidry replied, but Preacher knew better than to believe him. He hadn't trusted Guidry before, and now he resolved to keep an even closer eye on him in the future.

As the group spread out around the camp again, Mallory called several names and told the men they would be standing the first guard shift. Then he said to Preacher, "The rest of us better get some sleep."

Before the mountain man could reply, Alita stepped up to them and said, "We have something to discuss first, Señor Mallory. I know you want to find the gold coins that were stolen from the wagon train . . . and I can tell you where to start looking for them."

CHAPTER 13

As Mallory looked at her with quickened interest, Alita went on, "First, though, you must agree to my terms."

"And what would those be, señorita?"

"You must agree to take me with you."

Preacher wished she hadn't brought this up right now. The next morning would have been soon enough to hash it all out.

That wasn't going to happen, though. Alita had seen to that.

"You've got my attention, señorita," Mallory said. "Why don't you go ahead and tell me what you know?"

Alita shook her head. "First, your promise."

"Sure," Mallory said easily. "If you want to come with us, I don't reckon anybody's gonna stop you."

Preacher managed not to snort in disgust, but he had to make an effort. Mallory wasn't going to admit that he'd planned all along to take Alita with them. Not that it made any real difference in the long run.

"All right," Alita said, nodding. "Before I was taken prisoner by Black Horn's band, a large war party led by another chief called Twisted Foot passed through the village. They came from the north, and they had a prisoner with them, a white man with fair hair."

"If this happened before the Comanch' captured you and the old-timers, how do you know about it?" Mallory asked.

"I heard several women in Black Horn's village talking about it."

Mallory nodded and mused, "Injuns like to gossip, all right. You think the prisoner this hombre Twisted Foot had with him was Toby Harper?"

"I feel certain it was. And that means Twisted Foot and his warriors were the ones who attacked my father's wagon train and killed all the other men."

"That would seem to follow," Mallory agreed. "And they'd be the ones who looted the wagons and stole that gold, as well." He stroked the tuft of beard on his chin. "I never heard tell of Injuns goin' in for robbery much, though."

Preacher said, "Some of 'em have figured out how much store white folks set by money, especially gold. Maybe he's got some way to use it in mind."

"Could be," Mallory said. "Anyway, it's a place to start lookin'. Señorita, do you have any idea where Twisted Foot and his war party were headin'?"

Alita shook her head and said, "I'm afraid not. From what I heard in Black Horn's village, I know they were going south when they left, but that is all."

Mallory grunted. "South of here is nothin' but miles and miles of Texas . . . most of 'em empty except for rattlesnakes and redskins and buffalo. Findin' Twisted Foot's bunch is gonna be a long shot, but we don't have any other trail to follow." He looked at Preacher. "Is that the way you see it, too?"

"It is," Preacher said. "We're bound to run into some other bands of Indians. Maybe some of them will be peaceful enough to point us in the right direction."

"All right. First thing in the mornin', we'll keep headin' south and hope we run into old Twisted Foot before we reach the Gulf of Mexico!"

Preacher didn't trust Guidry to set aside his grudge against Pablo until they got back to Santa Fe—if they ever did get back—and he wasn't convinced the two prickly old-timers wouldn't start some new ruckus. But at least the rest of that night passed peacefully, and in the morning the combined group rode south through the Panhandle.

Alita was mounted on one of Mallory's spare horses now instead of riding double with Preacher. She rode with Laurenco and Pablo on either side of her and Preacher right behind her.

She had undone the braids and combed her fingers through her thick, raven-black hair, then put it up in a bun and used a broken stick to hold it in place. Even though her golden skin had a coating of dust and grime on it and her riding skirt and shirt were ragged and torn, she looked appealing enough to make most of the men gaze at her with raw hunger in their eyes.

Preacher saw that, and he knew Pablo and Laurenco did, too. Mallory had promised he would keep his men in line, but Preacher had his doubts about how long that would last.

Either way, he would continue to be ready for trouble.

That was a long, hot tiring day, and so were the next several as the group steadily pressed deeper into one of the wildest, most remote areas of the Republic of Texas. They were so far from Santa Fe now that there was no longer any thought of returning there any time soon.

The terrain was uniformly flat and either sandy or rocky, with tufts of hardy grass and occasional stretches of scrub brush. On the fourth day after the battle with Black Horn's warriors, they came to a place where the land suddenly dropped a hundred feet or more, forming an escarpment that zigged and zagged across the landscape. The slope was rugged, riven with cracks and washed-out gullies, but gentle enough in places that Preacher and the rest of the group were able to ride down to the lower level, which stretched out in front of them seemingly endlessly, just as flat as the land above.

That escarpment was known in these parts as the Caprock, Preacher recalled. It twisted its way for several hundred miles, dividing the plains to the north and west from the rest of Texas. He had seen it before, but not in this exact spot and not for a good number of years.

As they continued southeast from the Caprock, the land would become more rolling and vegetation more common. Eventually, if they went far enough—and it was starting to look like they would have to, in order to catch up to Twisted Foot—they would come to the much more rugged, thickly wooded hill country northwest of Austin, the new settlement that had become the Republic of Texas's capital less than a year earlier.

A few times during the journey, Preacher spotted Indians watching them in the distance. He pointed them out to Mallory, who nodded and said, "Yeah, I saw 'em, too. I reckon word of us travelin' through these parts is startin' to spread. Sooner or later, we'll have company."

Supplies were starting to run low, but they had seen plenty of wild game. One morning Mallory suggested that they remain camped where they were, on the bank of a small creek, while a hunting party went out after fresh meat.

"I reckon you and I have the most experience doin' that, Preacher," he said. "We lived off the land in the mountains plenty of times. So why don't we go?"

Preacher frowned dubiously. The idea of leaving Alita here with the rest of Mallory's men, even with Laurenco and Pablo to watch over her, didn't sound like something he wanted to do.

Alita must have seen his hesitation, because she spoke up, saying, "I will come with you as well, Preacher."

Mallory grinned at her. "Have you done a lot of huntin', señorita?"

"No, but I think I might enjoy it."

Guidry said, "This ain't no pleasure excursion. You ought to stay here with us where you'll be safe, señorita."

Alita regarded him coolly and said, "I always feel safe wherever Preacher is."

Guidry made a face at that and spat. Alita ignored him. Preacher was glad she felt that way, considering that they hadn't really known each other for very long. That sort of trust was gratifying.

Laurenco said, "If the señorita goes anywhere, so will Pablo and I."

"Now, dang it," Mallory said, "if we're after meat, we can't have a big bunch of folks trampin' around over the countryside. We're liable to spook all the game."

Preacher didn't want to leave the two old-timers alone with the rest of the bunch, either. Guidry still held a grudge against them both, and he might stir up the others against them.

"You don't need to worry about these fellas," he told

Mallory. "They told me about how they grew up in the rain forest in South America. They've probably forgotten more about stalkin' game than you and me know put together."

That was stretching things a mite, of course, but it had the desired effect. Mallory looked at Laurenco and Pablo with newfound respect and said, "Is that true? I thought you boys was Mexican."

"We have lived in Mexico for many years, señor," Laurenco replied, "but Preacher speaks the truth. We come from Brazil."

"All right," Mallory said with a shrug. "We'll give it a try. I'll loan you a couple of rifles, in case you get a good shot at a deer."

Guidry didn't look happy about that. Preacher wondered if he had hoped to stir up more trouble with Laurenco and Pablo while Mallory was gone, then blame whatever happened on the old-timers.

With the issue of who was going settled, the group of five walked out of the camp a few minutes later, leaving the horses and the rest of Mallory's men there. Dog trotted along with them.

Since coming down from the Caprock several days earlier, they saw that the country had grown more hospitable, although it was still rather arid in places. They had spotted both white-tailed deer and pronghorn antelope, as well as a few wild turkeys, but hadn't gotten close to any of the animals.

They hoped to change that today. If they saw any game, they would be stalking it.

As they walked along, Mallory said to Alita, "I hear you're engaged to marry that fella Harper, señorita."

Laurenco said, "The señorita's plans are no business of yours, señor."

"There's no need to be unfriendly, Laurenco," Alita said. "Yes, this is true, Señor Mallory. Toby asked me to be his wife, and I said yes."

"Lucky man," Mallory said with a smile, then held up a hand as Laurenco and Pablo scowled at him. "I don't mean nothin' improper. I'm just sayin' that the señorita is a very nice gal, and any hombre would be lucky to marry somebody like her."

"Neither of us can dispute that," Pablo said.

"While y'all were jawin'," Preacher said, "I spotted a couple of pronghorn up yonder a ways."

He pointed. About a quarter of a mile ahead of them, a small ridge jutted up. At the base of that ridge, a pair of pronghorn antelope grazed. The wind was light and out of the southeast, carrying the human scent away from the animals.

Dog growled quietly. Preacher said to the big cur, "I know you want to go after 'em, fella, but let us take care of that." He looked at the others, especially Alita. "We'd all best be quiet now."

Paying close attention to the wind, they walked quietly toward the antelope. Pronghorns had very good hearing and also excellent eyesight. If either of the animals lifted its head to look in this direction, it was liable to see the humans trying to sneak up on them.

Preacher and Mallory were good shots, but they were still too far away to be sure of hitting their targets. If they missed, that would be the end of this opportunity. The shots would alert the pronghorns, and they would be up and over that ridge in the blink of an eye. Preacher and his companions would never see them again.

They had cut the distance about in half when one of the antelope lifted its head. "Freeze," Preacher whispered. "Everybody stay as still as you can."

They all stood stock-still, but Alita was breathing harder than Preacher liked, maybe from the excitement and suspense of the hunt. Even though he knew it was unlikely at this distance, he worried that the antelope would hear her.

After a minute or so, the one that had lifted its head went back to grazing without ever glancing in their direction.

Preacher let out his breath and nodded.

"All right, slow and easy now," he whispered as he started forward once again.

They closed to good rifle range. Preacher and Mallory looked at each other and with gestures worked out that Preacher would take the antelope on the right while Mallory aimed at the one on the left. If they could bring down both animals, they would have plenty of meat to last them for a while. The men moved about ten feet apart and raised their rifles to their shoulders. They eased the hammers back to full cock, being careful that the clicks weren't too loud.

Before Preacher could squeeze the trigger, two things happened simultaneously: something hummed past his ear like a hornet, and a shot blasted elsewhere, probably fifty yards away.

That unmistakable hum had been a rifle ball, and he knew instantly that somebody had just tried to kill him.

CHAPTER 14

Preacher whirled toward the sound of the shot, but as he did, from the corner of his eye he caught a glimpse of the pronghorns bounding over the ridge and vanishing. They were gone, and now his attention was focused on whoever had just tried to blow his brains out.

He saw some brush in the area where the shot had come from. A thin haze of gray powdersmoke hung over the bushes. When they began to move, that confirmed the presence of the would-be killer. From the looks of it, the varmint was trying to light a shuck out of there as fast as he could, having missed the one good shot he would have.

He was about to find out what a bad mistake it was that his aim hadn't been better.

"Dog," Preacher said, "hunt!"

The big cur took off like a shot, racing low to the ground toward the brush where the ambusher had hidden. Preacher glanced toward his companions and said, "The rest of you stay here."

"I can come with you, Preacher," Mallory offered.

The mountain man shook his head. "Keep an eye on the señorita and her amigos."

He headed after Dog, his long legs carrying him quickly over the ground. The thought crossed his mind that Mallory might have been involved in the ambush. This could have been a way of getting rid of him. If that were the case, he might be playing into Mallory's hands by leaving him with Alita, Laurenco, and Pablo.

He didn't think that was true, though. He had caught a glimpse of Mallory's face when the shot rang out, and he had seemed just as surprised as Preacher was. Mallory might be a lot of things, but Preacher didn't figure that being a good actor was one of them.

Dog disappeared into the brush ahead. Branches waved wildly as he tore through the growth. Preacher didn't expect it to take long for the big cur to catch up, and sure enough, only a few moments had gone by before a startled yell sounded.

Preacher's heart slugged heavily in his chest as that shout was followed a second later by the boom of a pistol going off.

He didn't hear Dog yelp, though, so he hoped the shot had missed. He kept running. Branches crackled and clawed at his buckskins as he plunged into the brush. That obstacle slowed him down, but he steadily forced his way through the growth until it thinned somewhat and he was able to move faster again.

He saw a little knoll up ahead and climbed it with long-legged strides. Somewhere close by, a man cursed in a harsh, angry voice. Preacher reached the top of the rise and saw a man rolling around on the ground, wrestling with Dog. He managed to keep the cur's sharp teeth from tearing into his throat, which was more than a lot of men had been able to do. As Preacher watched, the man actually flung Dog off to the side and rolled after him before the cur could catch his balance and right himself. The man clawed a knife from his belt and raised it.

Preacher dropped his rifle and launched himself from the top of the knoll. He could have shot the man, but he wanted to find out what was behind the attempt on his life. In the dust and heat and flurry of battle, Preacher hadn't gotten a good look at the ambusher yet.

The mountain man crashed into him in a diving tackle, catching him around the shoulders. The impact drove the man to the side. He and Preacher rolled over on the ground. Both recovered quickly, came up on hands and knees, and surged to their feet.

Preacher recognized his opponent as a man named Carney, a member of Styles Mallory's party. He was tall and burly, with unruly black hair atop a rough-hewn face. Preacher had seen him talking to Goose Guidry on a number of occasions and supposed the men were friends.

While pursuing the man who'd fired the shot at him, Preacher had more than halfway expected that Guidry himself would turn out to be the ambusher. Now he figured there was a good chance Guidry had sent Carney after him.

Not that the motivation mattered right now, as Carney lunged at him, slashing back and forth with the heavy hunting knife he still held. Preacher darted one way then the other, and while Carney was a little off balance, he kicked the man in the belly and knocked him back several steps. That gave Preacher a chance to slide his own knife from its sheath.

"Don't know why you're doin' this, Carney," he said. "I thought you and me have been gettin' along all right."

"You set that dog on me!" Carney accused. "I thought he was gonna rip my throat out!"

In fact, Dog was waiting tensely nearby, watching for an opening to jump Carney again. His teeth were bared in a snarl, and his jaws dripped with anticipation.

"Dog, stay!" Preacher ordered. To Carney, he went on, "I only set him on you after you tried to kill me. That's what I want to know. Why'd you come after me like that?"

Carney's only response was to rush Preacher again. Sunlight flashed on the blades as they rang together, leaped apart, and then flickered forward again. It was as swift and graceful as any fencing match ever fought, and much more deadly. The slightest misstep or awkward stroke could mean instant death.

Preacher had fought many battles such as this, but chances were Carney had, too. The man didn't look like he was getting rattled as the fight swayed back and forth, each man attacking and giving ground in turn. Preacher didn't want to kill Carney. He still wanted the man to confess that Guidry had put him up to this. But he didn't know if Carney was going to allow him the luxury of that.

It looked very much as if this fight was kill or be killed . . .

Carney thought he saw an opening and darted in with a savage, gleeful grin on his face. The blade in his hand flashed at Preacher's face.

Suddenly the mountain man wasn't there anymore. He had spun away from the knife, and with a backhanded stroke, his own blade sliced deep into Carney's left side. Carney howled in pain and staggered back a step as he pressed his left hand against the wound. Blood welled between his fingers.

Preacher kicked him in the left knee, and since Carney was already leaning in that direction, when his leg buckled, he fell that way. He tried to push himself up with his right hand, the hand that held the knife, but Preacher's booted foot came down hard on his wrist, pinning it to the ground. Carney cursed through clenched teeth.

"Let go of it," Preacher said, "or I'll let you just lay there and bleed to death."

Carney's fingers opened. The knife dropped to the ground. With his other foot, Preacher kicked it out of Carney's reach. Then he stepped back and said, "Get up."

"I . . . I don't know if I can." Carney moaned. "You sliced my guts open!"

"You ain't hurt that bad," Preacher told him. "It's messy, but you won't die as long as that wound gets patched up. I'll see to that . . . as soon as you've told me why you tried to kill me."

"Because I didn't figure . . . I'd ever get a chance at that Mex girl . . . as long as you were around. I ain't afraid . . . of those two old greasers . . . but you . . ."

His voice trailed off, but he didn't have to finish what he was saying for Preacher to know what he meant. Preacher's reputation was impressive enough that most men—the ones with any sense, anyway—didn't want to get on his bad side.

"You mean Guidry didn't send you after me?"

"G-Goose? No, he didn't . . . know anything about it. I just slipped off . . . and followed you . . . on my own . . . Blast it, Preacher! My side hurts like blazes where you slashed me. You gotta help me!"

"What I ought to do is let Dog have you."

The big cur leaned forward and growled in anticipation at that.

"But I won't," Preacher went on. He sheathed his knife

and extended his hand toward Carney. "Come on. Let's get you up."

Carney took Preacher's hand, but then his treacherous nature came out. With the bloody hand that had been pressed to his wound, he struck upward in a vicious attack aimed at the mountain man's groin.

Preacher saw it coming and twisted aside enough to avoid the full force of the blow, but it landed with enough power to make pain shoot through him. Involuntarily, he bent forward. Carney lashed out with a leg and knocked Preacher's legs out from under him. He landed hard enough on his back to knock the air out of his lungs and leave him stunned for a few seconds.

Carney took advantage of the opportunity to scramble after the knife Preacher had kicked away. He scooped it from the ground and turned back toward the mountain man. He drew back his arm, ready to throw the knife.

A rifle roared, and Carney staggered. His arm didn't come forward. Instead, the knife once again slipped from his fingers and this time landed point first, digging the blade several inches into the ground. With a bloodstain rapidly spreading on the front of his shirt, Carney folded up beside the knife. His fingers clawed at the dirt for a moment before they relaxed, and the breath rattled in his throat.

Preacher turned his head and looked up at the top of the knoll. Styles Mallory stood there, slowly lowering his rifle. A wisp of smoke still curled from the muzzle. Alita crowded up behind him, and Laurenco and Pablo were there, too.

"I know you told us to stay back, Preacher," Mallory said, "but the little lady wouldn't hear of it, and it's a good thing. Carney can throw a knife plumb through a plank, and he's got good aim, too."

Preacher rolled onto his side and pushed himself up. He was still in some pain, but he didn't want Alita to see that. He said, "I'm obliged to you, Styles," even though he wasn't completely sure he should be.

At this point, he couldn't rule out the possibility that *Mallory* was the one who had told Carney to ambush him. Mallory could have shot him just to make sure Carney didn't reveal the plot to Preacher.

Maybe he was being too suspicious, Preacher mused, but he wasn't sure that was possible where Styles Mallory was concerned.

Alita was staring in horror at Carney's body. Laurenco put an arm around her shoulders and gently turned her away.

"Please, señorita, there is no need for you to look at such an awful thing. Come with Pablo and me."

As the two old-timers led her away, Mallory came down the slope and looked at Carney, too, shaking his head as he did so.

"Did he say why in blazes he tried to kill you, Preacher?"

"He claimed it was so he could have the girl."

Mallory frowned and said, "That girl's got to stay safe and sound until we get her back to her pa. He might not pay us the rest of what he promised if she told him she was mistreated after we got her away from those Comanch'."

"I was the one who got her out of Black Horn's village," Preacher pointed out.

"Yeah, but you know what I mean. We were the ones who pulled you out of that tight spot later on."

Preacher knew what Mallory meant, all right. Somewhere along the way, Mallory was going to double-cross him and try to kill him so he could claim sole credit for rescuing Alita. Preacher had figured from the start that Mallory was considering something like that. The slip Mallory had just made all but confirmed it.

Preacher pretended not to notice, though. Chances were, he wasn't in any danger from Mallory yet. Preacher was a mighty handy fella to have on your side in a ruckus, so Mallory probably planned to keep him around until they had found Toby Harper and recovered those gold coins.

Mallory went on, "You don't believe Carney was tellin' the truth?"

"He might have been," Preacher said. "I've seen him talkin' quite a bit to Guidry. I figured there was a chance Guidry put him up to it. When I threw that in Carney's face, though, he denied it."

"Yeah, I don't think they were good enough friends for that. Goose is proddy and hard to get along with, but I can't see him tryin' to pawn off his grudges on anybody else. When he's ready to settle things with you, he'll do it himself."

Preacher nodded. He turned toward Carney's body and said, "You plan to leave him here, or do we haul him back to camp and plant him?"

Mallory sighed. "Some of the boys might not take it kindly if we left him here for the buzzards and the coyotes, so I guess we'll have to take him back."

"Anybody going to be upset that you shot him instead of lettin' him kill me?"

"I don't think so. He didn't seem to be that close to anybody else." Mallory's mouth thinned to a grim line. "Anyway, it was my decision, and they all knew I was the boss when they signed on for this job. If they don't like it, they can take it up with me."

Preacher was nodding again when both men suddenly jerked their heads around at the sound of a shot from somewhere on the other side of the knoll.

CHAPTER 15

They charged up the slope and immediately spotted Alita standing with Pablo about a hundred yards away. Neither of them seemed alarmed.

Preacher didn't see Laurenco, but as he and Mallory hurried forward, the bald old-timer emerged from some trees carrying the rifle Mallory had loaned him. He waved at Preacher and Mallory, seemingly signaling them that nothing was wrong.

Preacher and Mallory reached Alita and Pablo at the same time Laurenco did. Laurenco waved toward the trees and said, "I saw a deer run in there and went after it."

"You get it?" Mallory asked.

"I did. Should we dress the carcass here or take it back to camp?"

"We'll dress it here," Mallory decided. "Good job, amigo. I reckon you really are pretty good at stalking game, like Preacher said."

Laurenco nodded in satisfaction. Leaving him and Pablo to look after Alita, Preacher and Mallory went into the woods to find the deer Laurenco had slain and carve as much meat off the carcass as they could carry.

"You don't have to protect me from the harsh realities of life," Alita called after them as they walked toward the trees. "I saw plenty of bad things in Black Horn's village."

"And if it was up to us, señorita," Laurenco said, "you would never have to suffer like that again."

Mallory had brought some canvas with him from their supplies. He and Preacher spread it out and piled meat on it from the deer Laurenco had shot. The animal was a good-sized buck, and they could eat off this bounty for several days.

They dragged this behind them as they rejoined Alita, Pablo, and Laurenco. Mallory said, "I'll get Carney and rig up something to drag him back to camp. Señorita, why don't you and the others go on ahead? You don't have to be around for this."

"Gracias. You are kind, señor."

Mallory grinned and said, "Well, don't go talkin' about that too much. I've got a reputation to maintain, you know. A pretty shady one, too, ain't that right, Preacher?"

"You said that, not me," Preacher replied. He wasn't going to disagree with Mallory's statement, though.

They started back toward the camp with Alita, Laurenco, and Pablo leading the way while Preacher brought up the rear with the load of venison. Mallory headed off toward the spot where they had left Carney's body.

Preacher knew the rest of the men would have heard the two shots, but spaced out as the reports had been, the men probably thought both shots had been taken at deer or other game. They wouldn't be expecting to find that their number had been reduced by one. Some of them might not take it well. Preacher could imagine Guidry using Carney's death as an excuse to start more trouble.

If he did, Preacher would deal with that when the time came.

They were within half a mile of the camp when a flurry of shots sounded up ahead. Preacher knew immediately that the others weren't shooting at game.

That was the sound of a battle.

He dropped the corner of the meat-loaded canvas he'd been pulling and told Alita and the old-timers, "The three of you stay here. Come on, Dog!"

The mountain man's long legs carried him swiftly toward the camp. Dog bounded ahead a short distance. The shooting had stopped abruptly after that first volley, and Preacher figured that wasn't a good sign.

He had to run through a line of trees before he came in sight of the camp. When he did, he stopped abruptly. The dozen men from Mallory's party were huddled together, surrounded by Indians. Some of the warriors had arrows drawn back on bows, ready to shoot. A few brandished old flintlock rifles.

One of Mallory's men had an arrow lodged in his shoulder. A couple of the others were helping him stay on his feet. All of them looked tense, angry, and scared—as well they should have been, since they were surrounded by enemies who seemed to be ready to slaughter them.

Preacher had stopped at the edge of the trees. Since none of the Indians had spotted him, he quickly eased back into cover. He estimated there were at least twenty warriors. Pretty high odds for four men to take on.

A frown creased Preacher's forehead as he considered the situation. He wasn't as familiar with the hairstyles, clothing, and decorations of the southwestern tribes as he was with those of the Indians who lived in the mountains and farther north on the plains, but even though at first glance he had thought these were Comanche, now something about them struck him as different.

There were other tribes that lived in Texas, and not all of them were as hostile as the Comanche. But even if these warriors belonged to some other tribe, they wouldn't take kindly to being shot at.

At least they hadn't massacred Mallory's men out of hand and seemed satisfied for the moment to keep them surrounded and disarmed. Preacher spotted a pile of rifles and pistols off to the side that the Indians had taken away from the group.

One of the warriors stepped forward and spoke to Mallory's men in a loud, harsh voice. None of them appeared to know what he was saying.

Preacher couldn't understand all of what was said, either, but he picked out enough words to know that the warrior wasn't spouting Comanche. That confirmed Preacher's hunch: these warriors were from some other tribe.

He had another hunch, and he was about to act on it when from behind him came a hissed voice.

"Psst! Preacher!"

He looked over his shoulder. Alita, Laurenco, and Pablo had caught up to him. Laurenco, slightly ahead of the other two, was the one who had gotten his attention.

"What is it?" the old-timer went on. "What's going on at camp?"

"Mallory's bunch is surrounded by Indians," Preacher replied. "One of them just warned them not to move or try anything tricky."

Alita stepped forward and asked anxiously, "Are these the Comanches we're looking for? The ones who have Toby?"

Preacher shook his head and said, "They ain't Comanch' at all. Lipan Apache is what I'd guess, based on where we are and what I heard that fella sayin'. I think they came to take a look at the strangers travelin' through their territory, then one of Mallory's men spotted them and took a wild shot at them. That set off the rest of the bunch. They're just lucky they didn't kill any of the Lipans."

"How do you know they didn't?" Laurenco asked.

"Because if they had, more than likely they'd all be dead by now, instead of prisoners," Preacher replied grimly. "Only one man's got an arrow stuck in him. It could've been a whole heap worse."

"What are we going to do?"

Preacher considered, then said, "The three of you stay here out of sight. When Mallory comes up, tell him to stay back, too."

"What are you going to do?" Alita asked. "You can't fight them by yourself."

"No," Preacher said, "but I can talk to them."

The three of them stared at him in surprise. Without waiting for them to say anything else, he told Dog to stay and then walked out of the trees, heading toward the camp with a bold and decisive stride.

The Indians spotted him coming right away and several of them exclaimed in alarm. Some continued covering the prisoners with their arrows while the others turned to face Preacher. They drew back their bows. All they had to do was loose the arrows, and he would look like a pincushion.

He didn't believe that would happen, but he was aware that he was betting his life on that hunch. He knew how curious Indians were, though. That was probably what had drawn them here in the first place. They would want to talk to anybody who walked so brazenly up to them like this.

Preacher lifted his empty right hand in the universal signal for peace. One of the warriors moved out slightly ahead of the others and studied him intently. The man was stocky and had a more elaborate arrangement of feathers in his hair than the others. Preacher suspected that he was the chief.

He wasn't very fluent in the Lipan Apache tongue, but he knew enough to say, "Greetings. We seek peace."

"Then why shoot?" the stocky warrior demanded.

"My friends were frightened. They believed . . ." Preacher searched for the words. "You came to attack them."

The warrior shook his head. "Why do white men come into our people's hunting grounds?"

Instead of answering the question directly, Preacher said, "You are Lipan Apache?"

The question surprised the man he was talking to. "You know our people?"

"I have heard much." Preacher was feeling a little more comfortable with the lingo now. "I know the Lipan Apache are fierce fighters but do not hate the whites."

A look of contempt came over the warrior's face as he said, "Some of these are Mexicans."

Preacher remembered hearing stories of how the Lipans raided Mexican settlements along both sides of the Rio Grande. In fact, their dislike of the Mexicans and the dictator Santa Anna had led them to consider throwing in with the Texans during the revolution a few years earlier, although they never actually had.

"These men come from Santa Fe, in Nuevo Mexico, far west of here. They are not the enemies of your people.

None of us are." Preacher played what he hoped would be a trump card. "We come in search of the Comanche, to do battle with a war chief called Twisted Foot."

The warrior stiffened. His jaw tightened into a hard, angry line. The Lipan Apache and the Comanche were enemies. The Lipans had roamed the Panhandle and farther north until the Comanche drifted south and began driving them off the plains and deeper into what was now the Republic of Texas. Like all the other tribes the Comanche had encountered, the Lipan Apache had not been able to stand up to their advance. However, their retreat had been marked by hard and bitter battles.

Preacher had heard men talking about that at Bent's Fort and elsewhere. The Comanche's establishment of their empire Comancheria was an epic, bloody story. Preacher didn't know where it would end. They had already clashed with the white settlers in Texas. Sooner or later, it would come to all-out war between the two sides.

But that lay in the future, and right now Preacher was concerned about the present.

"We know of this war chief called Twisted Foot," the stocky warrior said. "Why do you seek to do battle with him?"

"He has killed white men and stolen things that do not belong to him from a wagon train far north of here. He has a captive, a white man with yellow hair. Do you know anything of this?"

Preacher thought the warrior was going to answer him, but then the man shook his head impatiently.

"Too much talk," he snapped. "Your friends shot at us. They could have killed some of us."

"I apologize for that. They were frightened. They believed you to be Comanche." Preacher shook his head, like a parent despairing of a child. "They did not know any better. I give you my word it will not happen again." He gestured at the man who had the arrow stuck in his shoulder. "And you have already punished one of ours. Were any of your warriors hurt?"

The Lipan scoffed in contempt. "Your friends are not good shots."

Preacher had thought the same thing. In this case, though, they were lucky that they'd been spooked enough to miss.

"I hope we can make peace. My name's Preacher."

The warrior hesitated, then grudgingly said, "I am called Big Creek." He gestured toward the other warriors. "I am the leader of these people."

"It is good to know you, Big Creek. I would like to visit your village and speak with you about the Comanche and their prisoner."

Big Creek turned that idea over in his mind for a moment, then said, "These other men must stay here."

"They will agree to that."

"And I must have your word they will do no harm."

"You have it," Preacher said. "If you tell your warriors to lower their weapons and back away, I will talk to my men and make sure they understand."

After a second, Big Creek nodded curtly. He and Preacher walked toward the others together. It was obvious from their demeanor that they had reached a truce.

Big Creek stopped to talk to his men. Preacher stepped up to Mallory's men and said quietly, "All right, these Lipan ain't gonna kill you, which means you ought to thank your lucky stars their chief's feelin' reasonable."

Guidry—no surprise there—said angrily, "Those

redskins tried to kill us. They skewered Harlan with an arrow!"

"Only after you boys opened fire first. These fellas were just curious. They weren't lookin' for a fight."

"Then they shouldn't a'come skulkin' around like they did," Guidry responded in a surly voice. "What were we supposed to think when we spotted 'em sneakin' up on us like that?"

"I'm not gonna have this argument with you," Preacher said. "Get your wounded man patched up. Mallory will be back soon, and so will the señorita and the two old fellas."

"What are *you* plannin' on doin'?" Guidry asked.

Preacher nodded toward the group of Lipan warriors who had pulled back some while Big Creek talked to them.

"I'm gonna go have a parley with the chief and see if I can find out anything about Twisted Foot and that Comanche war party."

CHAPTER 16

The Lipan village was about a mile from the place where Mallory's group had camped. The lodges, maybe two dozen in number, were clustered at the base of a small hill. When Preacher walked up with Big Creek, he proved to be of great interest to the women, children, and dogs of the village. They all clustered around the tall, lean white man.

Big Creek sat down in front of one of the tepees and motioned for Preacher to join him. The mountain man sank cross-legged on the ground.

"It is said that Twisted Foot is a terrible chief who lives only to kill anyone who is not Comanche," Big Creek began without preamble. More of the Lipan Apache tongue was coming back to Preacher, so he didn't have any trouble understanding his host. "We have heard many stories about him but have never had to fight him. We have fought other Comanche dogs, though. There is a village a day's ride that way."

Big Creek gestured toward the south.

"But that's not Twisted Foot's village?" Preacher asked.

Big Creek shook his head and said, "The chief of that

band is called Broken Rock. He is bad, too . . . but not as bad as Twisted Foot."

"Do you know where Twisted Foot's village is?"

"Farther south. This many days' ride." Big Creek held up one hand with the fingers spread, indicating five. Then he added the other hand. "Could be this many."

Preacher took that to mean the chief really didn't know. Big Creek was just guessing.

"What about the prisoner Twisted Foot had with him when he came through this area a while back?"

For a long moment, Big Creek didn't answer. Then he said, "Some of my warriors watched the Comanche to make sure they did not travel toward our village. They saw the white man. Like you said, he had yellow hair on his head and his face. But that is all I know of him."

"He wasn't hurt?"

"Who can say? My warriors were careful not to get too close. But he was alive, they could tell that."

Preacher nodded. He didn't blame them for being careful. This band of Lipan Apache was on the small side. They wouldn't be much of a match for a big war party led by a chief with as fearsome a reputation as Twisted Foot.

As that thought crossed Preacher's mind, he went on, "What can you tell me about Twisted Foot? Where does he get his name?"

Big Creek looked at Preacher as if the mountain man were an idiot. He gestured toward his own moccasin-shod foot and said, "According to the stories we have heard, he was born with his foot twisted far to the side and down. It is a sign that evil spirits took root in him, even before he was born. But he has not let it stop him from fighting and killing." Solemnly, Big Creek added, "He is said to be very cruel, even for a Comanche."

When it came to cruelty, none of the tribes could hold a candle to some of Big Creek's Apache cousins who lived farther west, unless maybe it was the Yaquis across the border in Mexico. Preacher had heard about them but never tangled with them. For Twisted Foot to have the sort of reputation Big Creek was talking about, he had to be pretty bloodthirsty.

And that was the man, more than likely, in whose hands Toby Harper's life rested. *If* Harper was still alive. The more Preacher thought about it, the more he wondered if he ought to take Alita, Laurenco, and Pablo and head back to Santa Fe with them. He could deliver the girl safely to her father, and he could tell both Armando Montez and Daniel Eckstrom they should just forget about that stolen money.

If he tried to take Alita away from Mallory, though, it would force a showdown. Preacher was confident Mallory wouldn't let her go until he could deliver her himself and collect on the reward from her father—preferably without cutting Preacher in on it if he could get away with it. And Alita herself would never cooperate, as bound and determined as she was to find Harper. She had taken plenty of foolish chances already and was capable of doing it again.

So for the moment, until Preacher could figure out a way to turn things more to his advantage, he supposed the safest thing was just to go along with Mallory's plans.

"I appreciate your help, Big Creek," he said. "And I'm obliged to you for not killing those other fellas, even though you could have and they gave you reason to."

"My people would like to remain friends with the whites," Big Creek said. "As long as too many of them do not come with their tame buffalo and the thing that breaks the ground. Will you tell them not to do this, Preacher?"

Preacher knew the chief was talking about cattle and plows. He had seen how so-called civilization spread like wildfire in other parts of the frontier, and by now he wasn't sure anything could ever stop it completely.

But he didn't see how it would hurt to tell Big Creek what he wanted to hear, so he just nodded and said, "I will tell them, and I wish the same thing, my friend."

Preacher also promised Big Creek that Mallory's group would move on that day, away from the Lipan village. It was only early afternoon by the time he rejoined them, so they could still put some distance behind them.

The first thing Preacher checked was to make sure Alita was all right. He was relieved to see that she was sitting to one side with Pablo and Laurenco hovering around her, as usual.

Some of the other men glared at him when he walked up, looking even more unfriendly than usual. The sight of a long mound of freshly turned earth told him why. That would be Carney's grave. Judging by the looks Preacher was getting, the rest of the men blamed him for Carney's death just as much as they did Mallory, who had actually pulled the trigger. It didn't really make sense, but Preacher thought they acted like they blamed him *more*.

At least they had built a fire and were roasting some of the meat from the deer Laurenco had shot. Bellies full of hot food would help soothe the anger they felt.

Mallory came striding out to meet him and asked, "What in blazes were you thinkin', goin' off with those savages like that, Preacher?"

"The chief and me had come to an understandin' of sorts," Preacher explained. "I wanted to ask him about

Twisted Foot and that Comanche war party, and I figured he'd be more likely to talk plain sittin' in his own village instead of standin' around here with your boys and his warriors glarin' at each other, both sides spoilin' for a fight."

"Well, things *do* seem to have settled down a mite. Garza told me what happened. One of the fellas spotted a couple of Injuns lurkin' in the brush and figured they were about to pull an ambush. So he jumped up and took a shot, and that set the rest of 'em off. From the sound of it, they all missed—"

"And then the Indians rushed out and surrounded 'em," Preacher finished.

"Yeah. Harlan got that arrow in his shoulder when he tried to grab a pistol from his belt." Mallory spat. "He's lucky he didn't get it right through the heart."

"Yeah." Preacher added dryly, "From the looks of this bunch, I'd have figured they were better shots than that."

Mallory sounded defensive as he said, "Don't go underestimatin' these boys. They're good, tough hombres, every one of 'em. Those redskins just took 'em by surprise, that's all."

Indians nearly always took their intended victims by surprise when they attacked, Preacher thought. That was just the way it worked. And anybody who was going to survive for very long out here on the frontier had to be able to handle that.

Some of those fellas had spent too much time in Santa Fe's cantinas and brothels in recent months, he figured. They had lost their edge.

"I promised Big Creek that we'd move on, out of the Lipans' stompin' ground," Preacher said, "so after we've eaten some of that venison, we need to pack up and head on south."

Mallory's eyes narrowed. He said, "Are you givin' the orders now, Preacher?"

"Not so's you'd notice, but when we threw in with your bunch, I don't recall sayin' that you were in charge of me and those other three, either."

The two mountain men exchanged level stares for a moment, then Mallory shrugged.

"No need for us to wrangle about this," he said. "It so happens I agree with you. Best to move on. There's hard feelin's on both sides here, and it's a good idea to leave 'em behind. Did you find out anything about Twisted Foot from that chief, what was his name, Big Creek?"

"Some of them saw that war party moving through the area a while back. They still had the prisoner with him then. Fella with yellow hair and beard. It'd be too much of a coincidence if it was anybody besides Toby Harper, I'm thinkin'."

"Yeah, I agree," Mallory said. "Did he know where Twisted Foot's village is?"

"Five days' ride south of here." Preacher grunted. "Or ten. He wasn't sure. I don't figure he has any idea where it actually is, although he's probably right about it bein' south of here."

"So we keep headin' that way?"

"Seems like the thing to do," Preacher said.

Preacher sat next to Alita, Laurenco, and Pablo as they ate some of the venison. The meat was tough but not too gamy.

"I'm sorry it isn't better, señorita," Laurenco said.

"Much better than the scraps Little Duck threw to me back in Black Horn's village," Alita assured him. "Even with the hardships we have to endure, I'm happy to be away from there." She turned to Preacher and asked with a note of hope in her voice, "Did you learn anything about Toby when you visited that Indian village earlier?"

Preacher told her the truth. "They kept an eye on Twisted Foot's war party while the Comanches were passin' through these parts, and Toby was with them then, or at least a fella matchin' his description was."

"He was all right?" Alita asked eagerly.

"He was alive. That's all they could tell from a distance."

Alita's expression sobered. She said, "This was weeks ago, was it not?"

"Yeah."

"Then he may not . . . may not still be alive."

"I reckon you've got to prepare yourself for that possibility," Preacher said. "But he'd lasted for a while, and he wouldn't have if Twisted Foot didn't have a reason for keepin' him alive. Best thing to do is hope that hasn't changed."

"Yes. Yes, of course."

"We must all have faith, señorita," Laurenco said.

"You will see Señor Toby again, I am sure of it," Pablo added.

When everyone was finished eating, some of the men wrapped up the meat that was left. They made sure the fire was out, then they mounted up and headed south. Preacher thought they were lucky the Lipans hadn't demanded some of the horses as the price of being allowed to leave safely. Big Creek had seemed like a decent sort who really did want to get along, though.

Preacher brought Horse alongside Mallory's mount and said, "While I was at that Lipan village, Big Creek told me about another band of Comanch' who live a day's ride south of here. Chief's called Broken Rock. Evidently he's a bad sort, although not as bad as Twisted Foot. We'll need to watch out for them."

"Are there any Comanch' who *ain't* bad sorts?" Mallory asked.

"There must be," Preacher said, "but I'll admit I ain't ever run into 'em. Every one I've ever seen has wanted to fight, even the women and little kids."

"We'll keep our eyes open," Mallory said.

They traveled several more miles that day, until late in the afternoon they made camp again. Even with fresh meat, the mood was still tense and angry. As Mallory had said, Carney hadn't been all that close to any of the other men, but at the same time, he'd been one of them. Preacher saw Guidry talking quietly but intently with several of the others and had a pretty good idea what the scarecrow was up to.

He found Mallory and said, "I've got a feelin' that Guidry's tryin' to stir up a mutiny."

"I think you may be right," Mallory said. He stroked the tuft of beard on his chin as he frowned in thought. "I'd say I ought to just go ahead and kill him, too, but that'd turn the rest of 'em against me for sure." He shook his head. "Damn Carney for puttin' me in this spot."

"Thinkin' maybe you should have let him go ahead and kill me?" Preacher asked wryly.

"Too late for that now," Mallory said.

Preacher didn't know if he was joshing or not. And since he already expected Mallory to try to double-cross him sooner or later, it didn't really change anything.

Sooner or later, a showdown was coming.

CHAPTER 17

As always, Mallory posted guards to stand watch in shifts during the night. Preacher didn't fully trust Mallory or any of the other men in that bunch, so he, Laurenco, and Pablo took turns staying awake, too. They didn't let Alita know, because she was proud and stubborn enough to insist that she be given a turn at guard duty, too, and none of them wanted that.

The next day before they set out, Preacher caught a moment alone with the two old-timers and told them, "We're gonna be passin' through Comanche country again and might run into some of Broken Rock's warriors. Stay close to the señorita and keep your eyes open."

"Always, señor," Laurenco said.

As they pushed southward during the day, Preacher saw hills looming ahead of them in the distance. After traveling across so many miles of flat land, those heights looked bigger and more impressive than they probably were. Preacher would be glad to be among them. They weren't the mountains that he loved so much, but at least they were an improvement over those seemingly endless plains.

But they were also more dangerous in some ways. By

the middle of the day, the landscape had become more rolling, which meant that there were more places for enemies to hide. Preacher kept a close eye on the skyline, even though he knew that if Broken Rock's warriors were stalking them, the odds of spotting the Comanches were pretty slim.

After they had penetrated several miles into the hills, Mallory brought his mount alongside Horse as he and Preacher rode at the front of the group.

"Is the back of your neck startin' to feel a mite funny?" Mallory asked.

"Like all the hairs are standin' up on end?"

"Yeah, exactly."

Preacher nodded and said, "I've been feelin' that for the past mile or so."

Mallory rubbed the back of his neck, which he'd just been talking about. He looked from side to side and said, "I was hopin' we could slip past without anybody noticin' us, but those blasted Comanch' are out there, ain't they?"

"That's what I'm thinkin'," Preacher said.

"And there's not a thing we can do about it except keep ridin' and wait to see what they're gonna do."

"Nope. Maybe they'll decide there's enough of us, and we're well enough armed, that they don't want to mess with us."

Mallory glanced over at him and asked, "Do you really believe that?"

Preacher grunted and said again, "Nope. Not for a blamed second."

Mallory shifted the rifle he had resting across his saddle in front of him.

"Maybe I ought to ride ahead and scout a mite," he suggested.

"You'll lose your hair if you do. If there are any Comanch' out there, they wouldn't be able to resist a man riding alone. It's best we all stay bunched together as much as we can, even though I suppose that makes us a bigger target."

Mallory cursed quietly but bitterly and said, "I never dealt much with Injuns like these Comanche. I'm more used to Blackfeet, Crow, Shoshone, and the like. I've heard the Comanch' can ride and fight like devils, even more than the Sioux."

"I've fought 'em before, and I've heard plenty about them. There's nobody better at fightin' from horseback. Only ones who come close are some fellas called Cossacks, over there on the other side of the world in Roosha."

Mallory looked sharply at him. "How do you know anything about Rooshans?"

"I've palavered with quite a few fellas from Europe," Preacher said. "Wouldn't mind meetin' up with some of those Cossacks one of these days. They sound like the sort of hombres I'd like to know. Assumin' that I live long enough, that is."

"The way my nerves are jumpin' around right now, I'll be glad to live to see the sun set."

There were no real trails through this untamed land except for game trails, of course, many of them left by the buffalo herds that migrated down here every year, traveling from high on the great plains deep into Texas. Preacher and the others were following one such buffalo trail now, a wide area trampled flat by millions of hooves as it followed the easiest course through the hills.

When it entered a long, narrow, fairly straight valley that ran for a mile or more between two ridges, Preacher felt his instincts prick up even more.

"If this ain't a mighty fine place for a trap, I ain't ever

seen one," he muttered to Mallory as they continued riding forward slowly.

"I was just thinkin' the same thing. Maybe we should hurry up and get to those trees at the far end. They'd give us a little cover, anyway."

"If I was Broken Rock," Preacher said, "I'd have men hidden in those very trees. Then I'd send more warriors in from the ridges to close in behind us and drive us straight ahead."

"Well, then, what do you think we ought to do?" Mallory asked rather impatiently.

"I think we'd better back out of this trap as quick as we can," Preacher snapped as he drew rein. He didn't wait for Mallory to agree with him or discuss it further. He just wheeled Horse and called to the others, "Get back! Head back the way we came!"

All of them looked shocked. Mallory's men hesitated, as if they weren't going to obey any order Preacher gave.

Laurenco and Pablo reacted instantly, though, pulling their horses around. Laurenco reached out and grabbed Alita's reins in order to turn her mount, too. They dug their heels into the animals' flanks and sent them leaping back northward.

Preacher galloped past the other men. As he did, Mallory heeled his horse into motion and bellowed at them, "Don't just sit there! Go!"

Preacher heard hoofbeats pounding behind him as the men turned their horses and followed. Alita, Laurenco, and Pablo were still out ahead, although Preacher knew Horse could have caught up and passed their mounts with no trouble if he'd let the stallion have his head.

Movement to his left caught his eye. He glanced in that direction and saw half a dozen riders coming down the ridge as fast as they could. A quick look to the right showed him what he expected to see. More riders were galloping toward them from that direction, too, their swift ponies racing easily as they reached level ground. The bare, bronze chests of the riders confirmed that they were Comanche. Even though he couldn't hear them over the hoofbeats, Preacher knew they would be yelling and yipping in excitement as they tried to close in on their intended victims.

He looked back over his shoulder and saw Mallory and the others not too far behind. Beyond them, more warriors poured from the trees and joined in the chase. They had to be frustrated that Preacher had sensed their trap before they had a chance to spring it.

That didn't mean Preacher and his companions were going to get away. Their mounts probably weren't as fresh as those of the Comanches, and they had pack animals slowing them down, too. If they had to, they could abandon those pack animals. The Comanches might be satisfied with getting those supplies.

Preacher had a hunch that wouldn't be the case. Something told him that Broken Rock's warriors wanted blood.

They had still been close enough to the northern end of the little valley that the Comanches hadn't been able to close off behind them, as had almost certainly been the plan. As Preacher pulled up beside Alita and the two old-timers, he motioned for them to head toward a brushy hill about five hundred yards ahead of them. If they could stay ahead of the Comanches long enough to reach it, they might be able to take cover there and fight off the attack.

The only other alternative was a long, running fight, and Preacher was convinced they wouldn't win that in the end.

The warriors attacking from the flanks hadn't been able to choke off the group's retreat, but they were close enough that they started to fire arrows toward the fleeing riders. Preacher pulled Horse back a little, since he was confident Laurenco and Pablo knew to make for the hill and didn't need him to show them the way. As he fell back, he waved a hand to catch Styles Mallory's attention.

When Mallory looked at him, Preacher pointed to himself, then to the Comanche warriors to the left. He pointed at Mallory and then waved toward the Indians on the right. Mallory nodded curtly in understanding and veered his horse in that direction, pulling a pistol from behind his belt as he did so.

Preacher angled the other way and drew one of his pistols. An arrow whipped past his head. Bent low over Horse's neck, he charged at the warriors closing in on them.

The Comanches howled in fury as Preacher defiantly challenged them this way. More and more arrows flew around him. He was in pistol range now, so he raised the gun, pulled back the hammer, and squeezed the trigger as he lined the sights on a barrel-chested warrior. The pistol went off with a deafening boom.

The double-shotted load smashed into the warrior's chest and swept him backward off his pony. He landed hard, bounced once, and didn't move again.

Deftly, Preacher shoved the empty pistol behind his belt and pulled the other one. He and the Comanches were almost on top of each other by now. He saw a bronzed face twisting in lines of hatred before he shoved the pistol at it and fired again. The warrior's features disappeared in a red smear. He somersaulted backward.

Another warrior drove his pony in close and slashed at

Preacher with his bow, trying to knock the mountain man off the stallion. Preacher ducked under the sweeping blow and leaned to his right to strike hard with the empty pistol he still held. The gun crashed against the side of the warrior's head. Preacher felt bone shatter under the impact.

He swung Horse sharply away, and as he did, he saw Dog sail through the air in a mighty leap that sent the big cur crashing into another warrior. The Comanche toppled off his mount, and as he landed on the ground, Dog came down on top of him, sharp fangs ripping and slicing. The warrior let out a gurgling scream and thrashed his arms and legs as Dog tore his throat out. The cur whirled to look for another enemy.

Preacher saw one of the warriors drawing a bead on Dog with an arrow and flung himself at the man. Horse rammed hard into the Indian pony, and warrior and pony both went down. Horse reared up a little and brought his front hooves down on the Comanche's head, shattering his skull like an eggshell.

That old boy never should have threatened Dog, Preacher thought fleetingly.

Only one warrior was left in the bunch that had tried to close in from this side, and he whirled his pony around and headed to join his friends who were giving chase from behind. Preacher tucked the empty pistol away and took his rifle from the sling attached to the saddle. He lifted the long-barreled weapon to his shoulder and took aim.

The rifle roared and gushed flame. The fleeing warrior flung his arms out and pitched off his pony as the ball smashed between his shoulder blades and tore through his body.

Some men might hesitate at shooting an enemy in the back like that. Preacher figured that once some varmint had tried to kill him, he wasn't going to worry about *how* he sent the fella across the divide.

With no time to reload right now, Preacher hung the rifle back in its sling, called, "Come on, Dog!" and wheeled Horse to gallop after the others. As he looked across the valley, he saw that Styles Mallory was doing the same thing. Some of the Comanches Mallory had done battle with were down, but three of them were still on their ponies, racing after him.

Preacher grimaced as Mallory's horse suddenly tripped and went down. Mallory kicked his feet free of the stirrups and flew forward over the horse's head. He'd avoided the danger of being rolled on, but he was afoot with a trio of bloodthirsty Comanche galloping toward him.

Preacher turned Horse and yelled, "Stretch those legs, old son!" The stallion responded instantly and seemed to be flying over the ground, his legs moving in a gray blur as Preacher leaned forward in the saddle. Dog ran alongside as hard as he could, trying to keep up but falling behind the magnificent stallion.

Alita, the two old-timers, and the rest of Mallory's men had just reached the brushy hill where Preacher had instructed them to take cover. As Preacher cut across the valley toward Mallory, he was between them and the warriors giving chase. The forefront of the Comanche charge was about a hundred yards to his right.

This was going to be close, he knew. Already, some of the warriors were firing arrows toward him, but nearly all of them were falling short. A few came close, but not close enough for Horse to break his splendid stride.

Mallory's hat had come off in his fall, but he didn't seem to be hurt as he rolled over and came up on his knees with a pistol in each hand. He pointed the guns toward the warriors who had been closing in on him. They stopped and reached for arrows, obviously figuring it made more sense to sit off a ways and skewer him, rather than risk being shot.

"Come on!" Mallory shrieked at them. "Come and get it, you—"

His challenge trailed off in a burst of obscenities that failed to goad the Comanches into coming closer. But Preacher was still charging toward them, a fact that they seemed to have failed to notice.

That was unlucky for one of them, because Preacher pulled the tomahawk he always carried in his belt along with the brace of pistols. He drew back his arm and let fly. The tomahawk revolved swiftly through the air.

The throw was perfect, the tomahawk striking one of the warriors in the head just as he pulled back his bowstring. The sharp edge cleaved the skull and buried itself in the man's brain. He jerked upright, arched his back, and fell off his pony with the arrow unfired.

Their comrade's sudden and unexpected death alerted the other two warriors to the menace galloping toward them at breakneck speed. They turned away from Mallory toward Preacher, but that proved to be a mistake, too, as Mallory leaped to his feet and rushed them. Both his pistols roared. One of the warriors went down as blood and brains flew from his head.

The other Comanche had to fight to control his spooked pony. While he was doing that, Preacher dashed in, extended his left hand toward Mallory, and called, "Grab on!"

Mallory quickly stuffed his empty pistols behind his belt and reached up to catch hold of Preacher's wrist as the mountain man rode past him. Preacher clasped Mallory's wrist at the same time and grunted as he hauled the man up behind him on Horse's back. Mallory clamped his knees on the stallion's sides and got a grip on the back of Preacher's shirt to hold himself on.

Preacher pulled back on the reins and turned Horse to the left, intending to head for the hill where the rest of the party had taken cover.

But it was too late for that, he saw. Broken Rock's warriors had swept on past, and now they were between Preacher and the hill.

Four of the stragglers peeled off from the rest of the group and headed toward Preacher and Mallory.

"Blast it!" Mallory said. "We can't get to the others!"

"No," Preacher agreed, "and it looks like it's time for us to light a shuck outta here."

He turned horse again, called for Dog to follow him, and galloped east across the rolling landscape with the four howling Comanche warriors hot on his trail.

CHAPTER 18

When Preacher glanced back at the hill, he saw clouds of gray powdersmoke hanging over the brush and knew Mallory's men were putting up a good fight. He was sure Pablo and Laurenco were, too. There was nothing he could do to help them with so many Comanche warriors between him and them, but if he could get away from the ones pursuing him and Mallory, they might be able to circle around and get back in the main fight.

"I'm obliged to you, Preacher," Mallory said over the swift rataplan of Horse's hoofbeats. "Afoot like that, I wouldn't have stood much chance against those varmints on my own."

"You'd have done the same for me," Preacher replied, although he wasn't certain of that at all. He could easily imagine Mallory abandoning him and letting the Comanches do his dirty work for him.

Even carrying double—and both of them good-sized men—Horse's stride was steady and strong. The stallion's stamina had its limits, though, and Preacher knew he had already asked a lot of Horse. The Indians' mounts were fresher, and those ponies were wiry and resilient, too.

"Sooner or later we're gonna have to make a stand against those varmints," he told Mallory. "Better reload those pistols while you can."

"Good idea. Want me to reload yours, too?"

"Sure," Preacher said. "Let me know when you're ready."

Reloading while on the back of a galloping horse was a pretty tricky job, but Preacher had done it before and he knew Mallory was experienced enough to handle it, too. After several minutes, Mallory said, "All right, pass me one of your guns."

Preacher felt a little better when both pistols were loaded and charged and stuck behind his belt again. Reloading the long-barreled rifle was too awkward a chore for horseback, at least while the stallion was moving this fast, so that would have to wait.

Mallory tapped Preacher's shoulder, pointed ahead of them, and said, "Look over yonder! Some sort of ravine! Maybe we could get down in it and give 'em the slip."

Preacher looked where Mallory was indicating and saw the slash in the earth twisting a serpentine course. Treetops were visible in it, so it was wide enough for trees to grow. A creek probably ran through it during the rainy season.

Preacher didn't have any confidence that they could get away from the Comanches by venturing into the ravine, but maybe they could find a place to fort up, anyway. He had enough powder and shot that he and Mallory could put up a good fight.

And they were only outnumbered two to one, after all. The more Preacher thought about it, the more he felt like he and Mallory ought to be able to handle this.

He headed for the ravine, checked over his shoulder to see how close the Comanches were, and slowed Horse as they neared the drop-off. The ravine was twenty feet deep, about that wide, and Preacher's hunch about the creek was confirmed when he spotted a dry, rocky stream bed at the bottom.

"Keep an eye on those Comanch' and let me know if they get too close," he told Mallory as he rode along the rim. "As soon as I find a place where it's not so sheer—"

"Sorry, Preacher," Mallory interrupted, and Preacher knew instantly from the sound of his voice that he'd made a mistake by believing he could trust the man as long as they were fighting a common enemy. He tried to twist around and throw his elbow back to disrupt whatever Mallory was trying to do, but Mallory was quick and ruthless. The pistol in his hand smashed into the side of Preacher's head.

Pain and fire exploded through Preacher's brain. He felt himself falling. As he did, Horse reared up and whinnied shrilly. Dog snarled. A gun blasted. All that happened almost simultaneously. Preacher felt himself hit the ground, but only for a second. Then there was nothing but empty air underneath him again.

He barely had time to realize that he was plummeting into the ravine before blackness swallowed him up completely.

Something wet swabbed against his cheek. That was the first sensation he was aware of as he regained consciousness. Then he heard a low whine and realized that was Dog licking his face.

Preacher forced his eyes open and found himself looking into the big cur's anxious brown eyes from a distance of only a few inches. For a second or two he was confused, unable to figure out where he was or what was going on, but then the memory of Mallory's treachery and his tumble into the ravine flooded back into his brain.

He looked up and saw broken branches above him. That told him what had happened. He had plunged into one of the trees in the ravine and the branches had snapped under his weight. That had broken his fall enough so that it hadn't killed him.

Preacher quickly took stock of his situation, moving his arms and legs and then sitting up as Dog moved back to give him room. He had a number of aches and pains, but everything seemed to be working properly. Dog crowded in on him and licked his face again.

Preacher was glad to see that the big cur seemed to be all right. He remembered Dog's snarl, followed by the sound of a gun going off, and he'd worried that Mallory had shot his trail partner. Dog was in good shape, though, and obviously he had found a way down here into the ravine.

Then Dog turned his head sharply and growled low in his throat. That reminded Preacher of how they might still be surrounded by enemies.

His head had been ringing, probably from being walloped, but that faded and he heard gunfire in the distance. That would be the rest of Mallory's bunch, plus Alita, Laurenco, and Pablo, battling Broken Rock's warriors. Clearly, he hadn't been unconscious for very long.

He needed to get back to the others. He wondered what had happened to Mallory. It was unlikely that Horse would have allowed Mallory to remain on his back without Preacher. The stallion was a one-man horse and would tolerate others riding him only if the mountain man was on his back, too. So he'd probably bucked Mallory off, and the man had been left afoot again.

There was a good chance the Comanches had gotten him, Preacher realized. If that turned out to be the case, then Mallory had had it coming for the dirty trick he'd played on the man who had just saved his life.

If the warriors had seen Preacher fall into the ravine, they might venture down here to make sure he was dead. He needed to get back on his feet and see if he could figure out a way to get back to the others.

He stood up, feeling a few more twinges from sore, bruised muscles, and said quietly to Dog, "Show me how you got down here."

The cur turned, trotted along the dry stream bed for a few yards, then stopped and looked back at Preacher.

"Go ahead," the mountain man said with a small wave of his hand. "I'll follow you."

Dog started off again with Preacher behind him. Preacher had lost his hat in the fall; it was probably stuck up there in a tree somewhere. More than likely, his tomahawk was still lodged in the skull of the Comanche warrior he had struck down with that deadly throw. But he had both pistols and his knife.

Preacher and Dog went around several bends in the ravine. The banks got taller and were steep enough that they overhung the ground below. Preacher couldn't climb them. He thought about shinnying up one of the trees and trying to jump from a limb onto the top of the bank, but that seemed pretty unlikely to be successful. Dog had gotten down here *somehow* and found him, so he told himself to be patient.

That was difficult to do when he could still hear the

gunshots in the distance and knew Alita and the others were still fighting for their lives.

Dog stopped suddenly, whirled around, and growled as he looked past Preacher. Knowing that Dog must have caught an enemy's scent, Preacher crouched and turned swiftly, too, drawing one of the pistols from behind his belt as he did so.

A Comanche warrior stepped out from behind a tree. Preacher knew he hadn't passed the man, so the Comanche must have been stalking him for a while and now had closed to within good arrow range. He already had an arrow nocked and lifted his bow to pull back the string.

Preacher cocked the pistol as he raised it. He squeezed the trigger.

The hammer clicked down uselessly.

Blast Mallory's hide! Preacher realized in that instant that the man hadn't reloaded his pistols after all, only pretended to. Obviously, Mallory had already been planning to double-cross Preacher when he did that.

That thought flashed through Preacher's brain in a fraction of a second. In the next fraction, he flung himself forward and down as the Comanche fired. The arrow cut through the air mere inches above the mountain man's head as he dived to the ground.

Preacher surged back up and charged toward the warrior, but Dog was faster, flashing past him and leaping high to crash into the Comanche and drive him over on his back. The warrior dropped his bow and snatched at his knife as the big cur snapped and snarled at him.

Preacher got there a heartbeat later and lashed out with his foot. The toe of his boot connected with the warrior's wrist and sent the knife spinning away before the man could strike at Dog.

At that same moment, Dog got past the arm the Comanche had been using to ward him off. With the speed of a striking snake, Dog's jaws closed on the man's throat and clamped down, crushing his windpipe. The warrior writhed and jerked as Dog finished the job by tearing half his throat out in a spray of blood.

They weren't out of danger yet. Another arrow zipped past Preacher's head. A second warrior had come around the bend behind them in time to see Dog finish off this one.

Preacher dived and rolled to the side and snatched up the bow the first Comanche had dropped when Dog tackled him. He grabbed an arrow from the man's quiver and then it was a race to see which of them could get a shaft nocked first.

Although Preacher seldom used a bow, he was very good with one, and once he had acquired a skill, he never lost it. With blinding speed, he nocked the arrow, raised the bow, pulled back the string, and let fly.

The second Comanche was both fast and good, too, though, and he got his shot off at almost the same instant as the mountain man. Preacher felt the arrowhead graze his upper left arm as it went by, but it didn't penetrate his tough buckskin shirt.

The warrior reeled backward with Preacher's arrow buried in his chest. Preacher knew he had missed the man's heart, so the Comanche didn't die instantly. As the man staggered, he lifted his voice in a shrill cry that would alert any other warriors within earshot that he had found their quarry.

Preacher would have grabbed another arrow and planted it in the Comanche's body, too, but before he could do so, the man's knees buckled and he fell. When he collapsed

face first on the ground, that just drove the arrow deeper
into his chest. Preacher knew he wasn't a threat anymore—
but the warriors who had heard his cry would be.

Still holding the bow, he stripped the first man of his
quiver and slung it on his back. Then he said, "Come on,
Dog," and took off along the ravine in the other direction.

After a few more twists and turns, they came to a
narrow gully that branched off to the right and sloped
upward. Preacher figured that was how Dog had gotten
down here. He paused to consider whether he ought to
leave the ravine or stay down here and keep going. He
didn't want to get trapped, but as long as he was in the
ravine, Comanche warriors riding up above wouldn't be
able to spot him.

The sound of hoofbeats and harsh voices calling to each
other in the Comanche tongue helped make up his mind
for him. They were up there searching for him, all right. If
he came out into the open, they were bound to see him
right away. Even though a part of his brain was clamoring
for him to get back to Alita and the others, he let his instincts guide him and continued along the ravine, following the dry stream bed. Dog padded along behind him.

Even though Preacher was sore and tired and still a little
woozy-headed from being knocked out, he moved at a
good pace. At one point, he thought he heard warriors calling to each other far behind him, their voices a little hollow
from echoing against the banks.

That meant more of them were inside the ravine, too.
More than likely they had found the bodies of the two men
he and Dog had killed. That would just make them more
determined than ever to track him down and wreak
vengeance on him.

Preacher kept going. He didn't hear the riders above

him anymore and thought maybe they had moved off elsewhere.

But he didn't hear gunfire anymore, either. That made his jaw tighten and his lips compress into a thin, grim line. If there wasn't a battle going on anymore, did that mean the Comanches had overrun the defenders at the hill? Were Mallory's men dead now, along with Pablo and Laurenco? Was Alita a prisoner once more—or had she been killed in the fighting, too?

He didn't have any answers to those bleak questions, and he wouldn't until he eluded his pursuers and got out of this slash in the earth. If he could accomplish that, he was pretty sure he could find Horse. The big stallion wouldn't have strayed too far away, and if he was in earshot of Preacher's whistle, he wouldn't let anything on earth stop him from reuniting with the mountain man. Then Preacher could go in search of the others.

He pushed on, unsure if any of the warriors were still behind him. That question was answered when he heard a sudden howl and glanced over his shoulder to see that a couple of warriors had come around a bend about fifty yards back and spotted him. They raced toward him.

Preacher grabbed an arrow from the quiver on his back. He had only half a dozen of the shafts, but he wanted to use them if he could instead of firing his pistols, which he had reloaded while he and Dog were hurrying along the streambed. The sound of shots might draw too much attention.

The two Comanches split up as they pursued him. Preacher fired at the one on his right. The man tried to dodge the arrow, but it took him in the side, slowing him down. Preacher didn't think it had penetrated very deeply, though—not enough to put the warrior out of the fight.

The one on Preacher's left took advantage of the opportunity to launch a shaft of his own. It passed between Preacher's left arm and his side, clipping off a piece of fringe from his shirt as it did so. Preacher already had another arrow out and nocked. He drew back and loosed, and this missile flew true, thudding into the Comanche's chest. He rocked back, dropped his bow, and pawed futilely at the arrow's shaft for a few seconds before toppling over on his side.

The wounded man, even with an arrow in his side, managed to draw another arrow of his own and fit it on the bowstring. He tried to pull it back but grimaced as pain caused him to fail in that effort. Instead of persisting, he turned and dashed back around the bend before Preacher could launch another arrow at him. He shouted for help.

The mountain man turned and broke into a run in the other direction. If there were other Comanches around, it wouldn't take them long to come and see what all the yelling was about. With Dog at his heels, he charged around another bend.

Twisting and turning along with the ravine, Preacher fled. The fact that he was running away from trouble instead of charging straight at it grated at him, but at the same time, he had to be practical, at least until he found out what had happened to Alita and the two old-timers. He felt responsible for their safety. Fighting the Comanches when he was outnumbered and on foot wasn't going to help them.

He hurried along, keeping between the trees and the bank now so as not to be so visible, but then the ravine widened some and the trees thinned out. Preacher was in the open when he saw dirt clods suddenly rain down from the bank a few feet ahead of him.

He looked up just in time to see a Comanche warrior who had just leaped from the top of the bank hurtling down at him.

CHAPTER 19

The Indian's weight crashed on Preacher with such force there was no chance of the mountain man staying on his feet. He had caught a glimpse of a knife in the warrior's hand, so as he fell, he dropped the bow and flung up both hands to ward off the blade's thrust.

Preacher was on the bottom as they landed. The Comanche's knees rammed into his midsection and drove the breath from his lungs. He was half-stunned but had to force his muscles to work if he wanted to live. His left hand closed around the warrior's wrist and stopped the knife when the point was only inches from his throat.

His other hand slid along the man's arm and shoulder. He closed it into a fist and smashed it into the warrior's jaw. That knocked the Comanche to the side. Preacher heaved himself up and threw the attacker off him. Both men rolled and Preacher wound up on top this time.

He jabbed his knee into the warrior's groin and at the same time grabbed his wrist with both hands and twisted. As Preacher threw his weight forward, it drove the Comanche's own blade down into his chest. The warrior arched his back as his dark eyes opened wide in pain and shock, then dulled as death claimed him. His body sagged back to the ground.

Dog started growling. The Comanche's hand had fallen away from the handle of the knife buried in his chest. Preacher pulled the blade loose as he pushed himself to his feet. He listened and heard men calling to each other. Some of the voices sounded like they were down in the ravine while others were up on top.

All he could do was keep moving. He wiped the blood from the knife on the dead warrior's leggings, slid it behind his belt, and hurried along beside the dry stream bed.

He came to another gully like the one he had seen earlier. This one was choked with brush and dead wood that had washed into it over the years. The pile of thickly interwoven branches was at least a dozen feet tall and deeper than that.

Preacher stopped and looked at the gully for a long moment, then said quietly to Dog, "That's one of the snaki-est-lookin' places I've ever seen, pard, but I don't reckon we've got any choice. We got to find some place to hide before they find us."

He pulled some of the dead branches up to create an opening, then motioned for Dog to crawl up inside the pile first. He hated to make the big cur take the lead and possibly be the first to encounter any rattlesnakes or copperheads denned up in there, but he had to crawl in last so he could pull the branches back into place behind them and try to make it look like no one was in the gully.

Ahead of him, Dog twisted and squirmed and worked his way deeper. Preacher crawled behind him. When they had penetrated far enough into the pile that he couldn't see into the ravine when he looked back over his shoulder, he hissed at Dog, and the cur came to a stop.

Preacher moved a few more branches to thicken their concealment, then lay there, hearing his own heart slugging inside his chest and listening intently for any telltale sounds of their pursuers.

Minutes seemed like hours as they passed. A time or two, Preacher thought he heard voices, but he wasn't sure. Then he definitely heard horses passing by not too far away, but they never came too close and finally receded.

Then Dog started to growl. Preacher touched the big cur and the sound stopped instantly. Dog knew better; his instincts had just gotten the best of him for a moment. Both of them lay there, barely breathing, as harsh voices came from the ravine. Preacher understood enough of the Comanche lingo to know that two warriors were asking each other if they had found anything. Both men said that they hadn't.

Preacher was one of the best trackers on the frontier, so he had used all the knowledge at his command to try to *avoid* leaving any sign. Most Indians were pretty good hands at tracking, too, since hunting was so important to their survival, so Preacher knew there was a chance they would realize he and Dog were hidden in this gully.

If the minutes had seemed like hours earlier, the seconds now seemed like days as Preacher listened to the two warriors. They must have stopped right outside the gully mouth. They talked about how Broken Rock would torture the white man if they ever found him, since the white devil had killed so many of their warriors.

Then they said something that made Preacher's heart leap. He couldn't make out all the words, but he understood enough to know that Broken Rock had called off the attack on the rest of the group, and that the whites had fled back to the north. Before that, however, they had inflicted enough damage that Broken Rock had decided not to go after them, claiming that forcing the "invaders" to retreat was victory enough.

That meant there was at least a chance Alita, Laurenco, and Pablo were still alive, and Preacher knew he could find them again if he ever got out of this mess.

At last, the voices faded. The Comanche warriors moved on. Preacher breathed a little easier, but he didn't relax. Far from it. Instead, he maintained his vigilance for another hour after he didn't hear anything except the normal sounds of birds and small animals returning after the human searchers left.

He was about ready to risk crawling back out when he heard a slithering sound close by. He started to lift his head, then froze as he felt a weight on his left leg. It moved across that leg, then he felt it stretching across the right one as well.

There was no doubt in his mind that a large snake—probably a rattler—was crawling across his legs. As long as he didn't move, there was a good chance the critter would just ignore him and move on.

The trick was going to be not moving while a damn big snake crawled over him.

His jaw clenched so hard it seemed like his teeth might break. The snake was probably six or seven feet long, but it felt as if it took ten minutes for the sinuous burden to move across his legs. Finally the tail dropped off his right leg, and he heard a little rattle as it did. He'd been right about what kind of snake it was.

Preacher heard the varmint moving away through the brush. He let it get some distance between them before he said quietly, "All right, Dog, let's get outta here before something *else* comes along that'd sure like to kill us."

* * *

Half an hour later, Preacher put a couple of fingers in his mouth and blew a loud, piercing whistle that echoed across the rolling terrain around him and Dog. They had found another way up out of the ravine and carefully scouted around until Preacher was confident no Comanches were lurking in the area before he tried to summon Horse.

He waited a few minutes, then, seeing no sign of the stallion, he whistled again. Another couple of minutes went by. Turning to scan the landscape all around him, he searched in vain for what he wanted to see.

"Blast it," he said to Dog, "it looks like the big fella ain't around here after all—"

Dog's ears pricked up. The big cur was sitting down, but he leaned forward with a sense of eagerness about him.

Preacher looked the same direction Dog was looking. A familiar gray shape loped easily over the top of a ridge and started toward them. Relief flooded through Preacher.

A moment later, he felt surprise as well, as the two pack-horses followed Horse into sight. He wasn't sure where Horse had rounded them up or how the pack animals had avoided being captured by the Comanches, but Preacher knew better than to question good fortune. He was just glad to have the supplies back.

And very glad to be reunited with Horse, of course.

Dog let out a bark and ran to meet his friend. He dashed around Horse a couple of times, then fell in step beside the stallion as Horse continued trotting toward Preacher.

When Horse came up to the mountain man, he bumped his head against Preacher's shoulder several times in greeting. Preacher rubbed his nose and said, "It's mighty good to see you, old son." He didn't doubt for a second that Horse understood the sentiment, if not the words.

A quick check told him that the stallion was unharmed. Preacher patted him on the shoulder and went on, "I'll bet you bucked that varmint Mallory right off, didn't you? I wish you could tell me what happened to him. Did the Comanch' get him? I know you can't say, but I'm gonna figure that's what happened unless I find out different. Under the circumstances, he would've had to be one mighty lucky son of a gun to get away from them."

Even as he said that, an uneasy feeling stirred inside Preacher. Styles Mallory *did* seem to have an uncanny knack for getting out of trouble. It would be a mistake to assume that the Comanches had killed him, Preacher decided.

After petting Horse for a few more minutes, Preacher swung up into the saddle. With the packhorses trailing and Dog running ahead, he followed the ravine in its generally northward course toward the hill where Alita and the others had taken cover while Broken Rock's Comanches pursued them.

Preacher was east of the ridges where the group had almost ridden into Broken Rock's trap. He could see the easternmost of those ridges from where he was. The ravine gradually angled in that direction. Now that he was out of it and could get a better idea of where he was, he realized he had followed the slash in the earth farther than he had thought. He was a couple of miles from the brushy hill, although after a while he could see it, too.

It was getting late in the day by now. He hoped to pick up the rest of the group's trail, but he wouldn't be able to follow it for long before nightfall.

Since they had headed north—at least, according to

what he had overheard the two warriors in the ravine saying—that meant going after them would take him in the opposite direction from Twisted Foot, the stolen gold coins, and quite probably, Toby Harper—or the discovery of Harper's fate, anyway.

Despite that, Preacher couldn't abandon Alita, Laurenco, and Pablo to the mercies of Goose Guidry, Lupe Garza, and the rest of Mallory's men. Without Mallory riding herd on them, they would be more of a danger to the girl than ever, and when the two old-timers tried to protect her, as they inevitably would, those ruthless varmints wouldn't hesitate to kill them.

The sun was almost touching the western horizon when Preacher reached the hill where the battle had taken place earlier in the day. There were no slain Comanche warriors lying on the ground; Broken Rock and his men would have taken their dead with them. However, Preacher did find the bodies of a couple of ponies that had been killed in the fighting.

With his now-reloaded rifle in one hand, he rode slowly toward the hill. "Scout, Dog," he said softly.

Dog trotted toward the thick brush at the base of the hill. He nosed around outside it for a while, then disappeared into the growth. Preacher reined in and waited. After a few minutes, Dog started to bark.

There was no sense of anger or urgency about the sound, as there would have been if the big cur was about to tear into something or someone. Instead, he was just letting Preacher know that he had found something. Preacher heeled Horse into motion again and rode toward the hill.

He dismounted and let the reins dangle, then pushed some of the brush aside with the rifle barrel and followed Dog's barking. It didn't take him long to discover what was causing it. The big cur stood a few yards away from a dead man lying on his back with two arrows sticking up from his corpse, one in his chest and one that went all the way through his throat. His face was twisted and frozen in a look of agony, but Preacher recognized him. He was one of Mallory's men. After a moment's thought, Preacher recalled that his name was Abrams.

The others hadn't taken the time to bury him. If he was the only casualty—and a quick look around the area didn't turn up any more bodies, so more than likely he was—the rest of the group wouldn't have wanted to hang around here once Broken Rock called off the attack and pulled back. They would have lit a shuck out of here just as quickly as they possibly could.

It was a great relief to Preacher that he didn't find the bodies of Alita or either of the old-timers. That meant there was a good chance they were still alive, even though they weren't out of danger by any means.

Preacher wasn't sure he wanted to spend the time and effort to bury Abrams, either, but since it would be getting dark soon and he didn't intend to start out on the trail of the others until the next morning, he supposed he might as well. He had brought along a short-handled shovel in his supplies. It was still strapped to one of the packhorses. He got it and scooped out a shallow grave at the base of the hill as the shadows of twilight began to gather.

He broke the arrows off and rolled the body into the grave. It was an unceremonious burial, but Preacher didn't see any reason to stand on ceremony out here in the middle of this untamed land. Abrams was lucky, if you could call it that, to be laid to rest at all.

While Preacher was working at this grim task, he relied

on Dog and Horse to stand guard. They would let him know if anyone who might pose a threat came around.

He had just finished filling in the grave when Horse blew out a breath and Dog whined quietly. That was enough to alert Preacher. Without reacting suddenly, he straightened from what he'd been doing and listened.

The faintest of sounds, maybe a twig crunching in the dirt as someone stepped on it, came to his ears. Anyone without the mountain man's almost supernaturally keen hearing would have missed it.

But Preacher heard it and knew someone was in the brush behind him. He knew the lurker wasn't Alita, Laurenco, or Pablo. They would have spoken to him. And he didn't have any other friends out here.

He drew in a deep breath, then turned and dived at the thick growth, using the shovel to slash at the place where someone was skulking.

More branches crackled as whoever it was threw himself aside to avoid the attack. Strong arms wrapped around Preacher's knees and heaved. Preacher went over backward as a burly shape bulled out of the brush at him.

The man was big and fast and a good fighter, just like Preacher. He kicked the shovel out of the mountain man's hand and then tried to stomp Preacher's face. Preacher flung his hands up and grabbed the man's booted foot as it descended. He held it off long enough to scissor his own leg up and sweep it across the attacker's midsection, knocking him off his feet.

Preacher had seen that the man was wearing a broad-brimmed hat, although it went flying when Preacher knocked him down. That meant he wasn't a Comanche but more likely a white man, maybe a Mexican.

One of Mallory's bunch who had been left behind for some reason?

Preacher didn't know, but he intended to find out.

He rolled over, came up onto his hands and knees, and sprang to his feet. The other man rose just as quickly and was ready to fight. In the gray dusk, Preacher could see his rangy, rawboned form and hard-planed face. The features weren't familiar. This man was a stranger, not one of Mallory's group.

Preacher didn't have time to ask questions. The man leaped at him, big hands outstretched to grapple for a hold.

Preacher darted aside and tried to trip the stranger, but the man was too nimble for that, his reactions too swift. He caught his balance in an instant and spun, his left arm lashing out in a backhand that Preacher barely blocked before it smashed into the side of his head. The blow still landed with enough force to make Preacher take a quick step to the side before he caught himself.

The stranger bored in, trying to take advantage of that. He was too eager, though. Preacher already had his feet set again and snapped out a left fist in a short, sharp punch that landed on the man's mouth and rocked his head back. The man's momentum carried him forward. Preacher grabbed his right arm in both hands, hauled hard on it, and twisted to throw his right hip into the man at the same time. That gave Preacher enough leverage to heave the man off his feet and send him crashing to the ground.

That would have knocked the breath out of most men and put them out of the fight, at least momentarily, but not this hombre. He rolled and came up again, lifting an uppercut with him that landed on Preacher's jaw with smashing force. For a second, the mountain man's feet were off the ground, and then it was his turn to crash down with breathtaking impact.

The big fellow dived at him. Preacher jerked both knees up and planted his boot heels in the stranger's belly. With a grunt of effort, he straightened his legs and sent the man staggering wildly backward. The man windmilled his arms and tried to catch his balance, but he stumbled and fell again.

He was on his feet by the time Preacher could get up and reach him. Fists flew in the gloom as they stood there toe to toe, slugging away at each other.

Both men absorbed a considerable amount of punishment, and the battle swayed back and forth as the shadows thickened even more. Preacher knew he was pitted against one of the most formidable opponents he had ever faced. They were almost a match in size, reach, and strength.

Preacher could tell that the stranger was younger than he was, probably in his mid-twenties, but age didn't mean much to the mountain man. Ever since he had attained his maturity, the years had weighed very lightly on Preacher. Except for the touches of gray in his hair and beard, he could have passed for a much younger man.

Such an even bare-knuckles brawl like this could go on until both men were simply too battered and exhausted to continue, without a clear-cut winner. Or it could end in the blink of an eye, if either man made even the slightest mistake.

In this case, it was a misstep by the stranger that gave Preacher his chance. The man put his foot down on a rock that rolled unexpectedly underneath him. That caused him to drop his guard just for an instant.

Preacher's right fist rocketed over the lowered arms and landed on the stranger's jaw like a keg of blasting powder exploding. The man went over backward, his feet kicked high in the air as he fell, and he landed in a sprawl. For the first time in this epic battle, he wasn't able to spring right back up. He tried to lift himself but sagged back with a sigh, instead.

"Stay . . . right there . . . old son," Preacher said, panting with exhaustion himself. One of the pistols had remained tucked behind his belt during the ruckus. He wrapped his hand around its butt and went on, "I don't feel like . . . fightin' no more. I'd a whole lot rather . . . talk to you." He wanted to find out who this tall hombre was and what he was doing here. "But if you try anything else . . . we'll end this another way."

Dog suddenly growled, which made Preacher half-turn to see the big cur crouched and ready to spring into action. The hair on Dog's back was ruffled up in anger.

"Easy, Dog," Preacher said, because he saw the same thing that had caused the cur's reaction.

Men stepped forward out of the gloom, forming a half circle around them, and each of the shadowy figures had either a rifle or a pistol in his hands, aimed right at Preacher.

CHAPTER 20

One of the men stepped out a little in front of the others. He had a pistol in his hand, which was rock-steady as he said in a clear, commanding voice, "It might be a good idea for you to let go of that gun, friend. You're liable to make the rest of us a mite nervous."

The man sounded so icy-nerved that it was unlikely anything would make him nervous.

Outnumbered and outgunned the way he was, Preacher knew it would be foolish to do anything other than cooperate. Anyway, he wanted to find out what was going on here and who these hombres were, and if they really wanted him dead, they could have gunned him down easily by now.

"All right," he said as he let go of the pistol butt and moved his hand away from the weapon. "I'd be obliged if you boys would hold off on fillin' me full of holes."

The spokesman chuckled. "I reckon we can do that," he said. "Of course, somebody else might have an opinion on that." He leaned over slightly to look past Preacher. "What do you say, Private Wallace? What should we do with this fellow?"

Preacher looked back. The man he had knocked down had recovered enough to push himself up on an elbow. He lay there braced like that while he slowly shook his head, as if trying to get rid of the cobwebs in his brain.

Preacher was a little surprised to see that. He thought he had knocked the fella out cold.

The man called Wallace didn't answer right away. He gradually sat up and climbed to his feet while the others waited patiently. Then he lifted a hand, took hold of his jaw, and gingerly worked it back and forth.

"Don't seem to be broke," he drawled. "Which same is a mite surprisin'. Mister, I been kicked by mules that didn't hit as hard as you." He looked past Preacher. "Don't kill him, Cap'n, leastways not yet. Anybody who can scrap like this fella deserves a chance to be heard out."

"All right, Bill, if you say so." The man who was obviously the leader of this group lowered his pistol and then slid it into a sheath attached to his belt. "At ease, boys. I don't think our guest is going to cause us any more trouble. At least, I hope not."

"Guest?" Preacher repeated in a growling tone. "What in blazes makes me a *guest* of you fellas?"

"Well, you're not a Texian, are you? All of us are." The man paused, then added with another chuckle, "Most of us might not have been born here. I was born in Tennessee, myself. But we got here as fast as we could, didn't we, boys?"

That brought actual cheers from several of the men.

"No, I ain't from Texas," Preacher admitted. "I've been here a few times in the past." He remembered that the spokesman had called the man he'd been battling "Private Wallace," and Wallace had addressed the other man as

"Cap'n." Preacher went on, "Are you fellas the Republic of Texas army or some such?"

"We don't really have an army down here since we won our independence from Mexico," the leader replied. "We're what you'd call a ranging company. It's our job to patrol the frontier and keep the Indian troubles down. I'm the commanding officer of this company. Name's Hays. John Coffee Hays, but most folks call me Jack."

"Cap'n Jack," the big brawler called Wallace put in.

Hays said, "And that fellow you were just waltzing with is Private William Wallace. Bill, what started this little dustup, anyway?"

"This hombre jumped me," Wallace said. "He tried to stove my head in with a shovel."

"Because you were skulkin' in the brush like a Comanche," Preacher shot back at him.

"I didn't do a durned thing but watch you whilst you buried that other fella. Did you kill him?"

"Do I look like somebody who'd shoot arrows in a man?" Preacher responded, notwithstanding the fact that he had done exactly that a couple of times earlier today.

"Maybe not, but that still didn't give you cause to wallop me."

Captain Hays said, "All right, there's no point in wrangling about this. Mister, if you'll give me your word you won't try anything, we'll go ahead and make camp. That's what you were about to do, wasn't it? Then we can sit down and talk about this."

Preacher nodded and said, "All right." He had heard of the ranging companies down here in Texas. They were well-known as fierce Indian fighters and staunch defenders of the settlers, so he didn't figure he was in any danger from them.

"What's your name, by the way?" Hays asked.

"They call me Preacher."

"Preacher!" Wallace exclaimed. "The mountain man and fur trapper?"

"Reckon that's what I am."

"A ways south of your usual stompin' grounds, ain't you?"

"I suppose so, but I got a good reason for that."

"We'll talk about that later," Hays said. He turned to the others and went on, "Let's get that camp set up, boys. Jameson, Rivers, tend to the horses. It's a little late for a fire, so we'll have to make do with a cold camp tonight."

That caused a few grumbles from the men, but they went about their tasks with practiced efficiency.

Wallace looked at Dog and said to Preacher, "I'm glad you didn't set your wolf on me."

"He ain't a wolf. Well, not completely, anyway."

"I've heard a whole heap about you," Wallace went on. He motioned Hays over and said, "Cap'n, if this here fella really is the one I've heard tell of, he's just about the fightin'est son of a gun west of the Mississippi." He lifted a hand and rubbed his jaw. "I reckon I can testify to that, too, after tanglin' with him."

"I believe I've heard of you as well, Preacher," Hays said. "From what I remember of the stories, you've led a very adventurous life."

"I've gotten into my share of scrapes," Preacher admitted. "Maybe more than my share, when you come right down to it."

"But you never went looking for trouble, I imagine."

Preacher laughed and said, "Well . . . no, if I'm bein' honest, I've done that, too. Like the mess that led me to get mixed up with this deal down here in Texas."

"I want to hear all about that," Hays said. "We'll talk while we're having supper."

"I've got some supplies I can share . . ."

"No need," Hays assured him. "We're well provisioned."

Without a fire, the men had to make do with a sparse supper of jerky and some biscuits left over from that morning's breakfast. Two men stood guard while the others sat cross-legged on the ground and ate.

Full night had fallen by now, but Preacher's eyes had adjusted well enough to the starlight that he was able to make out something unexpected as a man jogged up to join the circle of Texians. A feather stuck up from the newcomer's hair, and his chest was bare in the faint glow from the stars.

"Son of a—" Preacher began as he tensed.

"Don't worry, he's a friend," Hays said. "Flacco of the Lipan Apache. His father is the tribe's main chief. He rides with us and scouts for us." To the Indian he said, "Sit down and have some supper, Flacco."

The scout grunted and sank cross-legged on the ground. One of the other men handed him a piece of jerky and a biscuit.

"Did you find anything?" Hays asked.

"A dozen white men camped south of here," Flacco replied in good English. "Or maybe white men and Mexicans, I did not get close enough to be sure about that."

Preacher's interest perked up quite a bit. Mallory's men had withdrawn to the north after the battle with Broken Rock's Comanches, but they could have circled around and pushed on south, risking another encounter. They might still harbor some hope of finding Twisted Foot and recovering the stolen money.

Flacco's next words confirmed that theory and made

Preacher sit up even straighter. "They had a woman with them," the scout said. "Young, with long dark hair. Probably a Mexican."

"And two old men?" Preacher asked sharply, prompting Hays to look at him with a curious frown.

"Yes," Flacco said solemnly. "Two old men who stayed very close to the girl."

"Sounds like you know who those folks are, Preacher," Hays said.

"I know," Preacher replied with a grim nod.

"Be obliged if you'd share that with us," Hays said, but there was an undercurrent of steel in his voice that made it clear the words weren't just a polite request. He wanted an answer.

Preacher didn't mind giving it to him. Fate had provided him with some unexpected allies—albeit at the cost of the bruises he had received in the fracas with Wallace—and he wasn't going to turn his back on this opportunity.

"That's the bunch I was traveling with before we got jumped by Broken Rock's Comanches. Me and another fella got separated from them. They made a stand here at this hill and fought off the Comanch', then retreated to the north when Broken Rock pulled back."

"If you were separated from them, how do you know that?" Hays asked, showing that he had a keen brain.

"I wound up hidin' in a ravine over yonder a ways," Preacher explained as he waved vaguely toward the east. "While Dog and I were buried up under some brush, a couple of Broken Rock's warriors came by lookin' for us, and I heard them talkin' about it."

Wallace said, "That fella I saw you buryin', he was one of the bunch you're talkin' about?"

"That's right. His name was Abrams. As far as I could

tell, he was the only one killed in the fight. From what Flacco just said, it's pretty clear the rest of the bunch went north a ways and then circled around."

"Back through Broken Rock's territory?" Hays said. "They must have a pretty good reason to risk that again."

"I'd say so," Preacher said. He paused to consider. From what Preacher knew of these Texas ranging companies, they were honest, forthright hombres, unlike the ruthless cutthroats Styles Mallory had recruited for the job. He decided his best course was to spill the truth of what he was doing here.

For the next few minutes, he did that, explaining about the attack on the wagon train, the murders of the men with it, and the disappearance of Toby Harper and the money. He told Hayes, Wallace, and the others about how Daniel Eckstrom had hired him in St. Louis to find out what had happened and how Alita Montez, in her love for Harper, had ventured into this dangerous wilderness accompanied by the two faithful old-timers, prompting her father to send Mallory and the others after her.

He spoke of the adventures he'd had along the way, how he had met the Kiowa chief Buffalo Bull, thrown in with Mallory's bunch, encountered the Lipan Apache chief Big Creek, and learned of Twisted Foot's war party and their white captive.

Flacco nodded solemnly and said, "My father and I know Big Creek. He is a good man, a good chief."

"That's the impression I had of him, too," Preacher agreed. "Anyway, it seems mighty likely that Twisted Foot's the one responsible for what happened to the wagon train, and Toby Harper's his prisoner, if he's still alive. We were headed south, hopin' to bypass Broken Rock's band, and locate Twisted Foot's village." The mountain man shrugged. "Things didn't work out that way so far, but I've still got a job to do."

"So do we," Hays said, "and it seems that our mission is connected to the one you're on."

"How's that?"

"We heard rumors about Twisted Foot and that big war party of his," the captain explained. "We don't know exactly where his village is, but my hunch is that that's not where he's headed."

Preacher frowned and said, "I ain't sure I follow what you mean."

"We also had word from one of our companies down along the border that a large group of Comancheros is headed in this direction."

"You mean Comanches?" Preacher asked.

"No, Comancheros. Mexican bandits who trade with the Comanches, although it's possible there are some gringos among their number, as well. They provide a steady traffic in guns, slaves, and liquor. This group we heard about is supposedly led by a man known as El Carnicero."

"The Butcher," Preacher translated. "Don't sound like a very friendly fella."

"No, he's not. His reputation is as a cruel, ruthless killer who always gets what he goes after."

For a moment, Preacher thought about what Hays had just told him, then he said, "You think Twisted Foot is on his way to meet up with El Carnicero and this bunch of, what'd you call 'em, Comancheros?"

"That's the way it seems to me," Hays said.

Wallace put in, "And there ain't nobody better at fig-urin' out things than the cap'n."

Preacher pondered some more, then said, "With the

money he stole from that wagon train, Twisted Foot could buy a heap of guns, couldn't he?"

With a solemn nod, Hays replied, "That's right. And armed with rifles, he could wreak a lot more havoc on the frontier than he already has."

"So you're out to keep that from happenin'."

"That's right. We rode up here from San Antonio to see if we could pick up Twisted Foot's trail and let him lead us to the rendezvous with El Carcinero." Wryly, Hays added, "From the sound of everything you've told us, we've over-shot our goal. Twisted Foot is already somewhere south of us and even has a prisoner he might be able to trade to the Comancheros for his value as a slave."

That made Preacher think of something that caused his backbone to stiffen. He said, "I expect a young, good-lookin' woman would be worth even more as a slave."

"You're right about that," Hays agreed. "This Señorita Montez you mentioned might be heading into even more trouble than she realizes . . . and from the sound of it, she was already in some danger from her so-called allies."

Wallace said, "What it sounds to *me* like is that you ought to throw in with us, Preacher. Come mornin', we need to light a shuck to the south, too. Maybe we can still catch up to them blasted Comanch' in time, and find those Comancheros, too."

"That's the plan," Hays agreed. "What do you say, Preacher?"

The mountain man didn't have to consider the question for long. His best chance yet to accomplish his mission lay with these men. He said, "You can count me in, Cap'n. I reckon for now I'm one of your Texas rangers, if you'll have me."

"Texas rangers," Hays mused. "I like the sound of that."

CHAPTER 21

Preacher didn't have to stand a guard shift that night, although Wallace warned him that since he had joined the ranging company, even on an unofficial basis, he wouldn't be considered a guest anymore.

"I reckon we'll just have to call you an honorary Texian," the big, rangy brawler said the next morning as he and Preacher sat side by side drinking coffee and eating flapjacks and fried salt pork.

"That's fine with me," the mountain man said. "As far as I can tell, bein' a Texian is an honorable thing."

"Dadblasted right it is."

"I've got to admit, though, I'm a mite surprised you don't hold any grudge against me because of that tussle we had yesterday."

"You mean because you whipped me?" Wallace sounded like he found the very idea astounding. "I don't mind admittin' you won that round."

"That round?" Preacher repeated.

"Why, sure. I figure maybe we'll have a rematch one of these days, when this trouble we're both mixed up in is all took care of. There ain't much in the world I like better than a good scrap with a fella who knows how to fight."

Preacher grinned. "You should've been a fur trapper. You'd fit right in at rendezvous, up in the mountains."

"Maybe sometime I'll take a *pasear* up there and see what it's all about."

Preacher pointed to the guns Wallace wore in leather holsters on his hips and said, "I don't think I ever saw a pistol like that before. I know that Cap'n Jack carries a couple like it, and so do most of the other boys. What sort of a weapon is that?"

Wallace pulled out the left-hand gun and held it up so Preacher could get a better look at it. It had wooden grips, but unlike the flintlock pistols Preacher carried, most of it was made of steel. From the end of the butt to the tip of the long barrel, it was a little more than a foot long. To Preacher, the thing looked rather ungainly, but when Wallace handed it to him and said, "See how you like it," he found the gun fairly well balanced.

"That there's a Colt Paterson, designed by a fella name of Sam Colt and made at a factory up in New Jersey," Wallace said. "It's a repeating revolver."

Preacher frowned and said, "You mean . . .?"

"Yep." Wallace tapped a metal cylinder that sat ahead of a hammer at the back of the frame. "There are five .36 caliber loads in there."

Preacher let out a low whistle of amazement. "You can shoot all five at the same time?"

"Well, no, you got to cock that hammer there between each shot. But still, if you're carryin' two of these beauties, you've got ten rounds before you have to reload."

"I never heard of such a thing," Preacher said, shaking his head. "It's a funny-lookin' critter, with the hammer on the back that way instead of the side. And where's the trigger?"

"It's folded up inside until you pull the hammer back," Wallace explained. "That makes it come down so you can shoot. Turns the cylinder, too, so that the next load lines up with the barrel."

"If that don't beat all," Preacher said as he studied the weapon. He looked up. "How do you reload?"

"You have to take the cylinder out. Push that lever down to loosen it. Most fellas carry a couple of extra loaded cylinders with 'em so they can swap 'em while in the saddle if they need to."

With Wallace tutoring him, Preacher fiddled with the Colt for several minutes until he started to become familiar with its operation. Then he asked, "How does it shoot?"

Wallace grinned and said, "Why don't you try it out?"

"You reckon I could?"

"Don't see why not. We've got plenty of powder and shot. Best ask the cap'n first, though, just to make sure." Wallace got to his feet, dusted off his rump, and said, "Cap'n, Preacher wants to try out one o' these Patersons of mine. That all right with you?"

Hays had been talking to Flacco, the Lipan Apache scout. He turned to Preacher and Wallace and said, "Have you seen any revolving pistols like that, Preacher?"

"Nope," the mountain man said. "Now that Wallace has told me more about 'em, I seem to remember hearin' some talk about such a contraption a few years ago, but I didn't think anything ever come of it."

"They didn't work that well starting out," Hays said, "and reloading them was so complicated and time-consuming that you lost most of the advantage you might have gained from a repeating firearm. However, once they were redesigned to make loading easier, we decided to give them a try. So far I've been pleased with the results." He gestured toward the one in Preacher's hand. "Go ahead, see what you think."

Preacher and Wallace walked out away from the camp a short distance. Hays and several of the other Texians followed to observe.

Wallace pointed and said to Preacher, "See that little nubby branch stickin' out from that oak tree yonder? See if you can hit it."

Preacher estimated that the tree was about fifty feet away. Far enough to be a challenging shot with a pistol, but not impossible by any means. He said, "Do I aim first and then cock the dang thing, or the other way around?"

"Go ahead and cock it," Wallace advised.

Preacher did so. The trigger swung down from where it had been folded up inside the body of the pistol. Preacher slid his finger around it carefully, since he didn't know how sensitive the trigger was.

There were no sights on the gun, so Preacher aimed without them. He had never believed in wasting time, so as soon as he had the pistol settled where he wanted it, he squeezed the trigger. The shot was loud, but not as loud as the boom of his flintlock pistols, nor was the recoil as strong.

He frowned as he saw that the short branch sticking out from the oak's trunk at eye level was still there, untouched. He wasn't used to missing a shot—and he didn't like it.

"Try again," Wallace urged.

Preacher was already drawing the hammer back. He leveled the Colt again, took a breath, and fired. This time, a section of the branch several inches long spun away through the air, clipped off cleanly by the ball.

"Whoo-eee!" Wallace exclaimed. "That's good shootin', Preacher."

Smiling, Hays said, "What you don't know, Preacher, is that it took all of us a lot longer than our second shot before we could hit what we were aiming at. You seem to have a natural talent for shooting."

"We'll see," Preacher said. He eared back the Colt's hammer again. "There's still a little bit of branch stickin' out from that tree."

Wallace said, "But that's too small to—"

The Colt blasted a third time. Wallace leaned his head forward to peer at the tree through the haze of smoke.

"It's gone! He shot it right offa there!"

Preacher turned the Colt around and extended it butt-first to Wallace.

"I'm obliged to you for lettin' me try it," he said. "I might have to get me one of them ree-volvin' guns some-time."

"I think we can do better than that," Hays said. "We have several spare guns and holsters, if you'd be interested in carrying a pair of them."

Preacher nodded and said, "I think I'd like that."

Wallace clapped a hand on Preacher's shoulder and offered, "I'll show you how to load. You'll be blazin' away with those things in no time."

That sounded good to Preacher. And if they ever caught up to Twisted Foot—especially if there were any of those Comancheros around—likely the more firepower, the better.

Flacco had already set out earlier to scout their route to the south. They were still in Broken Rock's territory, and there was a distinct possibility they might run into the same warriors who had jumped Mallory's bunch the day before.

They had no way of knowing how far Twisted Foot was ahead of them. Weeks had passed since the attack on the wagon train, but according to the information Hays had received, the group of Comancheros had crossed the border from Mexico only a week earlier. In all likelihood, Twisted Foot was camped wherever the rendezvous was supposed to take place, waiting for the Mexican traders to arrive.

However, Preacher knew that the survivors from Styles Mallory's group, as well as Alita, Laurenco, and Pablo, were less than a day's ride ahead. As the ranging company rode south, Preacher nudged Horse alongside Hays' mount and asked the captain, "What do you plan to do if we catch up to the bunch that has the girl and those two old-timers with them?"

Hays looked over at him shrewdly and said, "I have an idea you'd like to take that girl away from them."

"I don't figure she's rightly safe."

"Those men aren't outlaws," Hays pointed out. "They haven't broken any laws here in the Republic of Texas, have they?"

"Not that I know of, but I sure don't trust 'em. I wouldn't put it past 'em to try to sell Señorita Montez to those Comancheros."

"Yes, you mentioned that last night," Hays said, nodding. "We can't allow that to happen, of course. If we find that group and offer the señorita the choice of traveling with us instead, and they try to prevent her from doing so . . . well, that would give us a perfectly legitimate reason to take action, I believe."

"I've got a hunch they won't let her go without a fight."

"Then we'll deal with that when the time comes," Hays said. "I really can't afford to jeopardize our main mission, though. We can't let Twisted Foot get his hands on a bunch of rifles. No settlers would be safe anywhere between the Brazos and the Colorado Rivers, maybe beyond that. Twisted Foot might even be bold enough to attack the new capital at Austin."

Preacher understood the captain's position. For the time being, they were on the same side, but the time might come when Preacher would have to take off on his own again in order to do what he needed to do.

He hoped not. He felt an instinctive liking for these rough-and-tumble Texans.

The feeling deepened over the next few days as the ranging company rode south by southeast through a Texas landscape that grew steadily hillier and more beautiful. It was a different sort of beauty than the looming majesty of the Rockies to which Preacher was accustomed, but as he traveled through it with his new companions, he began to understand why these Texans felt so strongly about their homeland, whether it was native or adopted. This was a special place.

They didn't see any signs of the Comanches and began to hope that Broken Rock and his warriors either weren't aware of them or had decided not to risk attacking them.

In camp every evening, Preacher practiced with the Colt Paterson revolvers Captain Jack had loaned him. At first, the weight of the guns in the holsters on his hips felt odd to him, but he began to get used to it. He learned how to hold his hands close to the gun butts, ready to hook and draw. It was a new technique, not at all like pulling a flint-lock pistol from behind his belt, but he had always been a fast learner. By the time Preacher had been on the trail with the ranging company for three days, Wallace was quite impressed with the way the mountain man handled the Colts.

"You can get them Colts out and blastin' a lot quicker than I can, and you gen'rally hit what you're aimin' at, too," he said after watching Preacher practice with the revolvers. "I never thought about it before, but sometimes the speed of a fella's draw might be the difference between livin' and dyin'."

"It sure might," Hays added, having drifted up to watch the practice session. "You seem to have a knack that the rest of us are lacking, Preacher."

"Fightin's always come natural to me, I reckon," Preacher said. "This is just a new way of doin' it." As he holstered one of the revolvers and began loosening the cylinder loose to reload the other one, he changed the subject by saying, "I was hopin' we'd catch up to Mallory's bunch by now. They must be movin' pretty quick, like we are."

"You said you believe this man Mallory was killed by the Comanches?" Hays asked.

"Well, I figured he must've been, since they weren't far behind us and I know good and well Horse threw him off rather than lettin' him stay in the saddle. But when you get right down to it . . . I don't know. I mean, I was in a pretty bad fix just then, too, and I survived. Mallory always had a way of gettin' out of trouble, even when things looked plenty bad for him."

Wallace said, "If he did get away, where is he?"

Preacher shook his head. "No tellin'. He might've managed to get back to the rest of his bunch, although the chances of that still seem pretty slim to me."

The more Preacher thought about it, though, the more he realized that sounded exactly like something Styles Mallory would have done.

One thing was certain—if Mallory was alive, he would be wherever he believed he stood the best chance of making a profit.

The next morning, they pushed on through the hilly terrain, and after a couple of hours, Preacher noticed a long, craggy ridge in front of them, running east and west and notched by a deep gap that seemed to be their destination.

He pointed to it and asked Wallace, who was riding beside him, "Is that where we're headed?"

"Sure is," Wallace replied. "That's Bandera Pass. From what I've heard, Injuns have been usin' it for hundreds of years while travelin' in these parts. So did the Mexican army, and the Spaniards before that, when they'd send troops up here to try to pacify the redskins." Wallace snorted. "It don't seem like that worked out too well for 'em. I wouldn't call any part of this frontier pacified. Reckon it will be someday, though."

"It's been my experience," Preacher drawled, "that when a place gets *too* pacified, it ain't hardly worth livin' there no more."

Wallace threw back his head and laughed. "I can't argue with that! There'll be plenty o' time for peace and quiet when I get old . . . if I live that long!"

They rode on toward the pass. There was a visible trail now, and to Preacher's experienced eye, it appeared that riders had moved along here in the past day or two. He hoped that meant they were catching up to the group that included Alita, Laurenco, and Pablo.

Late in the morning they reached the pass and started through it. The trail dropped at a fairly steep angle, and the ridges on both sides thrust up sharply. A short time earlier, Flacco had come galloping back to the group after scouting ahead through the pass, prompting Hays to call a momentary halt, and Preacher had seen him talking intently with the captain while the rangers were stopped. Then Hays had waved them ahead, but Preacher could tell from the stiff set of his back that Hays was ready for trouble, perhaps even expecting it.

From where he rode alongside the mountain man, Wallace rumbled, "There seem like a funny feelin' in the air to you, Preacher?"

"Yeah, I'd say so," Preacher replied quietly. "It's one that I've felt plenty of times in the past, too."

"Like all the imps of Hades are about to bust loose and come howlin' over those ridges?"

"Could be," Preacher said.

The words were barely out of his mouth when Wallace's prediction came true—except it wasn't the Devil's minions who came howling over the ridges and poured down the slopes on both sides of the pass toward Preacher and the ranging company.

It was feathered and war-painted Comanches—hundreds of them, from the looks of it.

CHAPTER 22

Several of the men shouted in surprise or alarm, but Captain Jack's voice cut through the hubbub with its clear, powerful tone of command.

"Dismount and tie those horses!" he ordered. "We can whip them. No doubt about that!"

These Texians were iron-nerved men to start with. Any fleeting panic they might have felt at being set upon by such a large force of savages evaporated in an instant as their leader's calm but firm orders lashed through the air. Men swung down swiftly from their saddles and tied their mounts to sturdy bushes or even took the time to drive sturdy pegs into the ground and picket the animals.

Preacher tied his two pack animals to a bush but left Horse's reins looped around the saddle. The stallion wouldn't run off.

"Dog, stay close," Preacher said. He pulled his rifle out of its sling.

The Texians formed a ring around their mounts and got ready to fight. Preacher found himself between Wallace and a man named Ben Highsmith. He glanced back and forth at them, grinned, and said, "You boys ready for this?"

"More than ready," Wallace replied, and Highsmith gave a grunt of agreement. They each held a flintlock rifle, too.

"Open fire!" Hays called.

Smoothly, Preacher, Wallace, and Highsmith brought their rifles to their shoulders, cocked the weapons, and picked targets. There were plenty to choose from. Preacher settled his sights on a yipping warrior wearing a feathered headdress and squeezed the trigger.

The rifle boomed and kicked against his shoulder. Gray smoke gushed from the barrel, but the breeze moving through the pass cleared it away quickly. Preacher saw the Indian pony racing wildly along with the others now, while its former rider kicked and thrashed on the ground behind it. Then with a great shudder the Comanche went still as death claimed him.

Wallace and Highsmith fired their rifles, as well, and two more of the attackers pitched from their mounts as Texian lead found its target. With a rippling roar of sound, the other members of the ranging company opened fire, and on both slopes, Comanche warriors fell off their ponies or jerked under the impact of the bullets but clung to their mounts.

Preacher hung the empty rifle back in its sling and drew the two flintlock pistols he had left tucked behind his belt. The charging Comanches were in pistol range by now, so he cocked and leveled the guns and pulled the triggers. They kicked hard as the heavy powder charges detonated. Preacher had double-shotted both guns, as was his habit. With the clouds of dust and powdersmoke already in the air, he couldn't tell for sure what effect his shots had, but he believed at least two more of the warriors went down.

He shoved the empty pistols in his saddlebags and

reached down to pluck the Colt Patersons from their holsters. Now he could get down to some serious work, he told himself as he thumbed back the hammers and raised the revolvers.

He fired the right-hand gun first, then the left, going back and forth between them. Recoil made the barrels come up a little each time he fired. Preacher settled into a steady rhythm, squeeze the trigger, thrust the other gun forward and fire while he was bringing the first one back down and cocking it, and then the whole thing over again. Left, right, left, right—and the storm of lead that erupted from the Colts scythed through the front lines of the attacking warriors and mowed them down.

The other men were doing the same thing. A circle of bloody slaughter surrounded the ring of men and horses in the center of the pass. Warriors and ponies alike rolled in the dust, never to rise again.

Clearly, the Comanches hadn't expected such a terrible, deadly defense. They had known that a few of them would die, there was no way to avoid that, but then they would wash over the Texians like a tide and wipe them out.

That had been their plan, but instead dozens of them had died in the first moments of the battle, and in their shock and surprise, the survivors howled their outrage and turned their ponies and fled toward the slopes on both sides of the pass. A spattering of shots from the Texians sped them on their way and knocked a few more off their ponies.

"Reload!" Captain Jack called into the echoing silence that fell. "Reload, and fall back to those rocks and trees!"

A short distance up the pass stood a clump of live oaks with a cluster of boulders near them. The scattered rocks were about the height of a man's waist, which meant that

Preacher and the others could kneel behind them and have some decent cover. The horses and the ranging company's pack mules could be tied in the trees where they would be reasonably safe.

The Texians moved quickly to take advantage of this shelter. Preacher untied his two packhorses and led them while Horse and Dog trotted alongside him.

The Comanches had withdrawn over the ridges so the Texians couldn't take potshots at them with their rifles, but none of Hays's men doubted that the Indians would be back soon. Even with the damage they had done to the ambushers, the Texians were still outnumbered at least four to one. Because of that, the Comanches had to believe they were destined to win this battle.

Preacher reloaded his rifle and flintlock pistols, then told Dog to stay in the trees with Horse and the other animals. The big cur whined, and Preacher said, "I know you want to be smack-dab in the middle of the fracas, old son, but this ain't your kind of fight. If it gets down to hand-to-hand, I'll whistle for you, I give you my word."

Wallace overheard that and asked, "Does that wolf of yours understand what you're sayin'?"

"He's a dog, at least mostly," Preacher said, "and since I don't speak his lingo, I can't say for sure he knows what I'm tellin' him. But he acts like he does, and I reckon that's all that matters."

"Yeah, I suppose so." Wallace switched out the cylinders on his Colts and started reloading the ones he had emptied. He let out a grim chuckle and went on, "Those Comanch' were plumb shocked when we fired that first volley . . . and then went right on a-shootin'."

Preacher followed suit in getting his revolvers ready to

fire again. "Good chance that was the first time they'd ever come up against repeatin' guns."

"I don't think they ever got a chance to even fire any arrows at us!"

Hays walked up in time to hear that excited comment from Wallace and said, "Don't get overconfident, Private. I think there's a good chance that before this is over, there *will* be a few arrows coming our way."

"I don't doubt it, Cap'n. But we'll make those varmints pay for shootin' 'em."

"Yes, I expect we will."

The sun had climbed a little more in the sky and was directly overhead now. Hays directed a couple of the men to build a fire in a clear spot in the trees and start boiling a pot of coffee.

"Keep it going," he instructed. "We're all liable to need plenty of coffee this afternoon. Break out the biscuits left from breakfast this morning and pass around strips of jerky, too. We should keep our strength up."

"You sound like you figure this to be a long fight, Cap'n," one of the men said.

Hays nodded. "With their superior numbers, I don't expect the Comanches to withdraw until nightfall. We'll have to hold out until then."

Wallace said to Preacher, "You reckon that chief you tangled with . . . what was his name?"

"Broken Rock," the mountain man replied.

"Yeah, him. You reckon this is his bunch?"

"I wouldn't be surprised if he's part of it, but I'm not sure he had this many warriors. This may be several different bands teamin' up to ambush us."

"Including Twisted Foot?" Hays asked.

"No way of knowin'," Preacher said, "but it don't seem

likely to me. He hasn't shown any signs of bein' interested in anything except trailin' south, and if the word you got is true, we know why. He's out to meet those Comancheros and trade with them."

Hays nodded. "And using that stolen money, arm himself well enough to do more damage than any other war chief in Texas. I'm going to stop him from doing that, no matter what it takes."

"We got to get outta here first," Wallace drawled. "Reckon we could just make a run for it the rest of the way down the pass, Cap'n?"

"I think we'd be playing into the Comanches' hands if we did that. They probably have warriors hidden at the bottom of the pass, too, just waiting for us to try it."

That seemed likely to Preacher. The course of action Hays had laid out, trying to hold off the Comanches until darkness fell, seemed like the best way to proceed. Indians would fight at night when it was necessary, but they were a lot less likely to. If the Texians could hold out until then, the Comanches might well decide that the "medicine" wasn't on their side in this fight after all.

Preacher gulped down a cup of hot coffee and put a piece of jerky in his mouth to soften up and gnaw on. With his borrowed Colts reloaded, he loaded all four of his flint-lock pistols as well, then carried them and the rifle over to one of the rocks and sat down behind it. He had two loaded spare cylinders for the revolvers, as well, and during the past few days he had practiced swapping them out and could perform the task pretty quickly.

That gave him twenty-five shots at his disposal. That ought to be enough to send quite a few of those painted and feathered varmints across the divide, he told himself.

That thought had barely gone through his mind when

an arrow seemed to come out of nowhere and whip past his right ear, so close that he felt it disturb the air.

"Here they come!" a man shouted.

Preacher lifted his rifle as he saw that some of the Comanches had worked their way stealthily down the slope, slipping through the thick brush until they were close enough to loose arrows at the Texians. A yell of pain from somewhere in the circle of defenders indicated that at least one of the arrows had found its target.

As one of the warriors stepped out from behind a small tree to pull back his bowstring, Preacher drew a bead on him and pressed the trigger. The rifle boomed before the Comanche could loose the arrow. The ball smashed into his chest and drove him over backward. The arrow from his bow arced high in the air as his dying fingers involuntarily released it.

Preacher set aside the rifle and picked up two of the flintlock pistols. Instead of attacking on horseback this time, the Comanches were able to charge at the Texians on foot because they had gotten closer without being spotted.

They must have hoped that the sudden volley of arrows would kill some of the defenders and throw the others into chaos. But the Texians were too icy-nerved to spook like that. Rifles and handguns blasted, and once again the wall of lead shredded the first wave of attackers. The Comanches kept coming, though, leaping over the bodies of their fallen comrades and screeching in fury.

Preacher fired one of the flintlock pistols into the wide-open mouth of a warrior and saw a grisly pink spray explode behind the Comanche's head as the ball blew out the back of his skull. The man stumbled a couple more steps and then pitched forward on his face so the hideous wound was on full display.

Preacher didn't bother looking at it. He was already aiming with the other pistol and ripped a shot through a warrior's throat. Blood fountained in the air from a torn jugular as the man collapsed.

Preacher set the empty pistols aside and snatched up the other two flintlocks. He fired them at the same time and saw two more Indians go down.

Now it was time for the Colts again. The smooth walnut grips already felt familiar and comfortable in his hands as he pulled the guns from their holsters, eared back the hammers, and commenced to killing with them, smoothly, rapidly, and efficiently. Almost every time Preacher pulled a trigger, a Comanche died.

Behind another rock to his right, Wallace was having almost as deadly an effect. One of the warriors got close enough to vault over the small boulder, though, and tackle the big Texian. Wallace went over backward from the impact and hit his head hard on the ground. He seemed to be stunned. The Comanche raised a knife and was poised to bring it down into Wallace's chest.

Preacher still had one round in his right-hand gun. Without turning his body, he extended the revolver toward the warrior about to kill Wallace and pulled the trigger. The gun boomed and bucked, driving a .36 caliber ball all the way through the Indian's head. He dropped the knife and toppled off Wallace.

"Obliged to you," Wallace called as he scrambled upright, shaking the cobwebs out of his head. "Maybe I can kill one of the varmints for you sometime."

The assault had slowed, but the Comanches were still all around the rocks and the grove of trees. Arrows zipped through the air. Preacher crouched low to switch out cylinders in the Colts. When he raised up again, an arrow struck his hat and swept it off his head. He spotted the Comanche who had fired it about fifteen yards away. The warrior grabbed desperately for another arrow, but Preacher shot him before he could pull one from the quiver.

Preacher thumbed and fired the Colts until they were both empty again. By that time, the Comanches had started to retreat again, hurrying back up the slopes as fast as they could. Preacher pouched the irons in his hands and grabbed his rifle again. He had it reloaded in time to lift it to his shoulder and squeeze off a final shot.

One of the fleeing warriors arched his back and flung his arms out as the rifle ball smashed into his back. He managed to stay on his feet until he toppled over backward and tumbled several yards back down the ridge before coming to a stop in an ungainly sprawl.

The rest of the Comanches disappeared before Preacher could reload and try again.

Captain Hays walked around quickly, checking on his men. When he came to Preacher and Wallace, he said, "I'm glad to see that you fellows are all right."

"I came mighty close to *not* bein' all right," Wallace said. He prodded the dead Comanche's body with his foot as he went on, "This red devil was fixin' to knife me when Preacher blew his lights out."

"How many men did we lose?" Preacher asked. He figured the Texians couldn't have come through unscathed with so many arrows flying around.

"One man dead," Hays replied grimly, "and several more wounded, but none of them appear to be seriously hurt. I'd say that all things considered, we came through that skirmish pretty fortunate."

"Yeah," Preacher said as he squinted up at the dark, wooded ridges overlooking the pass, "but we still got plenty of time for our luck to change."

CHAPTER 23

It got hotter in the pass as the Texians tended to their wounded and waited for the next attack from the Comanches. They wrapped the dead man's body in a blanket and placed it respectfully in the woods.

Wallace wasn't as respectful of the Comanche who had made it into the rocks and tried to knife him. He and another man picked up the corpse and slung it outside the cluster of boulders.

That annoyed Preacher slightly, but considering how bitter the conflict between the settlers and the Comanches had been for decades now, and how cruelly captives had been treated by the Comanches, that callous attitude wasn't surprising. He felt the same way toward the Blackfeet, the mountain man reminded himself. Not that long in the past, he and his son Hawk That Soars had spent a considerable amount of time dedicating themselves to the task of seeing how many Blackfeet warriors they could kill, and they hadn't been respectful about it, either.

Wallace gazed up toward the ridge on the east side of the pass and spat.

"Wish the varmints would go ahead and get on with

it," he said. "I never did care for sittin' around and waitin' to fight."

"I reckon they know that," Preacher told him. "They want to get our nerves good and tight before they come at us again. Besides, they're probably palaverin' about what to try next. They've attacked two different ways, and all it's gotten 'em is a heap of dead warriors."

"Close to fifty, I'd say," Wallace grunted. "But we lost a man, too, and one Texian is worth more than fifty of them filthy savages."

Preacher didn't say anything. Again, he understood the hatred on both sides.

The waiting lulled some of the men into not paying as much attention as they might have. Preacher remained alert, though, and he was one of the first to see a flaming arrow arching out from the slope above the pass. The burning brand flew high in the sky and then hurtled down toward the trees.

Preacher yelled a warning, but by the time the words were out of his mouth, more arrows had joined the first one. The shafts with their blazing heads fell like rain for a long moment. Men ducked for cover as some of the arrows were short in their flight and landed among the rocks.

Most of the shafts landed in the trees, though, and several of them started fires in the undergrowth. It wasn't as easy to set the live oaks ablaze. Men reached up with their rifle barrels, knocked the arrows they could reach out of the branches, and stomped out the flames. Others battled the fires in the brush, slapping at them with blankets. The smoke spooked some of the horses, so a few of the Texians worked to calm them.

All that was a considerable distraction. Preacher knew that was exactly what the Comanches intended. He was watching as warriors suddenly charged from all directions. Again, they had crept up close enough to attack on foot.

"Here they come!" Preacher bellowed as he threw his rifle to his shoulder and planted a heavy lead ball in the center of a charging Comanche's forehead.

He knelt behind one of the rocks, set the rifle aside, and emptied all four of the flintlock pistols, one after the other. With each blast a warrior fell. He pulled the Colts and opened fire with them, keeping track of the shots in his head so he didn't waste any time cocking the guns again on empty chambers.

He wouldn't be able to swap cylinders this time, he saw. The Comanches had swarmed too close for that. He rammed the revolvers back in their holsters and pulled his knife from its sheath, rising to meet the attack as one of the warriors leaped over the boulder.

Preacher's legs were braced, so he didn't go down or even give ground under the impact. His left hand shot up and grabbed the Comanche's right wrist as the warrior tried to slash at him with a knife.

Preacher thrust with his own blade. The Indian caught his wrist, but the mountain man was too strong to be stopped. He tore free and drove the knife into the warrior's chest, angling the blade up so the tip pierced the man's heart. The Comanche's eyes widened in shock. His strength ran out of him like water. Preacher ripped the knife free and slashed it across the man's throat, finishing him off.

Preacher flung the dead warrior aside. As he did, another of the warriors bounded on top of the boulder and launched at him in a diving tackle. Preacher twisted out of the way, and as the warrior landed belly-down on the ground, the mountain man dropped on top of him, ramming a knee into the small of his back to pin him there.

Swiftly, Preacher reached around with his left hand, cupped it under the warrior's chin, and jerked his head back so the skin of his throat was taut as Preacher raked the bloody blade across it. More crimson spurted as the Comanche flailed in his death throes.

A howl warned him. He threw himself to the side, but not in time to completely avoid the next attack as a third Comanche dived at him. The man caught him by the shoulder and drove him to the ground.

Preacher rolled over and lashed out with his right leg. The heel of his boot caught the warrior on the jaw and drove his head back with such force that a loud crack sounded as the man's neck snapped. He went limp.

Preacher rolled again and came up on his feet, still holding the knife. He was ready to use it, but the Comanches were already breaking off their attack and heading back up the slope. Some of the Texians fired after them to speed them on their way.

Preacher wiped the blood off his blade on the leggings of a dead Comanche and slid it back in its sheath. He set to work reloading all his guns while he had the chance. That process was automatic enough that he was able to look around while he was doing it and get an idea of how much damage the defenders had suffered in this assault.

Wallace had a cut on his arm that dripped blood, but he also had the bodies of three warriors at his feet. One had been shot, another looked like Wallace had crushed his skull with something, and the third Comanche's face was dark with blood and his tongue stuck out. Clearly, Wallace had choked him to death.

"You hurt?" the big Texian called over to Preacher.

"Not at all," the mountain man replied. "Looks like you picked up a little scratch."

"This?" Wallace looked down at the bloody sleeve of his homespun shirt and snorted. "This ain't nothin'. I've cut myself worse than this shavin', plenty of times."

Several more of the Texians were wounded, too, Preacher saw, but they were all on their feet, most busy reloading. The fires started by the flaming arrows had all been put out, but the smell of smoke lingered in the air. It had been a good tactic by the Comanches, and they had come closer to overrunning the Texians this time than ever before. But in the end the attack had failed and they had been driven off again.

Preacher glanced at the sky and saw that the sun was still high. The Comanches had lost enough men that they might consider withdrawing without waiting for nightfall, but Preacher's instincts told him that wasn't going to happen. Those warriors were proud enough that they would want to avenge their losses. And the hate they felt for the whites was a powerful thing, too.

No, Preacher thought, like it or not, he and the Texians were still going to have to hold out for a while longer.

Another of the defenders had been killed in the latest attack. One of the Comanches had gotten to him, and both men had died plunging their knives into each other, again and again. The Texians wrapped this fallen comrade in a blanket, too, and placed the body with the man who had been killed earlier.

This time, they left the bodies of the slain Comanches where they had fallen. There were too many to toss them back out of the rocks. It seemed almost like the pass was filling up with corpses, Preacher mused, and he wasn't the only one to notice that.

When he glanced up, the sky was dark overhead with circling buzzards. Some of the ugliest birds in the world when they were on the ground, they were almost eerily graceful as they swooped in front of the sun, cutting smoothly between the heavens and the earth below.

Captain Hays came over to Preacher, Wallace, and Ben Highsmith, who were still grouped together on the east side of the perimeter.

"Are you all right, Bill?" he asked Wallace as he nodded toward the big man's bloody sleeve.

Wallace assured the captain that he was, just as he had told Preacher earlier. Then he asked, "What do you reckon those varmints will try next, Cap'n?"

"They've attacked us every way I can think of so far," Hays said, "and none of them have really worked. I think they're probably having a council of war right now, trying to decide just how much our scalps are worth to them."

"You mean whether they want to keep fightin' or light a shuck outta here?"

"That's right."

"They won't give up," Preacher said with flat certainty. "We've hurt 'em too bad for them to do that, and not bad enough yet to make 'em quit. We've still got more killin' in front of us."

Hays sighed and nodded. "I'm afraid you're right about that. And when they come at us next time, they may not try anything fancy. Since things have gone this far, they may believe it's better just to rely on superior numbers and keep coming until they overwhelm us, even if we inflict terrible losses on them."

"That's probably the only way for them to salvage their

pride," Preacher said. "From what we've seen, I reckon they still outnumber us somewhere between two and three to one."

Wallace said, "Yeah, but every Texian is worth more than three of those varmints."

"Bluster has its place, Private," Hays said, "but it doesn't win battles. Powder and shot, cool nerves and cold steel . . . that's what we have in abundance. And that's what will allow us to whip our enemies today."

Several of the men heard that calm declaration, and it moved them to let out cheers. The rest of the Texians took it up without knowing why, but the enthusiasm was contagious.

The Comanches up on the ridges would have heard that defiant outburst, too, Preacher thought. And if they'd had any doubts or difficulties in making up their minds, that would have banished them.

They would be coming soon, more determined than ever to punish these intruders and water the Texas soil with their blood.

While he had the chance, Preacher checked on Dog and Horse and spent a few minutes visiting with his trail partners. He gave in to impulse and told the big cur, "You can come with me this time, Dog. I got a hunch we're gonna be busy with your kind of fightin' pretty soon."

Dog's tongue lolled out. He looked for all the world to be grinning in anticipation.

Taking the cur with him, Preacher returned to the cluster of rocks. Wallace said, "Gonna cut loose your wolf on 'em, eh?"

Preacher didn't bother to correct him this time. He just said, "In more ways than one."

Captain Hays came over and held out a pair of the Colt Paterson revolvers to Preacher.

"These belonged to one of the dead men," he explained. "You handle them as well or better than most of us, so it makes sense for you to have the extra ten rounds. I'd tell you to use them wisely . . . but I know you will."

"Thank you, Cap'n," Preacher said as he took the guns from Hays. "I'll try not to disappoint you."

"I'll not be disappointed in you or any of my men. Not after the way you've all fought today. This is the sort of battle that could be in the history books someday, gentlemen. Whether it actually will be or not, who can say? I suppose that depends on how the battle ends and whether we survive. But I know this . . . I'm proud to have fought alongside all of you. You're the finest bunch of Texians any man could ever hope to know. And that includes you, Preacher."

"Durned right," Wallace said with an emphatic nod. "You can forget what I said about you bein' an honorary Texian, Preacher. After today, it don't matter where you was born. You're a Texian down to the bone, just like the rest of us."

"And I'm mighty proud to be considered one," Preacher said honestly as he returned Wallace's nod.

"Cap'n!" one of the men yelled. He pointed to the ridge. "Look up yonder!"

Preacher, Wallace, Hays, Highsmith, and all the others tilted their heads back to gaze up at the crest. A long line of riders had appeared there, stretching almost all the way from one end of the pass to the other. Hays quickly stepped out to where he could look in the other direction and said, "They're up there on the west side, as well."

Wallace let out a lot whistle. "I didn't realize there were that many of the varmints still alive. Yeah, I'd say we're outnumbered, all right."

"But not outgunned," Hays said. "Don't forget that." He began walking briskly around the perimeter, calling to the men to get in position and be of stout heart. "We're going to whip them," he declared firmly, more than once.

Preacher didn't know about that, but he had never given up before, and he sure as blazes wasn't about to start now.

On each ridge, one of the warriors raised a lance above his head and screamed a command. Yelling at the top of their lungs, the Comanches charged down the slopes in two waves, destined to meet in the middle of Bandera Pass.

CHAPTER 24

Preacher knelt behind the rock with Dog standing close beside him, ready to leap into battle. The rifle butt was snug against the mountain man's shoulder as he drew a bead on one of the Comanche warriors racing down the ridge. Holding his breath, he squeezed the trigger.

The heavy lead ball flew true and struck the warrior in the chest. The man leaned far back, and Preacher thought he was going to fall off his pony that way.

But then the warrior recovered enough to straighten for a second before the pain made him sag forward. He pawed at the hole in his chest as blood welled from it, and then he lost his balance. He slipped from his pony's back and fell under the animal's flashing hooves. The pony tripped and catapulted forward, tumbling down the slope in a welter of flailing legs. The warriors right behind the fallen man and horse tried to swerve around them, but a couple of those ponies tripped, too, and went down. It was a ghastly tangle, and Preacher felt sorry for the ponies.

Not for the Comanches, though. This was war, and Preacher hadn't called the tune.

He set the rifle aside as more shots rang out from the defenders. Several more warriors fell, but Preacher estimated at least a hundred and twenty were charging from the eastern ridge, maybe more. If there were as many on the other side—and he suspected there were—that meant the odds were around four to one.

The Texians' superior firepower *might* be enough to offset that advantage, but only if they could stay alive long enough to use the Colts.

The Comanches were close enough to fire arrows from horseback. The deadly missiles whipped through the air around the defenders. Preacher heard a man cry out in pain, then another. The arrows were taking a toll.

He picked up the first pair of flintlock pistols and waited a couple of heartbeats for the leading edge of the charge to come within good range. Then he lined up his shots and squeezed the triggers, and through the smoke he glimpsed two warriors flying off their ponies. He set the empty pistols down and picked up the other pair.

Beside him, Dog growled deep in his throat.

"Soon, old son," Preacher breathed. "Soon."

A moment later, the second pair of pistols boomed and two more warriors crossed the divide as Preacher's lead blew them off their ponies. He picked up the extra Colts Hays had given him and rose from his crouch as if defying the Comanche arrows to strike him.

"Come on, you sons of Lucifer!" he bellowed. He began firing the revolvers as he swung from left to right, creating a lethal swath of ground in front of him.

Even so, the next wave of howling, yipping death was almost on top of him as he dropped the empty Colts and shouted, "Dog, hunt!"

Preacher's hands swooped to the holsters on his hips and came up filled with Colts belching flame and smoke.

It was an awesome display of shooting, the sort of thing that could be accomplished only by a man with an almost supernatural ability to handle firearms. Preacher blasted ten rounds, and ten warriors fell, each dead from a shot to the head or heart by the time he hit the ground.

Dog leaped onto one of the rocks and from there launched himself at the nearest warrior. The big cur's weight drove the Comanche off his pony. He landed hard on his back, and before the warrior could even begin to struggle, Dog had ripped his throat out.

Whirling, Dog clamped his incredibly powerful jaws on the ankle of another warrior riding past. The man yelled and tried to kick him loose, but Dog held on grimly until the warrior lost his grip on his pony and slid off, waving his arms wildly.

As soon as he hit the ground, that was the end for him, as Dog let go of his mangled ankle and lunged for his face. Jaws opening wide, Dog's fangs clamped shut like a bear trap and did just about as much damage to the Comanche's features. The big cur practically tore his face off his skull.

Meanwhile, Preacher had holstered the empty Colts and now had a knife in each hand as he waited for the charging warriors to come closer. He swayed a little back and forth to avoid arrows that flew toward him.

Two of the Comanches wielding lances aimed their galloping ponies toward the rock behind which Preacher waited. When they were ten feet away, they veered their mounts sharply away from each other so they could race by on both sides of the boulder and skewer Preacher at the same time.

The mountain man took them completely by surprise,

bounding onto the rock and leaping into the air so that their thrusts with the lances missed him. At the same time, he flung both arms out as far as they could reach and let the Comanches' momentum slash their own throats on the knives as they charged past him.

Preacher landed nimbly on the rock, ducked another lance, and leaned over to disembowel the warrior who had missed that strike.

Then the tide of Comanches washed over the rocks and Preacher was in the middle of them, spinning and slashing and kicking men off their ponies. It was sheer madness amid the shrieks of horses and men and the constant booming of pistols. Some of the Texians had saved their shots for close range, and those .36 caliber rounds took an incredible toll on the attackers. The air filled with the acrid stench of powdersmoke and the coppery tang of freshly spilled blood—a lot of it.

Preacher's arms, in fact, were red to the elbows as he descended deeper and deeper into the carnage. He knew he was suffering some wounds, but he didn't actually feel them. His blood was surging too hard in his veins, his heart slugging too madly in his chest, for him to be aware of anything other than the hostile faces screaming at him as he slashed at them.

Something bumped his legs. He came to his senses enough to look down and see that Dog was fighting alongside him. The big cur's coat was streaked with blood from his own injuries—and plenty that had splattered on him from the devastation his fangs were wreaking. A savage grin plucked at Preacher's mouth. If he was going to go down at last after all his adventures . . . if the dead Comanches piled up around him until he could no longer withstand their weight . . . if this was his day to die . . . he could think of no better way to leave this world than with his loyal friend at his side and those bloody blades in his hands . . .

The shadows of dusk were gathering over Bandera Pass as the Texians loaded the blanket-shrouded forms of their dead over saddles and got ready to depart this grim notch in the hills. Although nearly all the defenders had suffered wounds of some sort, only five of them had been killed before the Comanches broke off the attack and retreated for the final time.

A short time earlier, Flacco had confirmed that the Comanches were gone after scouting both sides of the pass. Nobody had bothered to count the dead warriors, but it was easy to see, even at a glance, that well over a hundred of them had been slain in the fighting. That was as high a price as the Comanches were willing to pay, especially with night coming on.

Preacher finished tying a rag around Wallace's leg as a makeshift bandage, one of several that the big Texian sported. Earlier, Wallace had patched up Preacher's wounds, which were numerous but not serious. The same was true for Dog.

Captain Hays came over to Preacher and Wallace and said, "We're about ready to move out. But I have to tell you something, Preacher, and I don't believe you're going to like it."

"No rule says I have to. Go ahead, Cap'n."

"I'm under orders to report any significant hostile encounter with the Indians, so we'll have to ride to Austin and let President Lamar and the Secretary of War know what happened here."

Preacher frowned. "I thought you boys got sent to find those Comancheros and keep Twisted Foot from tradin' with them."

"Those were our orders," Hays agreed. Preacher could tell from the taut line of the captain's jaw that he didn't particularly care for what he was saying, either. "But the other order takes precedence. It won't take that long to reach Austin, and then we can get back on the trail. Of course, you're not under my command, so you can proceed however you please."

"Thank you most to death for that," Preacher muttered. "I'll be pushin' on south, then."

Wallace said, "Not by yourself, you won't." He faced Hays and went on, "Cap'n, I'm requestin' a leave of absence."

A faint smile touched Hays's lips. "I take it you intend to go with Preacher?"

"Yes, sir, I surely do." Wallace glanced at the mountain man. "If that's all right with you."

"Be glad to have the company," Preacher assured him.

Two more members of the ranging company had been listening to the conversation and stepped forward now.

"Mose and I want to take leaves of absence, too, Cap'n," one of them said.

Hays frowned. "Am I about to have a mutiny on my hands, Howard?"

"No, sir," the young man said. "We just want to go with Preacher to hunt for them Comancheros. You've done said plenty of times how important it is to keep the Comanch' from gettin' their hands on a bunch of rifles."

Hays sighed, nodded, and said, "That's sure enough true." He looked around at the other men. "Anybody else want to leave the company for the time being?"

"I would," Ben Highsmith said. "It's been a plumb honor to fight alongside Preacher. But I reckon I'm too shot up with arrows."

Highsmith was pale from loss of blood and had a couple of bandages wrapped around his middle where arrows had penetrated, luckily not deep enough to prove fatal.

Several other men spoke up, expressing much the same sentiment as Highsmith. The company was in bad shape after the nearly daylong battle with the Comanches. Some of them needed better medical attention than they could get out here in the middle of the untamed frontier.

After a moment, Hays nodded and said, "All right, I'll grant those leaves of absence to the three of you. Besides, since you're all good Texians, I suspect that if I *didn't* give you permission, you'd just go ahead and do what you want to anyway." He chuckled. "It's never wise to stand between a Texian and a fight."

"Truer words were never spoke, Cap'n," Wallace said.

"Be sure and take enough supplies and ammunition with you," Hays went on. "And when you're finished with this little lark, I'll expect you to rejoin the company. You'll find us in either Austin or Bexar. Unless we've already been sent back out to those Comancheros and run into you along the way."

"We'll sure be watchin' for you, Cap'n," the young man called Howard promised.

Hays shook hands with all three of them, then clasped Preacher's hand.

"It was an honor fighting alongside you, sir."

"Same goes for me," Preacher said. "If there's anybody who can tame this wild country, it's you Texas rangers."

The men all mounted up. A few of them had to ride double, since some of the horses had been killed in the fighting even though they'd been in the cover of the trees. Horse was fine, and so were the mounts belonging to Wallace, Mose, and Howard, along with Preacher's pack-horses.

They all rode together to the bottom of the pass, where Preacher and his companions headed on south while Captain Jack Hays and the rest of the ranging company swung off to the east. Preacher wasn't sure exactly where the new capital city, Austin, was in relation to Bandera Pass, but he knew he was headed in a different direction.

Preacher hadn't spoken to Mose and Howard much since throwing in with the ranging company, but he had picked up a little about them. He looked over at the young men and said, "You fellas are brothers, ain't you?"

"Yes, sir," Howard replied. "I'm Howard Strickland, and this here is my little brother Mose."

Despite being the "little" brother, Mose was almost a head taller than Howard. He was the tall, lanky, soft-spoken and taciturn sort, while Howard was short and stocky and had a general air of feistiness about him.

"We're obliged to you for lettin' us ride with you," Howard went on. "We'd sure hate to see how bad things might turn out if those Injuns get their hands on a bunch of rifles. Texas is plumb dangerous enough with them just havin' bows and arrows and lances!"

"Yep," Mose agreed.

"I'm glad to have you along," Preacher said. He paused, then added, "When you get right down to it, though, the job that brought me here ain't stoppin' the Comanches or the Comancheros. It's findin' that fella Toby Harper and recoverin' the money Twisted Foot stole, if I can. And I've given myself the job of seein' to it that Señorita Montez gets back to her pa safe and sound."

"And settlin' the score with that Mallory varmint who double-crossed you, I expect," Wallace said.

"If he's still alive, that'd make a nice bonus," Preacher admitted. "We'll likely find out, I reckon, once we've located ol' Twisted Foot. I expect Mallory's bunch will be somewhere in the vicinity."

They rode on in silence for a while as twilight settled down over the Texas landscape. Preacher had decided they would try to put several miles between themselves and Bandera Pass before stopping to make camp for the night.

"Where are you fellas from?" he asked the Strickland brothers.

"We come from a town in Arkansas you never heard of called Gravette," Howard answered. "Our folks had a farm near there. But it's up in the Ozarks, and that's mighty hard country for farmin'. So they decided to come down here and brought the whole family along." He chuckled. "Got here in 1835."

"Just in time to go to war with Mexico," Preacher said.

"Yep," Mose said.

"Yeah, we was part of the Runaway Scrape. Mose and me got enough size on us to fight at San Jacinto when Sam Houston whipped ol' Santa Anna. The two of us and a couple of friends of ours name of Bo and Scratch were right in the thick o' things. That was a good scrap. Pert near as good as the one today."

Wallace said, "So you see, Preacher, none of us was born here, but that don't keep us from bein' Texians now. Same goes for you."

"I appreciate the sentiment, Bill."

That brought a hoot of laughter from Howard and a smile from Mose. "Cap'n Jack's the only one who calls him Bill," Howard said. "The rest of us call him the name he's been known by ever since he was a young'un."

"What's that?"

Wallace took his right foot out of the stirrup and stuck it out. Grinning, he asked, "With clodhoppers like that, what do you reckon they call me? Bigfoot Wallace!"

CHAPTER 25

Preacher and his companions couldn't rule out the chance of running into more Comanches, so they took turns standing guard that night and for the next several nights as they rode south through the hill country.

They passed well west of San Antonio de Bexar, according to what Wallace and the Strickland brothers told Preacher. It had been quite a while since he had been to that settlement, the largest in Texas, and he wouldn't have minded visiting it again, but he had other chores to tend to.

As they traveled, they kept an eye out for any signs of Styles Mallory's bunch. That group shouldn't have been too far ahead of them, even with the delay of the nearly daylong battle with the Comanches.

On the afternoon of the third day, Dog ran ahead and dashed back and forth, sniffing the ground, then turned and hurried back to Preacher. He whined a couple of times, then repeated the process.

"What's gotten into that wolf of yours?" Wallace asked.

"He's picked up a familiar scent," Preacher said, not bothering to correct the big Texian this time. "And there's only one explanation for that."

He motioned for the others to stop, then reined in and swung down from the saddle. Leaving Horse's reins dangling, Preacher walked ahead until he came to the area where Dog was running around. He kept his eyes on the ground, so he had no trouble spotting the hoofprints that appeared to have been made in the past day or so.

Dog was especially interested in an old log, rearing up to put his front paws on the thick trunk of the oak that had fallen sometime in the past. It was just about the right size, Preacher reflected, to have served as a seat for somebody.

"Who do you smell, Dog?" the mountain man asked. "Alita or those two old-timers? Or all three of 'em?"

Dog barked sharply as if answering the question. Preacher didn't doubt that he was.

When the big cur had started acting like this, Preacher's first thought was that he had picked up the girl's scent. Dog would have remembered it from the time they had all spent with Mallory's bunch. Although she had been frightened of him at first because of his fierce appearance, Alita and Dog had become friends, and she had spent quite a bit of time rubbing his ears and scratching his head. Dog wouldn't have forgotten her scent in the days they had been apart.

Preacher studied the tracks scattered around and then told the others, "They were here, all right. I'm sure of that."

"Mallory's men?" Wallace asked.

"Yeah. The horses that left these prints were shod, and it ain't likely that another party this size was travelin' through these parts, headin' south."

"How long ago do you reckon they came through?" Howard asked.

"Sometime yesterday, I'd say."

"So if we push a little harder, we might catch up with them tomorrow," Wallace said.

Preacher nodded. "More than likely. Might be a good idea not to push *too* hard, though. If we ride up on 'em in broad daylight, they're liable to start shootin' as soon as they recognize me. I wouldn't trust any of that bunch any farther than I can throw 'em."

"From what you've told us about that varmint Guidry, I don't blame you. You're thinkin' we'll locate their camp and do some scoutin' tomorrow night?"

"That's what I had in mind," Preacher said.

"We have an actual trail to follow now," Howard pointed out. "As long as we don't lose it, it should take us right to them."

Preacher nodded toward Dog and said, "Once this big fella's got the scent, there ain't much chance of us losin' the trail."

Preacher's prediction turned out to be true. They were able to follow the hoofprints left by the numerous riders, and any time they came to a stretch where the prints disappeared, Dog tracked their quarry by scent.

During the next day and a half, they left the hills behind and traveled over grassy, gently rolling countryside crossed regularly by creeks and dotted with clumps of mesquites and live oaks. Preacher knew the terrain would continue leveling out gradually all the way to the Gulf of Mexico.

He didn't think they would have to go that far. His instincts told him that the spot picked for the rendezvous between Twisted Foot and the Comancheros wasn't that far ahead of them.

Late in the afternoon, Preacher called another halt, dismounted, and knelt to study the hoofprints they had been following.

"These ain't any more than a couple of hours old," he told his companions. "We'll push on for a while, but take it easy. This ain't the time to be crowdin' the fellas we're after."

The landscape still had enough of a roll to it that seeing for long distances was difficult. Preacher, Wallace, and the Strickland brothers might come up on the larger group without much warning. Preacher kept Dog close instead of allowing him to range ahead; he didn't want the big cur being spotted and recognized.

They stopped when night fell. Preacher told the others, "Cold camp tonight, boys. We don't want anybody seein' or smellin' a fire."

As they sat around and gnawed jerky, Preacher took his boots off and replaced them with high-topped moccasins he took from his saddlebags.

"You goin' somewhere, Preacher?" Wallace asked.

"Thought I'd scout a mite," the mountain man replied. He took off his hat and tossed it onto his saddle. He rubbed dirt on his cheeks and forehead to keep them from shining in the moonlight. His dark beard, still a lot more pepper than salt, covered his jaws and chin. In his dark brown buckskins, he would be able to blend into the shadows without much trouble.

"You want some company?"

"No offense, Bigfoot, but Dog and me are used to doin' this sort of thing by ourselves."

"Anyway, Bigfoot," Howard said, "you may be a fightin' fool, but you ain't exactly the quietest fella in the world."

Wallace scowled and said, "I can be quiet when I need to."

"I don't doubt it," Preacher assured him, "but it'd be better if you and Howard and Mose stayed here for a spell."

"We'll be here," Howard promised. "But if you need us, Preacher . . ."

"I'll holler," the mountain man said.

With Dog at his side, he stole off into the gathering shadows. Within moments, he couldn't see his three companions anymore, and he was confident they couldn't see him, either.

He moved at a swift but stealthy pace, trotting along like a big cat. He estimated that he had covered about a mile from the spot where he had left the others when he came to a sudden stop.

Dog pressed against his leg. Preacher felt the big cur trembling with eagerness. The faintest of growls came from him.

Preacher drew in a deep breath, then knelt beside Dog and slipped his arm around the hairy neck. He leaned close and said, "Yeah, I smell it, too. That's a campfire, no doubt about it. They ain't far away now."

The only question was . . . were the people camped up ahead Mallory's bunch, including Alita, Pablo, and Laurenco? Or was it Twisted Foot's big war party or even the Mexican traders the Comanches were supposed to meet?

Preacher didn't know, and there was only one way to find out.

"Let's get a mite closer," he breathed to Dog.

Preacher rose and padded onward. The smell of woodsmoke grew stronger. He had no trouble following his nose on a course that took him a little west of due south now. He hadn't spotted the glow of a fire yet, but that came as no surprise. Whoever had built it could have dug a small pit first, to keep the flames from being so obvious.

Preacher stopped, put a hand on Dog's back, and pressed down lightly. Dog knew that meant to stay. He dropped into a sitting position. Preacher made a slight gesture, reinforcing the order. Then he slipped forward and after a short distance dropped to his hands and knees to creep forward.

This reminded him of sneaking up on those Blackfoot villages when he was a young man, although the landscape in these parts was a lot more wide open than it was up in the mountains. The star-dotted vault of night seemed incredibly vast above him. A quarter-moon was visible, not too high yet in the eastern sky.

He crawled up a grassy slope, hoping that he wouldn't put a hand down on some night-roaming rattlesnake. When he reached the top, a hunch made him stretch out on his belly and push ahead on his elbows and toes just enough for his head to rise above the crest.

On the other side of the rise, about a hundred yards away, a dark line of trees and thicker vegetation marked the course of one of the numerous creeks. Not far from it was a slowly shifting mass that Preacher realized was a group of horses picketed and grazing. A dim glow between the horses and the trees told him that was the origin of the smoke he'd been following. That was the campfire, and he saw a few shadowy figures moving around it.

He had to get closer. At this distance, he couldn't make out any details. Judging by the number of horses, though, which appeared to be fairly small, this had to be Mallory's group. Twisted Foot's war party and the band of Comancheros from Mexico would have needed more mounts.

Preacher eased forward, moving slowly and carefully.

The breeze was blowing from the camp toward him, so the horses wouldn't smell him and get spooked. He could hear low voices talking, but he couldn't make out the words yet.

He froze as a man suddenly walked away from the fire, straight toward him. The man stopped after he'd gone several yards, though, and as Preacher watched, he could tell the hombre was just relieving himself. After a minute, he turned and walked back to the others.

The man was thin as a rail, and the disjointed way he moved was familiar. Preacher knew he was looking at Goose Guidry. That confirmed his hunch that this was the bunch Styles Mallory had brought from Santa Fe to Texas.

He wanted to make sure Alita and the two old-timers were still with them and unharmed, but he was going to have to get closer for that. He started forward again—angling to the side so he wouldn't have to crawl over the spot where Guidry had watered the grass.

He had made it to within twenty yards of the camp when a man stood up and said in a voice loud enough for Preacher to understand, "Hollis, you and Weston will take the first turn on guard duty tonight."

Preacher stiffened, and his jaw tightened into a hard line. He not only understood the words, he recognized the voice.

It belonged to Styles Mallory.

Mallory hadn't just escaped from those Comanches a long way north of here. He had made it back to the group and taken command again.

Preacher forced down the anger he felt bubbling up inside him. Yeah, Mallory had double-crossed him and tried to kill him, and that score would be settled sooner or later, but for now Preacher had more important things to worry about. Still moving slowly and silently, he began circling the camp and gradually working his way closer at the same time.

After a few minutes, he was able to discern a dark figure stretched out on the ground with a man sitting on each side of it. That patch of shadow was the right size and shape to be Alita Montez, wrapped up in a blanket against the night chill, maybe. The men flanking her—guarding her—would be Laurenco and Pablo. It was too dark for Preacher to be absolutely certain that was who he was looking at, but he had a hunch he was correct.

He would have liked to make sure of their identities and confirm that they were all right, but he couldn't reach them tonight without alerting the others to his presence. Although it chafed him to do so, he began backing away from the camp.

He had to leave as stealthily as he had approached, so it was half an hour before he reached the spot where he had left Dog. The big cur had sensed him coming and was standing up, waiting, when he got there.

"Come on," Preacher whispered. "Let's get back to Bigfoot and the Strickland boys."

When Preacher and Dog were close to their camp, he called out softly to announce their arrival. He didn't want to take the others by surprise and have them start shooting.

They found Wallace, Howard, and Mose on their feet, holding rifles.

"We figured we'd better be ready if anybody was chasin' you," Wallace said. "Did you have any luck?"

"I found 'em," Preacher said. "Not just Mallory's bunch, but Mallory his own self, too."

"So he *did* get away from the Comanches."

"Yep, and he's still givin' the orders. I'm pretty sure that the gal and the two old-timers who've been takin' care of her were with them, too."

"It must have been a relief to see them," Howard said. "I know you were worried about 'em."

"I couldn't get close enough to be certain they were all right, but I didn't see anything to indicate they weren't. Actually, the fact that Mallory's still alive is a good thing. I trust him to keep the girl safe more than I trust Guidry and the rest of that bunch." He paused. "Mallory won't let anything happen to her that'd hurt her trade value with the Comancheros."

Wallace said, "You really believe he'd be low enough to swap her to those varmints?"

"I don't doubt it for a second, if he thought he could make a bigger profit that way," Preacher declared flatly.

"Well, then, we've got to take her away from them."

Preacher nodded and said, "That's my plan. We need to figure out some sort of distraction, so I can slip in and grab her and the old-timers."

Howard nudged his brother's ribs with an elbow and said, "We can be pretty distractin' when we want to be, can't we, Mose?"

"Yep," Mose replied.

"Question is," Preacher said, "do we make our move now, or do we risk waitin' for Mallory to lead us to the rendezvous between Twisted Foot and the Comancheros? If Toby Harper's still alive, I'd like to rescue him, too. Assumin' that he wasn't workin' with Twisted Foot all along, and there's really only one way to find out about that."

"It'd be takin' a big chance," Wallace said. "Lots more

enemies to deal with." He grinned in the starlight. "But there's somethin' to be said for gettin' a bunch of folks that need killin' together in the same place. Makes dealin' with 'em simpler."

"I always did like the simple life," Preacher said.

CHAPTER 26

Now that they knew where Mallory and his group were, that made following them easier. The trail led south by southwest for another day and a half. To Preacher's surprise, because he had never traveled through this part of Texas before, the landscape actually grew more rugged, broken up by limestone hills and ridges covered with thick brush and scrubby trees. The ridges often overlooked sparkling blue creeks. It was pretty country, no doubt about that.

As they rode along at an easy pace, following Mallory's group but not getting too close, Wallace said, "You can see why folks feel the way they do about Texas, Preacher. All you got to do is look around."

"It's mighty nice," the mountain man agreed. "I reckon the Rockies will always be home to me, though."

"I'd like to see 'em someday. I hear tell there's some good-sized mountains here in Texas, 'way out west toward Nuevo Mexico, but they probably ain't that big compared to what you're used to."

Howard said, "Maybe after this is all over, Preacher, we

could go up to the Rockies with you and you could teach us about fur-trappin'."

"Yeah," Mose agreed. "That sounds like somethin' I'd like to do."

That was a long speech for the tall, laconic Texian. The other three looked at him.

"I got a Crow Indian friend called Nighthawk," Preacher said. "I ought to introduce you to him, Mose. The two of you would just flat talk each other's ears off, I reckon."

The idea of his brother talking anybody's ears off struck Howard as funny. He laughed, slapped his thigh, and said, "I'd sure like to see—"

He stopped short as they all heard a sudden burst of gunfire in the distance.

The four men sat up straighter in their saddles as the shooting continued. Wallace said, "That ain't somebody huntin' game. That's a fight!"

"And a good-sized one, too," Preacher agreed. The shots came from in front of them, the area where they knew Mallory and the others were.

That meant Alita, Pablo, and Laurenco probably were in danger. Preacher heeled Horse into a gallop and called for the others to follow him.

They rode hard around ridges and clusters of boulders, up rises and down the other side, all while the gunfire went on. They topped another slope and reined in abruptly.

Several hundred yards in front of them, a group of riders had taken cover in some rocks while a large force of mounted Comanches rode around them, whooping and firing arrows. It was a situation similar to what had happened in Bandera Pass, but these defenders didn't have the lethal Colt Paterson revolvers, only one-shot flintlock rifles and pistols.

The rocks obscured the people who had taken cover among them, but Preacher had no doubt this was Mallory's bunch. That was confirmed when he spotted Styles Mallory himself crouched behind one of the boulders. Mallory thrust a rifle barrel over the rock and fired.

A few yards away, Goose Guidry battled alongside Lupe Garza. Preacher recognized them, too. He searched intently among the rocks for some sign of Alita or the two old-timers but didn't see them. He could only hope that Laurenco and Pablo were keeping Alita close to the ground and shielding her body with their own. Knowing the two of them, that was what he expected.

"That's the bunch we been chasin', ain't it?" Wallace asked as the four of them sat and watched the battle.

"Yeah," Preacher said.

"Are we gonna try to help them?" Howard asked.

Preacher frowned. Every instinct in his body wanted to race down there and jump into the battle with both feet—or both Colts, rather—but there were at least fifty Comanche warriors surrounding the defenders in the rocks. Even with their revolvers, Preacher and his companions wouldn't be able to swing the odds in their favor.

The mountain man said harshly, "We'd just get ourselves killed if we did, and it wouldn't help those folks. Best we can do now is hope that Mallory's got enough sense to surrender."

"Surrender?" Wallace repeated as if he couldn't believe it. "If they do that, those Comanch' will just kill 'em!"

"Maybe, maybe not. Not right away, anyway. We've left Broken Rock's band a long way behind. There's a good chance those are some of Twisted Foot's warriors, and if they take prisoners, they're likely to lead us right to that rendezvous with the Comancheros. They might want to use captives to give them more leverage in tradin'."

Wallace glared at Preacher for a moment and then said, "That's a mighty cold-blooded way of lookin' at it. What about that girl and the two old pelicans with her?"

"If they make it through this battle, I don't reckon the Comanches will kill them. They'll know that the girl is valuable to the Comancheros, too, even more so than the others."

Howard shook his head and said, "It sure rubs me the wrong way to stay out of a fight, but I suppose you're right, Preacher. Maybe we can do the survivors some good later on."

"If there *are* any survivors," Wallace said in a surly voice.

"We'd best back off a mite," Preacher suggested. "We don't want those Comanch' spottin' us up here."

They moved back down the rise and dismounted. Howard and Mose held the horses while Preacher and Wallace took off their hats and stretched out on their bellies just below the crest so they could watch the battle.

From the looks of it, the fighting wouldn't be going on too much longer. Fewer and fewer shots came from the defenders in the rocks. The circle of warriors racing around on their ponies as they fired arrows into the rocks steadily tightened. In less than ten minutes, the shooting stopped entirely. The Comanches pulled back a little, as if waiting to see what was going to happen.

A moment later, somebody stuck a rifle up from behind the rocks. The barrel had a white rag tied on it. The Comanches knew what that meant. Several of them let out triumphant whoops. They closed in on the rocks, yipping in excitement.

Within minutes, the Comanches had dragged out ten prisoners. Preacher's breath hissed between tight-clenched teeth as he saw Alita being shoved roughly back and forth between two of the warriors. One of them laughed, hooked his hand in the front of her shirt, and tore it open. Alita tried to tug the ripped garment closed, but the Comanche swatted her hand away.

Wallace muttered and growled in anger and exasperation. Preacher knew exactly how he felt. He wanted to put a rifle ball in that warrior's head, and he might have been able to do it from here. But that wouldn't help Alita in the long run.

Relief went through the mountain man when he spotted Laurenco and Pablo among the prisoners, too. They didn't seem to be hurt, although it was difficult to tell at this distance.

Styles Mallory, Goose Guidry, and Lupe Garza were all still alive, too, along with several of the other men. The Comanches herded all the prisoners together, poking at them with lances. Some of the warriors went into the rocks, laughing and shouting, and started mutilating the bodies of the men who had been killed in the fight. Preacher didn't have much sympathy for them—he knew any of them would have killed him without a second thought if it meant more money for them—but still he had to grit his teeth again at the knowledge of what was being done in those rocks.

The Comanches rounded up all the horses belonging to Mallory's group and then started off to the south, driving horses and prisoners alike. They left Alita alone for now.

She stumbled along between Pablo and Laurenco, with the two old-timers supporting her.

"Now what?" Wallace asked.

"Now we follow 'em," Preacher said.

The party of Comanches was a large enough group that following them was no problem. They didn't move very fast since the captives were stumbling along on foot. Preacher and his three companions stayed back far enough that they weren't likely to be spotted.

Anyway, the Comanches acted like the lords of this country—which they pretty much were, Preacher supposed—and didn't pay much attention behind them. They didn't figure anyone would dare to follow them.

The ride gave Preacher the chance to come up with a plan. It had plenty of risks to it, but overall it seemed like the best bet for him to accomplish his goal of rescuing Alita and the two old-timers and finding Toby Harper and the money. The idea depended on where they were going, though, and how soon they would get there.

They stopped to make camp for the night, which was what Preacher wanted. He, Wallace, Howard, and Mose climbed to the top of a brushy knoll to watch as the Comanches built a good-sized fire and tended to their ponies while the prisoners sat down with several warriors guarding them.

Preacher could tell how tired Alita, Laurenco, and Pablo looked, but other than exhaustion they seemed to be all right. Some of Mallory's men were wounded and in worse shape. They might not make it all the way to wherever the Comanches were taking them. Mallory himself, along with Guidry and Garza, appeared to be unharmed.

"What are we gonna do?" Wallace asked. "Slip in there tonight and grab the girl?"

"I'm gonna slip into their camp, all right," Preacher said, "but not the rest of you."

Howard said, "You want the rest of us to make a ruckus so you'll have a chance to free the prisoners?"

Preacher shook his head. "Come mornin', I intend to *be* one of those prisoners."

The three Texians stared at him. Wallace found his voice first and asked, "What in blazes are you talkin' about?"

"The Comanches standin' guard will be watchin' to make sure none of the prisoners try to escape. They won't be expectin' somebody to sneak in. I want to make sure Señorita Montez is all right, and then I'm gonna stay with 'em until they get back to wherever Twisted Foot has met up with the Comancheros. Bigfoot, you'll trail along behind us and stay close by in case I need some help."

"What do you figure on me and Mose doin'?" Howard asked.

"You go along with Bigfoot," Preacher explained, "until you know where the rendezvous is. As soon as you do, light a shuck for Bexar and find Cap'n Jack and the rest of his company, and then bring 'em all back to the rendezvous as fast as you can."

"Preacher, you're loco," Wallace said bluntly. "There ain't no way of knowin' where the cap'n will be, and Texas is a mighty big place!"

"Yeah, but he said he'd be headin' in this direction as soon as he reported to the president about that fight at Bandera Pass and got medical attention for the fellas who needed it. I'm countin' on Howard and Mose runnin' into him somewhere along the way. That'll speed things up."

Wallace rubbed his angular jaw as he frowned in thought. "Maybe," he allowed slowly. "And maybe you'll wind up gettin' staked out on an anthill by those Comanch'."

"I'll take that chance." The mountain man shrugged. "Worst comes to worst, I'll grab the señorita and the old-timers and make a break for it. I plan on takin' a couple of pistols and some spare cylinders with me."

"That'd take the Injuns by surprise," Howard said. "Maybe not the Comancheros, though. We don't know how well they're armed."

"That'd be another good thing to find out, I reckon."

Wallace pondered on Preacher's plan as evening settled down over the landscape. Finally, he nodded and said, "It all sounds mighty risky to me . . . but I don't reckon there's any way to tackle somethin' like this without takin' a lot of chances. We need some sort of signal, though, so if you get too deep in a hole, I'll know to come bustin' in to pull you out."

"If you hear these Colts blazin', that'll be the signal," Preacher said. "That'll mean I'm tryin' to kill as many of those varmints as I can, as fast as I can."

CHAPTER 27

Preacher waited until it was good and dark to make his move, and while he waited, he gnawed some jerky and washed it down with water from one of the canteens.

Dog sat beside him with his rear end butted up against Preacher's hip. From time to time, with no warning, he turned his head, leaned closer, and licked Preacher's ear or cheek, bringing a chuckle from the mountain man each time it happened.

"You're gonna have to stay with Bigfoot, old son," he told the cur as he rubbed Dog's ears. "I'm hopin' those Comanch' won't notice they got one extra prisoner, but I don't reckon there's any way in the world they wouldn't notice you."

Dog whined quietly.

"I know. But if Bigfoot has to come a-runnin' to help me, that'll be your signal to jump right in, too. I feel a whole heap better about the whole thing knowin' that the two of you won't be far away."

Dog leaned against Preacher's shoulder. He was fierce enough to terrify strong men, and his snarl could turn their guts to water, but at moments like this, he was just a big, overgrown pup to Preacher.

He hugged Dog, stood up, scratched the big cur's ears again, and then said firmly, "Stay with Bigfoot. Do what he says."

"You reckon he'll actually do it?" Wallace asked.

"He will. Horse won't give you no trouble, either."

"I hope so. I got to admit, that wolf makes me a mite nervous."

Preacher laughed. "I didn't figure much of anything could make you nervous, Bigfoot. But don't worry about Dog. He knows what to do."

He left his hat and boots on but took off the holstered revolvers. He stuck two of the Colts in his waistband at the small of his back and covered them with his buckskin shirt. Loaded extra cylinders went in his pockets. With any luck, they wouldn't be too noticeable. He tucked his sheathed knife into one of his saddlebags for safekeeping.

"All right, fellas, I'll be seein' you. Actually, *you'll* be seein' *me* before I see you again, if all goes accordin' to plan. When those Comanch' move out in the mornin', I ought to be with them as one of the captives."

"Good luck, Preacher," Wallace said as he stuck out his hand. Preacher shook with him, then with the Strickland brothers, who echoed Wallace's encouraging words, even the normally taciturn Mose.

Preacher moved off silently into the shadows and disappeared within seconds.

Earlier, while it was still light enough to see, he had studied the surrounding countryside and decided on his best approach to the Comanche camp. The site was under some large trees sitting in the open, except on the west where some brush came within a few yards of the trees.

Preacher circled in that direction, catfooting through the darkness.

He used all the stealth he had learned in the decades of adventurous living on the frontier to move through the brush in almost complete silence. That meant he had to proceed very slowly and judge every move, even the smallest one, before he committed to it. But there was no rush, he told himself. He had all night if he needed it.

He didn't know how much time had passed when he reached the edge of the brush. He stretched out on his belly so he could study the camp by the flickering light of the fire, which was dying down now and would soon be just embers.

The captives were gathered in a tight knot under one of the trees. Laurenco, looking haggard in the unsteady light from the flames, leaned against the trunk while Alita leaned against his chest and appeared to be asleep. Pablo was beside Laurenco, also nodding off. Styles Mallory was on Laurenco's other side.

Preacher felt a surge of anger as he looked at Mallory. The man had double-crossed him and tried to kill him, and Preacher wasn't going to forget—or forgive—that treachery.

Right now, though, if he could get among the prisoners as he intended, he and Mallory would be allies for the time being. *Unless* Mallory tried to betray him again and call the attention of their Comanche captors to him.

Preacher couldn't rule that out, just because of Mallory's nature. A lowdown scorpion just has to sting.

But he couldn't see how it would gain Mallory anything, either, and he didn't believe the man would make such a move unless it benefited him somehow. Turning Preacher over to the Comanches wouldn't really curry any favor with them. They would just do whatever they already planned to do with the captives, anyway.

Preacher was convinced they were taking the prisoners to Twisted Foot, and wherever Twisted Foot was, by now El Carnicero and the rest of the Comancheros probably were, too.

The next move for him was to join the prisoners. Only two warriors were standing guard over them now, and both of those men were watching the captives themselves, alert for any sign that they were about to make a break for it.

Preacher didn't like the idea of crossing the ten or twelve feet of open ground between the brush and the trees, but at least the moon hadn't risen yet. Carefully, he lifted himself on hands and knees and eased forward out of the brush.

The few moments it took for him to reach the trees seemed much longer than they really were. When he was hidden in the thick shadows again and no outcry had arisen in the camp, he stopped where he was and allowed relief to wash through him.

He indulged that feeling for a couple of heartbeats, then it was time to get on with what he was doing.

Again taking it so slowly and carefully that he was able to move without making more than the faintest of sounds, he worked his way closer to the tree where Laurenco leaned with Alita resting against him. Most of the prisoners seemed to be asleep now, but Preacher could tell from the way Laurenco held his head that the older man was still awake.

When he was on the other side of the tree, he pushed himself up and pressed against the trunk. He whispered, "Laurenco. Don't react. It's me, Preacher."

Despite being told not to react, Laurenco lifted his head

and his whole body stiffened. It wasn't much, though, and neither of the warriors standing guard seemed to notice.

"Preacher?" Laurenco said, barely moving his lips. "How can that be? Mallory told us you were dead, that the Comanches killed you."

Mallory was sound asleep now, slumped over on the ground. Preacher swallowed the anger that welled up in his throat at the sight of the treacherous varmint. He said simply, "He was wrong." He could explain the details later. "Is the señorita all right?"

"Yes. Frightened and exhausted, and humiliated by the disrespectful treatment some of those savages gave her, but unharmed. So far."

"What about you and Pablo?"

"The Indians pushed us around some, but no worse than Mallory's men did before the Comanches ever attacked us." The old-timer paused, then added, "I am not sure which group is more deserving of being called savages."

"I agree with you there," Preacher said.

"You have come to rescue us? You have help, perhaps?"

"I do, but not enough to tackle these Comanch' head-on. Instead of rescuin' you . . . I've come to join you."

"What?"

Laurenco's startled response was enough to wake up Alita. She lifted her head and murmured, "What is it?"

"Shhh," Laurenco said. "Nothing, señorita. Go back to sleep."

"No, something is going on," she insisted. "Tell me what it is. I am not afraid."

Laurenco sighed and said, "You must not cry out or do anything to make the savages look more closely at us. Do you understand?"

"I do."

"Very well. Preacher is alive, and he is here to help us."

"Oh!"

Preacher winced at Alita's exclamation. Laurenco quickly tightened his arm around her shoulders to try to stop her from doing or saying anything else. She didn't make a sound after the first gasped word, but she was stiff now and after a moment sat up straighter.

"Where is he?" she whispered.

Preacher reached around to where he could grasp Alita's arm and squeeze it reassuringly. She turned her head and peered back over Laurenco's shoulder into the darkness on the other side of the tree.

"Careful, señorita," Laurenco whispered.

"How did you . . . Mallory told us . . ."

"I know," Preacher said, interrupting Alita's confused words. "It's a long story, and I'll tell you about it later. Right now, I want you to understand, I'm not here to rescue you. I'm going to pretend to be one of Mallory's bunch and go with you to wherever the Comanches are taking you."

Alita was smart enough to grasp instantly what Preacher had in mind. "You still want to rescue Toby and recover the money my father sent to Señor Eckstrom?"

"That's the idea," Preacher said. "I've got some friends trailin' us, and once we get to the rendezvous, they'll try to fetch help in time to do us some good."

Laurenco said, "It sounds as if there's a good chance this plan won't accomplish anything except to get *you* killed, too. You should take the señorita and try to escape. Leave Pablo and me here. We would only slow you down."

"No," Alita said. "I would never desert the two of you like that, Laurenco."

"But you must—"

"Stop arguin', blast it," Preacher said in as urgent a whisper as he could manage. "Those Comanch' are gonna start watchin' you closer if you keep it up. Makin' a break now would just get some of us, or all of us, killed and wouldn't help nobody. Let's just wait and give this plan o' mine a chance to work."

"Yes. Yes, of course, you're right," Laurenco said. "Señorita, lean your head against me again and go back to sleep. You need your rest." He paused, then sighed and added grimly, "Tomorrow, like all the others, will be a hard day."

Alita didn't respond for a moment, but then she said, "You are right, Laurenco. I will try to rest. And Preacher . . . I am very glad you are not dead."

"So am I, señorita, so am I." Even under these bleak circumstances, a chuckle escaped from the mountain man's mouth. "Mallory over there may not feel the same way, though. He's liable to be a mite surprised when he sees me, and we might as well go ahead and get it over with."

Preacher told Laurenco to wake up Pablo, carefully, and fill him in on what was going on. While Laurenco was doing that, Preacher crawled around to the other side of the tree where Mallory now lay on his side with his knees pulled up.

Preacher slid his arm over Mallory's shoulder and as quietly as possible clamped his forearm across Mallory's throat to choke off any outcry. He let his weight down on Mallory and pinned him to the ground so the man couldn't thrash around and attract the attention of the guards.

"Mallory!" he breathed into the man's ear. "Mallory, don't fight me, blast it. It's Preacher. I'm here to help you."

Mallory went still. Preacher glanced at the Comanche

guards. They appeared bored and sleepy. They were the lords of this realm, they far outnumbered the prisoners, and if anybody had told them that an enemy had just slipped *into* the camp, they wouldn't have believed it.

"If I let go of you, are you gonna stay still and quiet?" Preacher whispered. "I know you figure I got a grudge against you, but believe me when I say that don't mean a damn thing right now. We're on the same side."

Those words tasted bad in Preacher's mouth, but he said them and meant them. The score he had to settle with Styles Mallory could wait for another day—and if that day never came, then Preacher figured he'd have more important things to worry about.

"How about it?" he went on. "We gonna work together?"

Mallory nodded, his chin pressing down against Preacher's forearm.

Preacher eased off on his grip, and when Mallory didn't try anything, he let go entirely. He slid off so that he was lying next to Mallory, close enough that they could whisper back and forth.

"Tell me that you got a couple hundred good men out there just waitin' to jump these filthy redskins," Mallory said.

"Nope, but I met up with some fellas who are helpin' me out. When we find out where Twisted Foot is meetin' with those Comancheros, a couple of 'em are gonna try to fetch help for us."

"Wait . . . we're not gonna try to escape? That's not why you're here?"

"No. I'm gonna pretend to be one of your bunch, and we'll let these Comanch' take us where we want to go." Preacher paused, then played another card. "Remember, there's still the matter of that money Twisted Foot stole."

"Yeah," Mallory mused, "but he may have already paid it to the Comancheros."

"Well, then, if he has, we'll just have to steal it back from the varmints."

Mallory didn't say anything for a moment, then he breathed, "You're a crazy man, you know that, Preacher?"

"So I've been told," the mountain man said.

CHAPTER 28

Over the next few minutes, Preacher explained his plan to Mallory, although he didn't tell the man exactly how many allies had accompanied him, only that they were members of a Texian ranging company.

If Mallory knew that Preacher only had three men with him—and two of those would be leaving to search for Captain Jack Hays and the rest of the company as soon as they knew where the rendezvous was—he really would believe that Preacher had lost his mind.

"Have you heard those Comanch' sayin' anything to back up my hunch that they're takin' you to Twisted Foot?" Preacher asked.

"Hell, I don't know what they're jabberin' about," Mallory replied. "A couple of 'em speak barely enough English to boss us around. Lupe's heard 'em talking to each other in Spanish, though, and he says they've mentioned Twisted Foot and somebody called El Carnicero. That means the butcher."

"I know what it means. He's the leader of the Comanchero band that crossed the Rio Grande from Mexico and headed in this direction a while back."

"How do you know that?" Mallory asked with a frown.

"I told you, I ran into a Texian ranging company. The fella in charge of it told me about El Carnicero."

"I reckon that makes sense. We don't know that him and Twisted Foot have got together yet, though. Or whether they've already had their rendezvous and the Comancheros are on their way back to Mexico."

"No, we don't," Preacher admitted. "From what I've heard, though, whenever a band of Comancheros comes across the border and meets up with a war party, they have a big fiesta that lasts for several days, maybe even more, before they get down to any serious tradin'. The Comancheros usually bring a wagonload of tequila with them. I reckon they figure they can make a better deal for themselves if they get the Indians drunk first."

Bigfoot Wallace had told Preacher about those celebrations while they were traveling together. Admittedly, Wallace was just conveying rumors he had heard. He had never witnessed one of those rendezvous between Comanches and Comancheros.

Probably not many white men *had* witnessed such an occasion—and lived to tell the tale.

"I guess maybe there's a chance you're right, then," Mallory admitted. "And more than likely, that would be the best chance we'd have to get our hands on that dinero."

"And Toby Harper," Preacher added.

"Yeah. Montez wanted him back, too, or at least wanted to know whether the fella had betrayed him. The thing of it is, even if you're right and we find ourselves in the middle of that rendezvous, we're gonna be outnumbered by Comanches and Comancheros alike, with odds higher than I can count. You're hopin' those reinforcements will show up in time to give us a hand. But what if they don't?"

"Will we really be that much worse off than we are right now?" Preacher wanted to know. "What do you figure the chances are we could get away from *this* bunch?"

Mallory was silent for a moment, then sighed.

"Mighty slim," he said. "All right, Preacher, we'll play it your way. In the mornin', I'll talk to the other fellas and let 'em know we need to pretend like you've been among us all along. Maybe those Comanch' won't notice." He paused again. "You know who's not gonna be happy about this, at all?"

"Guidry?" Preacher guessed.

"That's right. He hates you so much that I ain't sure what he might do."

"If he tries to give me away to the Comanches, I'll just do what I planned on doin' if *you* took a notion to betray me." Preacher shrugged. "I'll just kill him and be done with it."

Since Pablo was awake now, too, and Laurenco had explained everything to him, Preacher crawled back over and eased forward until he was sitting beside the old-timer as if he had been there all along. He kept his head down and didn't look at the guards. During his talk with Mallory, he had asked if the Comanches had counted the prisoners. Mallory didn't know, but he didn't recall seeing them do anything that looked as if they were. They had just rounded up the ones who hadn't been killed in the fight and started marching them relentlessly to the south.

If that was true, it would help Preacher keep up his deception until they got where they were going. He didn't intend to draw attention to himself.

While he was doing that, Mallory reached over to Lupe

Garza and carefully shook the burly Mexican awake so he could explain in whispers how Preacher was joining them and might be able to have reinforcements show up in time to help them. Mallory would tell Garza to pass along the news to one of the other men, who would pass it in turn to another.

The trick would be to spread the word slowly, so the Comanches wouldn't notice the prisoners buzzing about something. Each man would be instructed to wait a while before talking to one of the others.

The plan was filled with plenty of danger and it wouldn't take much to ruin it, but Preacher couldn't see any better way to play the hand he'd been dealt.

Anyway, if all hell broke loose, he knew Bigfoot Wallace and the Strickland brothers would come galloping in to help, and the prisoners would give a good account of themselves. He hadn't mentioned to any of them that he had two fully loaded Colt Paterson revolvers with him. He figured that if it came down to it, he could kill eight or ten of those Comanches before they knew what was going on.

He watched through slitted eyes from under his lowered hat brim as the word spread slowly among the prisoners. Several of them glanced toward him, but they didn't do it so blatantly as to tip off the guards that something was going on.

Goose Guidry cast a murderous glare in his direction. Preacher ignored that, but he told himself that once trouble broke out, as it inevitably would, he would probably be wise not to let Guidry behind him.

The rest of the night passed peacefully. Preacher even got a little bit of sleep, although his slumber was light, and he would have been fully awake again in an instant if there had been any sign of trouble.

He was fairly optimistic when the Comanches roused the prisoners the next morning by yelling and kicking at them. None of them seemed to be paying any more attention to him than they were to the others. They were given a short drink from water skins but no food. Alita was allowed to retreat behind a bush to tend to her personal needs, although one of the warriors watched her with a smirk on his face.

Preacher was glad they gave her that much consideration. Everybody else had to take care of their business out in the open.

After the Comanches had eaten, they swung up onto their ponies. Warriors carrying lances herded the prisoners into a compact group and forced them to start walking, poking at the captives but not hard enough to draw blood.

"They don't feed us, eh?" Preacher muttered to Laurenco, who walked beside him. Alita was right in front of them, flanked by Pablo.

"They tossed us scraps from the rabbits they roasted last night," Laurenco explained. "They seem to believe that will be enough to sustain us until we get where we're going." He shrugged. "Perhaps it will be, if the journey isn't too long."

"I wonder how far it is from here to the border."

Laurenco shook his head and said, "I have no idea. I have never been in Texas before. It seems to be a vast land."

"It does, at that," Preacher agreed.

They trudged along all morning through country that would have been mighty pretty under other circumstances. When they came to a creek running from northwest to southeast, they turned and followed it southeastward. It was a clear, sparkling stream that bubbled along merrily over a wide, rocky bed. On the other bank, an almost sheer limestone bluff reared up, about twenty feet high. Trees grew along the rim.

On this side was a mostly clear, grassy strip with more trees off to the left. The Comanches seemed happy and excited as they rode along, which made Preacher suspect that they were getting close to their destination. A few of them raced ahead on their ponies, whooping exuberantly.

For the past few miles, Alita hadn't been steady on her feet as she walked along, and now her knees buckled abruptly. Laurenco had been keeping an eye on her. He sprang forward, still nimble despite his age and worn-out, battered condition, and caught her under the arms to keep her from falling.

Pablo was there instantly, too, helping support her.

"Señorita, you must rest," Laurenco said. "I will tell the savages—"

"No," Alita said as she breathed heavily. "No, you cannot, Laurenco. We must keep going. If we displease them, they might punish us."

Preacher said, "I've got a hunch we ain't too far from where we're goin'. The señorita's right. If she can make it, it's best that we keep movin'."

"Yes, I . . . I feel better now." Alita managed to stand up straighter, although clearly her legs were shaky underneath her as she continued taking one step after another. "I will be all right."

Preacher could tell that she wouldn't be for much longer, though, and from the worried glance Laurenco sent toward him, he knew the old-timer felt the same way. If Preacher was wrong about them nearing the end of this forced march, Alita would soon collapse and wouldn't be able to keep going.

He wasn't sure how the Comanches would react to that. They might be angered enough to take it out on her, and then the old-timers would try to protect her, and there was every chance in the world the whole thing would end badly . . .

It might draw unwanted attention to him, but if she started to fall again, he might just have to carry her, Preacher decided. He wasn't as worn out as the others were, and his lean, wolfish frame packed a lot of strength. He could tote Alita for a good long way if he needed to.

He wasn't going to have to worry about that, he saw a short time later, because the whole group went around a bend in the creek and he saw that they had reached their destination.

He would have liked to stop and study the layout for a few minutes, but their Comanche captors weren't going to allow that. They kept the prisoners moving. Preacher held his head up now and took a good look as he continued walking.

The creek bank to the left rose to a broad, level area some eight feet higher than the area right along the stream. This bench extended for at least a half mile and was a quarter of a mile deep. Sitting in the middle of this large open area were the ruins of what had been an impressive adobe house surrounded by a crumbling stone wall. Most of the house's walls were still standing, but the roof had collapsed in places and Preacher could tell that the insides had been gutted by fire at some time in the past. The outer wall had had wooden gates at the entrance. One of them lay on the ground rotting while the other hung crazily askew from one hinge.

Outside the wall around the house and its yard, more ruins were scattered. One structure was large enough that

Preacher figured it had been a barn. The smaller ones likely would have been used for storage, probably a blacksmith shop, and quarters for the workers.

Preacher could tell that this had been a *rancho* built by some daring pioneer who had come out here from San Antonio de Bexar, more than likely. It was difficult to tell how long the ruins had been here. Maybe as long as a hundred years, which would have put the ranch's establishment well before the revolution that had ended Spain's rule over Mexico. Some rich Spanish grandee must have had dreams of starting an empire here in the Texas wilderness.

Those dreams had smashed head-on into the threat of the Comanches, as the burned, devastated state of the buildings made perfectly clear. Preacher figured the ambitious but foolish grandee, his family, and his workers had all been wiped out, maybe in a series of raids, maybe in one big massacre.

Currently, the *rancho* was occupied again, though. Pole corrals that appeared to have been built fairly recently had a lot of Indian ponies and good-looking saddle horses in them, as well as the mules that had pulled the half-dozen covered wagons parked inside the compound's wall.

There were a lot of people around, too—bare-chested Comanches in buckskin leggings and feathers, Mexicans in tall sombreros, linen shirts, and tight trousers with gaudy embroidery down the sides of the legs, even a few white men in buckskins and homespun. Those had to be gringo outlaws who had thrown in with the Comancheros. Even at a distance Preacher heard shouts and laughter. One of those fiestas Bigfoot Wallace had told him about was going on.

A couple of the Comanches bringing in the prisoners galloped ahead, no doubt to bring word of the group's arrival. Preacher heard some of the warriors calling to each other and understood enough of the lingo to know that they were talking about Twisted Foot.

The captives were so tired and in bad enough shape that some of them struggled up the rise, even though it wasn't that steep. Laurenco and Pablo each held one of Alita's arms. Since she was in good hands, Preacher drifted over to walk beside Styles Mallory.

"Looks like your hunch was right all the way down the line," Mallory muttered. "This is a rendezvous if I've ever seen one. Hell, it sounds like the greasers have even brought along some whores."

Mallory was right. Preacher heard female shrieks as they approached. He hoped they were cries of ribald laughter and not caused by anything else.

Once they reached level ground, all the haggard prisoners were herded toward what had been the main entrance in the stone wall. Through that opening, Preacher saw that a brush arbor had been erected in front of the double doors of the *hacienda*. Those doors were gone, destroyed in the fire that had gutted the house.

The arbor created a shaded area, and in that shade were several chairs that must have come from one of the wagons. None of the furniture in the house would have survived the flames. From what Preacher could see of the ruin's interior, it must have been an inferno in there.

Two of the chairs were occupied. A tall, broad-shouldered Comanche warrior sat in one of them, while a moonfaced Mexican with a close-cropped black beard lounged in the other. As the prisoners tramped through the opening where the gates had been, some of their captors yipped and yelled. He heard Twisted Foot's name in the Comanche tongue, but he didn't need that to realize they were being taken before the brutal war chief.

That meant the man sitting beside him was probably El Carnicero, the Butcher, the leader of the Comancheros.

Under his breath, Mallory said, "I hope that help you were talkin' about ain't far off, Preacher."

The mountain man knew better than to hope for that. They were going to have to survive for a few days, anyway.

And judging by the hostile glare on Twisted Foot's face as the war chief stood up, that might be a long shot.

CHAPTER 29

Sitting down, Twisted Foot was quite an imposing figure. When he rose from the chair, his height and his brawny frame continued to give that impression.

It was only when he started to walk toward them that his deformity became obvious. His right foot was turned far in and twisted so that he actually walked on the outside of that foot, rather than the sole. On horseback, it wouldn't hinder him in the least from being a great warrior, but when he walked, it made his gait awkward and lurching. Even so, the expression on his face was one of proud, cruel arrogance.

El Carnicero, on the other hand, appeared amused as he got to his feet and sauntered after the Comanche war chief. He was about as wide as he was tall and was something of a dandy in fancy trousers and a charro jacket. A quirt dangling from its loop around his left wrist brushed against the ornate trim on his trousers leg. His sombrero had little balls dangling from the outer edge of the brim. The jovial grin on his face didn't really jibe with the nickname "the Butcher."

Appearances could be mighty deceptive sometimes, though, the mountain man knew.

As the prisoners were marched across the courtyard, Twisted Foot came to a stop and crossed his arms as he waited for them to reach him. El Carnicero ambled up beside him and hooked his thumbs in his gunbelt, which had two holstered Colts attached to it. Preacher was interested but not surprised to see that the Comanchero boss had somehow gotten his hands on a couple of the revolvers.

Two of the warriors who had brought in the captives dismounted and stood in front of Twisted Foot. Preacher was able to follow enough of what they were saying to know that they were reporting their encounter with Mallory's bunch a couple of days' ride northwest, while scouting to make sure none of the Texian ranging companies were in the area.

They had assumed at first that Mallory and his men were rangers, but then they had seen Alita and the two old-timers and decided that wasn't the case. Then they took the men to be slavers and figured they might as well steal the girl and bring her to Twisted Foot so he could trade her to the Comancheros. The men who survived the battle could be traded as slaves, too, or tortured to death if El Carnicero didn't want them.

Mallory leaned closer to Preacher and asked quietly, "How much of that heathen jabberin' can you make out? It sounds pretty ominous."

"It is," Preacher said, "but really, it ain't any more than what we expected." Quickly, he filled Mallory in on what the Comanches were saying.

The warriors had used their lances to prod the prisoners into a line so Twisted Foot and El Carnicero could inspect them. The Mexican shuffled forward and leered at Alita, who stood between Laurenco and Pablo with them helping her stay on her feet.

"Step back, you old fools, and let me look at this pretty bird," El Carnicero said in Spanish.

"You will leave the señorita alone," Laurenco said stiffly. "She has been mistreated and is exhausted and should be allowed to rest, if there is any comfortable place."

Preacher didn't figure El Carnicero would pay any attention to Laurenco's demand, unless it was to be angered by it. At first, the Comanchero continued grinning and looked like he wasn't going to react.

Then his left arm lifted quickly and whipped from left to right. The quirt slashed across Laurenco's face and made him let go of Alita as he staggered. She screamed, and Pablo started to step forward, but Laurenco quickly thrust out an arm to keep his friend from charging at El Carnicero.

"No," he said sharply. "No, *mi amigo*, see to the señorita." He straightened and lifted a hand to the blood-dripping cut on his cheek that the quirt had opened up. The cold glare he gave El Carnicero would have been enough to make some men nervous. The grinning Comanchero didn't seem bothered by it, however.

"Next time you defy me, *viejo*, I will kill you," El Carnicero said. The grin on his lips didn't extend to his eyes as his gaze swept over the other prisoners. "This is true for all of you. Better yet, *I* will not kill you. I will give you to my friend Twisted Foot and tell him that he is free to do whatever he wishes with you."

In fluent Spanish, Twisted Foot said, "I am already free

to do whatever I wish. These pitiful dogs are no more *your* prisoners than they are mine."

"I did not mean to imply otherwise, my friend," El Carnicero said smoothly. When Twisted Foot didn't say anything else, he returned to his scrutiny of Alita.

Stepping closer to her and ignoring the glares from Laurenco and Pablo, he lifted his right hand and stroked her cheek, then cupped her chin and tilted her head back and forth.

"Muy bonita!" he declared. "A girl this pretty will fetch a small fortune." He looked at the old-timers. "You two must be her duennas." They flushed at the insulting comparison to the elderly female governesses who often accompanied young ladies, then looked even angrier as the Comanchero leader went on, "Tell me, is she unspoiled? That would increase her value."

Laurenco began, "You should not—", but Alita stiffened her spine, stood up straighter, squared her shoulders, and jerked her chin away from El Carnicero's grasp. She slapped him across the face, just as he had slashed Laurenco with the quirt.

"Such things are no concern of yours," she told him coldly.

For a second, he scowled darkly, then his cocksure grin returned as he said, "My apologies, señorita. Surely you realize I could simply discover the answer to my question for myself."

Alita paled but didn't say anything.

El Carnicero waved a hand dismissively and went on, "No matter. We will discuss that another time. Let me look at these gringo dogs." He started along the line of captives, then laughed as he came to the burly Lupe Garza. "Oh, ho!

Not all are gringos. But you are still a dog, amigo, if you run with dogs."

He came to Preacher and Mallory. His gaze passed fairly quickly over Mallory but stopped at Preacher. The grin went away. His forehead creased in a frown as he studied the mountain man.

"This one," he mused. "Something about this one worries me . . ."

Preacher looked down at the ground and didn't meet the Comanchero's eyes. Humbling himself like that wasn't easy. It went against the grain for him to treat an enemy with any attitude other than defiance. But after a moment, El Carnicero shrugged and moved on, evidently ignoring the instincts that warned him about the mountain man.

The next time he stopped was in front of Goose Guidry. The rail-thin hardcase glared at him.

El Carnicero chuckled and said, "You would like to kill me, eh, amigo?"

"You're damn right I would, you dirty greaser," Guidry practically spat. "And I don't care what you do to me afterward, if you try to whip me with that quirt, the way you did that old pelican, I'll make you eat the blasted thing."

"Oh, ho!" El Carnicero exclaimed again. "Bold talk! Can you back it up?"

"You think I can't?" Guidry sneered. "Reckon there's only one way to find out, ain't there, greaser?"

"Indeed," El Carnicero agreed. Eager anticipation appeared on Guidry's face, but it vanished as the Comanchero turned his head and called, "Pepito!"

With a name like Pepito, the man El Carnicero summoned should have been small, even tiny. Instead, he was towering, a rawboned giant, his face too small for his head, which resembled a block of stone. He stepped from a group of Comancheros who had been watching this confrontation and shuffled over to his leader.

"Que, jefe?"

El Carnicero had to reach up to clap a hand on the giant's shoulder. With a nod toward Guidry, he said, "This hombre has threatened me. What do you think I should do about that?"

"Let me have him, *jefe*," Pepito urged. "I will teach him respect."

"I knew I could count on you, my good amigo."

Even the sight of Pepito lumbering over hadn't been enough to wipe the sneer off Guidry's ugly face. He said, "If you think I'm scared of this big, dumb brute, you're wrong, mister. I'll take him on. I'll take on as many of those greasers as you send at me. It just proves you're too scared to tackle me yourself."

Preacher didn't know whether to admire Guidry's boldness or be astounded at his stupidity. He didn't waste any time debating the question. Like everybody else, he just waited to see what was going to happen next.

Pepito struck with surprising speed. His open hand came up and cracked across Guidry's face. That finally succeeded in getting rid of his sneer. The blow also knocked him off his feet and sent him sprawling in the dust.

Pepito charged after him, clearly intending to kick and stomp him to death. The prisoners and the Comanche warriors surrounding them broke apart to create room for what inevitably would be a short-lived battle.

That was what Preacher believed, anyway. From the looks of it, Pepito ought to be able to break Guidry in two like a brittle branch.

However, Guidry rolled away from the attack, and the

vicious kick Pepito aimed at him missed. That threw the giant off balance. Guidry caught hold of Pepito's upraised foot and heaved with all the strength in his wiry frame.

Pepito went down like a felled tree crashing to earth in a forest.

Guidry was up in the blink of an eye, and the kick he launched didn't miss. It slammed home in Pepito's groin. The giant screamed and curled up in a ball as he clutched himself.

"Goose, look out!" Mallory called.

Guidry tried to turn as El Carnicero stepped up behind him. The heavyset Comanchero was pretty quick for his bulk, too, though, and the gun he had drawn rose and fell in a chopping motion. The butt crashed against the back of Guidry's head. Guidry's knees buckled. He collapsed and landed on his face in the dirt, out cold.

El Carnicero pouched the iron. He turned to Twisted Foot, pointed to the unconscious Guidry, and said, "I want that one. He is a stubborn fool, but he has spirit."

Twisted Foot nodded solemnly in agreement.

El Carnicero went on, "I want the girl, too, of course, and her two *duennas*. And these others." He pointed to Preacher, Mallory, Garza, and a couple of the other men. That left a handful of prisoners. El Carnicero waved at them and said, "Your warriors can have them. Some good sport, eh?"

The men who had just been so casually condemned to an agonizing death yelled in fear and anger and tried to charge at the Comanchero leader, but the warriors surrounding them reacted quickly. They swung their lances, using the butt ends to hammer the prisoners about the head and shoulders and drive them to the ground. Lupe Garza scowled and took a step forward, but Mallory caught hold of his arm and said, "Forget it, Lupe. There's nothing you can do for them."

Twisted Foot turned to El Carnicero and said, "The ones you want, how many rifles will you give me for them?"

"We can discuss that later. Tomorrow, we get down to business, eh?" El Carnicero shrugged. "Or the next day, perhaps. For now, it is time to celebrate."

Twisted Foot didn't look like he cared about celebrating, but if he was a good leader, he would know that his men needed to blow off steam from time to time. That appeared to be what was going on here at the abandoned rancho, so he'd probably be willing to let it continue for a while.

The longer the better, Preacher thought. By now, the Strickland brothers ought to be fogging it away from here, back toward Austin. With any luck they would run into Captain Hays and the rest of the company and lead them right back here.

Pepito still lay curled up on the ground, whimpering as he clutched his privates. El Carnicero motioned impatiently toward his men, and when a couple of them hurried forward, he said, "Help Pepito up and tend to him."

"What can we do to help him, *jefe*?" one of the men asked.

"Tequila!" El Carnicero roared. "It heals everything, no?"

The men took hold of Pepito's arms and struggled to lift him to his feet. Another of the Comancheros had to come help them.

Other men took charge of the prisoners. These were armed with flintlock rifles and pistols. The brace of Colts carried by El Carnicero appeared to be the only repeating firearms among the Comancheros.

Preacher wondered what sort of rifles were in the wagons. He was confident that was where El Carnicero's trade stock was kept. Probably had some barrels of gunpowder in there, too. That was something that might be handy to keep in mind for the future . . .

El Carnicero told his men, "Take them into the hacienda and put them in the room with the other one. Watch them carefully."

Preacher saw hope leap to life in Alita's eyes at the Comanchero's mention of "the other one." Was he talking about Toby Harper? It was certainly possible. And they would find out soon, because the guards, poking at the prisoners with rifle barrels, forced them toward the big, fire-gutted house. A couple of men picked up the still-unconscious Goose Guidry by his shoulders and ankles and carried him after the others.

Alita's step was stronger now, Preacher noted, probably because she hoped she would soon be seeing her fiancé.

While the Comancheros herded the captives toward the house, Twisted Foot's warriors dragged away the luckless members of Mallory's group designated for torture. Some cried in abject terror, others looked too stunned to even react anymore. Preacher had never liked or trusted any of them, but he felt a pang of sympathy anyway. He had run into plenty of varmints who deserved a swift pistol ball in the head, but he wouldn't consign his worst enemy to what was waiting for those fellas.

As they neared the house's entrance, some instinct made the mountain man turn his head and glance back across the creek at the limestone bluff rising there.

What he saw there made his heart beat a little faster. Standing at the top of the bluff, looking straight across the creek at him, was Dog.

CHAPTER 30

The sight of the big cur lifted Preacher's spirits. If Dog was nearby, then chances were that Bigfoot Wallace was, too. It helped a lot knowing that he had a couple of allies he could depend on close by. Sure, they were still outnumbered more than a hundred to one . . . but sooner or later, these Comanches and Comancheros wouldn't know what hit 'em.

Preacher didn't give any sign that he had spotted Dog on the bluff, and none of the others seemed to have noticed the big cur, who whirled and dashed off as soon as he knew that Preacher had seen him. The mountain man didn't say anything about it to the others as they entered the house. He'd had to tell Mallory and the others what his plan was so they wouldn't give him away to the Comanches when he joined them. From here on out, though, he would play his cards even closer to the vest, not trusting anyone except Alita and the two old-timers.

The roof had collapsed and rotted here in the front part of the house, but there were several rooms in the back where, despite damage from the long-ago fire, the roof was still largely intact. Preacher and the other captives were taken to one of those rooms. The door was gone, but a pair of guards stood just outside it, armed with rifles and pistols.

The Comancheros prodded the captives to enter, and as they did, a hollow voice croaked, "Alita! Is . . . is it really . . ."

"Toby!" Alita cried. Her exhaustion forgotten, she flung herself toward a shadowy figure that stepped forward from one of the room's dim corners. She threw her arms around him and hugged him tightly. The man lifted a trembling hand and patted her awkwardly on the back.

There were no windows in the room, but thin rays of light slanted down through the holes in the roof. One of those rays illuminated the man's face enough that Preacher got a fairly good look at it over Alita's shoulder. The man's blond beard wasn't enough to hide how haggard his features were. His face was bruised and had scabbed-over cuts on it, vivid evidence that he had been treated roughly.

Preacher had a hunch the Comanches had some sport with him while they traveled across Texas to the rendezvous with the Comancheros. Nothing bad enough to kill him, but plenty to dispel the notion that he had been Twisted Foot's partner in the attack on the wagon train. Toby Harper had survived the massacre somehow, and Twisted Foot had decided to take him along as a captive. Preacher was certain of that now.

Harper put his hands on Alita's shoulders and moved her back a step. "Let me look at you," he rasped. "I . . . I can't believe it's really you . . . I must be . . . imagining this. Dreaming . . ."

"It is truly me, *querido*," she said.

His face crumpled with grief, and tears rolled from the

deep hollows in which his eyes were set, trickling down into the scruffy beard.

"You shouldn't have come," he said. "You shouldn't . . ."

She gripped his arms and told him, "I had to find you, my love. I had to prove that you would never betray my father and . . . and me."

"But now you'll just die here, too . . . or worse!"

In Spanish, one of the Comancheros who had brought them here ordered harshly, "Get on in there, all of you." He punctuated the command with a blow from the butt of the rifle he carried. He drove it into the back of one of Mallory's men and sent him stumbling forward.

The other captives moved into the small, windowless room. The men carrying the still-unconscious Goose Guidry pitched his limp form at their feet.

"Laurenco! Pablo!" Harper exclaimed. "You're here, too."

"Take heart, my young friend," Laurenco said as he squeezed Harper's shoulder.

"We always knew you bore no blame in this tragedy," Pablo added as he clapped a hand on Harper's other shoulder.

That encouragement, plus the smile that Alita summoned up, seemed to put a little stiffness back in Harper's spine. He straightened from his dismal, despairing stance and looked at the others in the room.

"Who are these men?" he asked.

"We came to find you," Mallory said. He nodded toward Alita. "And the señorita. Her father hired us."

"Same for me," Preacher said, "only it was Daniel Eckstrom in St. Louis who hired me. At the time, I didn't know about Señorita Montez being missing, too."

"I don't guess it matters how you all got here," Harper

said. "I . . . I'm just sorry for what's going to happen to you . . . to all of us."

Mallory said, "Don't give up yet. We're—"

"We're not gonna lose hope," Preacher interrupted. The Comancheros had withdrawn outside the room, but probably several of them were standing guard right outside the door and would hear anything said in here. They didn't need to know about the plan Preacher had shared with Mallory.

At first, Mallory had looked annoyed when Preacher broke in on what he was saying, but now he glanced at the doorway and understanding dawned in his eyes. He said, "That's right, Harper. We'll pull through somehow."

There was nothing in the room except the hard-packed dirt floor. The prisoners all sat down and leaned against the walls. Alita had Harper on one side of her, Laurenco on the other. Pablo sat on Harper's other side, with Preacher next to him and then Mallory and Garza.

Even though the day had been warm outside, the thick adobe walls kept the heat from building up too much inside the ruined house. The lack of a door and the holes in the roof allowed air to move through the room, so it didn't get stuffy. But with so many people crowded into the chamber, which wasn't very big to start with, the smell of unwashed flesh made for an oppressive atmosphere. Some of Mallory's men broke wind now and then, which didn't help.

At moments like this, Preacher sure missed being back in the mountains with all that clean, high country air.

Exhaustion caught up with the captives. Several of them dozed off, including Alita. She leaned against Toby Harper this time. He put his arm around her shoulders. After she had been breathing deeply and regularly for a few minutes, he looked over at Laurenco and said quietly, "You shouldn't have let her come looking for me."

"And how would we have stopped her, Señor Harper? You know as well as any and better than most that the señorita has a mind of her own and no qualms about following it."

"Her father should have forbidden it."

"He did that very thing, señor," Laurenco said solemnly. "For all the good it did."

"Then he should have locked her up in their *casa*. In her room, if he had to."

With a gloomy look, Pablo said, "If he had done that, she would have found a way to escape. You know this, señor."

"When she told us that she was going, no matter what her father said, we decided it would be better if we went with her and tried to keep her safe," Laurenco explained. He sighed. "To our everlasting shame, we failed. Savages caught us and turned us into slaves. There is no way of knowing what terrible thing might have happened eventually had not Señor Preacher helped us escape."

Harper turned his head to look at the mountain man and said, "You did that?"

"Preacher shouldn't get all the credit," Mallory said. "He might've gotten you away from the redskins, but they would have caught up and wiped you out if me and my boys hadn't come along at the right time."

"This is true," Laurenco allowed. "We owe a debt of gratitude to you as well, Señor Mallory." The old-timer paused. "Now tell me, what were your intentions once you believed Preacher was dead? Did you not plan to trade us to the Comancheros yourself?"

Mallory scowled and sat up straighter. "That's a

dadblasted lie! We just wanted to rescue Harper, here, and find out what happened to that money from the wagon train, too."

"What about that, Harper?" Preacher said. "Why don't you tell us what happened when Twisted Foot and his bunch jumped the wagons?"

Harper looked at Alita, who was still sleeping soundly, overcome by everything she had gone through. Having her with him seemed to have lifted him out of the doldrums that had gripped him earlier, when they first arrived, because there was a trace of anger in his voice now as he said, "I don't like being asked to explain myself."

"That ain't what I'm askin' for," Preacher said patiently. "The señorita's insisted all along that you never would've double-crossed her pa, and I don't have any reason not to believe her. Now that I've seen how the Comanch' have been treatin' you, I reckon it's pretty clear that you weren't workin' with them."

Mallory said, "Unless *they* double-crossed *you*."

Harper shook his head. "That's not the way it was. Señor Montez has always been mighty good to me, the whole time I've been working for him. And I'm engaged to marry his daughter. Does that sound like I'd ever betray him?"

"Some fellas will do a lot of things that'd surprise you, if the money's right."

"Well, not me," Harper said coldly. "I had nothing to do with Twisted Foot attacking that wagon train. In fact, I wish I'd been killed along with the others." He glanced at the girl sleeping with her head on his shoulder. "If I had been, Alita never would have come out here. She'd be safe back in Santa Fe."

"Safe, maybe, but grievin' for you," Preacher said. "Go on with the story."

"There's not much to it. We'd been hit by Indians before, going through that part of the Santa Fe Trail, and we'd always been able to fight them off. Never as big a war party as the one Twisted Foot had, though. They were hidden behind Devil Horn Buttes. I'd sent a man to scout that area, because other bands had used it as cover to ambush us in the past, and when he didn't come back, I knew something was wrong. I told the men to get the wagons circled up . . ."

Harper sighed and shook his head.

"But it was too late. Twisted Foot and his warriors were on us before we could get ready. If it had been a normal-sized war party, I think we might have had a chance, but there were just too many of them . . ."

Harper's voice trailed off as a haunted look came over his face. Preacher knew he was reliving those terrible moments when death had charged at them, whooping and howling.

Harper drew in a deep breath and went on, "We put up a good fight, though. I was standing on the seat of the lead wagon, trying to draw a bead on one of the devils with my rifle, when an arrow hit me in the head—"

"In the head?" Mallory broke in. "If you got shot in the head with an arrow, how come you ain't dead?"

"It hit me at just the right angle to glance off, I suppose." Harper touched his right temple to indicate where the arrow had struck him. "But it hit me hard enough to knock me backward over the seat and into the wagon bed, and knock me out. I guess if any of the Comanches saw me topple over like that, they thought I was dead. But I wasn't."

Again Harper had to pause and gather his resolve to go on.

"When I came to, I heard screaming and . . . and laughing. I managed to pull myself up and look out of the wagon. Most of the men who'd been with me were already dead, but some of them . . . some of them were still alive . . . and the red devils were . . . were . . ."

"I reckon we've got a pretty good idea what they were doin'," Preacher said quietly. "No need to describe it."

Harper nodded, carefully so as not to disturb the still-slumbering Alita. He said, "I went a little crazy, I guess. I still had my rifle, so I jumped out of the wagon and was about to shoot at one of the Comanches when another warrior galloped up on his pony and kicked me in the back, knocked me down. All of a sudden, they were all around me, and I'm sure that in another second or two I would have been dead . . . if Twisted Foot hadn't ridden up right then. He ordered them to leave me alone and then questioned me in Spanish. He wanted to know if we had any money."

"It was money he was after all along?" Preacher asked.

"Well . . . I think mostly he just wanted to kill white men and Mexicans," Harper said. "But he's pretty smart. He knows what we use money for, and he figured if we had any, he could steal it and use it to buy guns from the Comancheros." The young man paused. "I didn't quite follow all of this at the time, of course. I was too shaken up for that. But I came to understand it while we were on our way south to rendezvous with El Carnicero."

That made sense to Preacher. He nodded and said, "So Twisted Foot asked you about the money, and you told him . . . ?"

"To go to hell," Harper replied without hesitation. "I'm

sure he figured he could torture the information out of me, but he didn't have to." He sighed again. "The way they were tearing those wagons apart, it wasn't long before they found all the gold coins anyway. At least I didn't have to betray Señor Montez's trust."

"I'm surprised they didn't go ahead and kill you once they had what they wanted," Preacher said.

"No more surprised than I was. I was going to try to fight, but I knew there was no hope. Then Twisted Foot told his men to make me a prisoner and said they were going to take me with them to meet the Comancheros. I can't be sure, but I think he believed that fate had spared my life for some reason, and he didn't want to go against that. He's a superstitious man, perhaps because of his deformity. He believes he's been touched by the spirits and is destined to be the greatest war chief the Comanches ever had." A dry, humorless chuckle came from Harper. "*And* he figured he could trade me as a slave and maybe get another rifle or a keg of powder out of El Carnicero. Twisted Foot prides himself on being a shrewd bargainer, too."

"And since then?"

"Since then they've treated me pretty roughly, as you can see, but I wasn't really afraid for my life. Twisted Foot had ordered his warriors not to kill me."

Mallory said, "You didn't try to escape?"

"I watched for any chance, believe me. There just wasn't any. Twisted Foot had me closely guarded all the time."

Lying in front of the other prisoners, Guidry began to stir, and a faint moan came from him. As he slowly regained consciousness, one of the men scooted forward and helped him sit up.

"Wha . . . what happened?" Guidry managed to say after a few moments. He shook his head as if to dislodge the cobwebs from his brain.

"You durned near got yourself killed by bein' such an arrogant ass," Mallory said.

Guidry grimaced. "But I kicked that big greaser's *cojones* to mush, didn't I?"

That brought grim chuckles from several of the prisoners. Mallory said, "Yeah, you did, so I reckon you can take some comfort from that when they've got you staked out on an anthill in the hot sun."

The prospect of that made even Guidry lose some of his confidence. He frowned and said, "You think that's what they'll do to me?"

"I don't know," Mallory said, "but whatever they do, I figure you can count on it not bein' anything good."

CHAPTER 31

Shortly after that, things got worse, because the captives were able to hear the tormented screams that began somewhere outside. The thick walls muffled those screeches of agony somewhat but didn't shut them out entirely. Everyone inside the room knew what was going on out there, and they knew as well that if not for El Carnicero's whim, that it just as easily could be them shrieking their guts out.

Alita woke up and sat wide-eyed and trembling with both of Toby Harper's arms around her, offering her comfort but not able to provide much.

Mallory leaned close to Preacher's ear and whispered, "Those fellas you sent for help better be lucky enough to find it and get back here in a hurry. Once those red devils run outta victims, they're liable to come for us, and I don't figure the greaser will try to stop them. We ain't worth more than the business deal he's already got cookin' with Twisted Foot."

Preacher nodded. He knew Mallory was right, but there was nothing he could do at the moment.

He still had those Colts hidden at the small of his back, though. By sneaking into the Comanche camp after the others had been taken prisoner, the warriors had just assumed that he'd already been searched and disarmed, too. He'd had to pull his belt in extra tight to keep the weight of the guns from dragging down his trousers, so it wasn't exactly comfortable—but at the same time, the weight of the Colts was *extremely* comforting.

The screaming went on all afternoon, and eventually the prisoners almost became numb to it, as bad a thing as that was. The human mind could withstand only so much horror before it simply refused to take in any more.

Preacher kept track of the time by watching the angle of the sun's rays move across the makeshift cell. He knew when it grew late in the afternoon, and sure enough, not long after that the light began to fade.

From time to time during the afternoon, he had heard the Comanchero guards talking to each other in low-toned Spanish. As the shadows in the room started thickening, footsteps approached through the ruined *hacienda*. One of the Comancheros stepped into the room and, without saying anything, pointed a shotgun at the prisoners.

Another man followed him. This one carried a corked jug in one hand and a stack of tortillas in the other. He set the jug on the floor and tossed the tortillas down beside it.

"You can fight over them like dogs," he said in heavily accented English as he sneered at the captives. Then he told his companion in Spanish, "Have them toss the jug out when they are finished. Don't leave it in here. They might try to use it as a weapon."

"Sí, Alphonso," the shotgunner replied with a nod.

The man who had brought the food and drink went out. On hands and knees, with the scattergun still menacing him, Mallory crawled forward to get the jug and tortillas and bring them back to the others. There were enough tortillas for each prisoner to have a couple of them. They were stale and a little moldy, too, but at least they were food.

Mallory pulled the cork in the jug and tilted it to his mouth.

"Blast it," he said when he lowered it. "I was hopin' that'd be tequila in there, but it's just water."

"That's better," Preacher said. "We need our wits about us."

"Tequila don't fog up my brain." Mallory shrugged. "But I reckon you're probably right."

They drank sparingly as they passed the jug around, making sure that everybody got some of the water. Laurenco and Pablo tried to convince Alita to drink more, saying that they didn't need as much, but she refused.

"I won't have you giving up any of your share for me," she said. She looked at Harper, adding, "And don't you try to do that, either."

"Why are they even feedin' us?" one of the men asked. "They're just gonna kill us, aren't they?"

Mallory said, "I think El Carnicero's got in mind takin' us across the border into Mexico and sellin' us as slaves. I've heard there are gold and silver mines down there in the mountains, and the fellas who own them use Yaqui Indians and anybody else they can get their hands on to work in them. They work those poor varmints to death, too."

"I ain't spendin' the rest of my days swingin' a pick down in some hole in the ground," Guidry said. "I'll force 'em to kill me first."

Preacher hated to agree with the rail-thin hardcase about anything, but in this case, Guidry was right. Preacher wasn't going to accept such a dismal fate, either.

The guard with the shotgun stood in the doorway watching them until they finished eating and the jug was empty. He backed away and, with a jerk of the shotgun's twin barrels, motioned for one of the prisoners to toss the jug back out.

Lupe Garza picked it up and seemed to be weighing it in his hand, as if he were thinking about flinging it at the guard. Mallory said, "Forget it, Lupe. At this range, if he pulls those triggers he's liable to kill all of us."

"His boss won't like it if he does," Guidry said.

"I reckon El Carnicero would rather see us dead than let us escape."

Guidry just shrugged. After a few seconds, Garza rolled the empty jug through the doorway. The shotgunner bent down and picked it up, then walked off through the house.

The two guards who were still just outside the door leaned in to grin at the prisoners, as if to remind them that they still had no chance of getting away.

As it grew darker, one of the guards lit a candle. Its faint, flickering glow didn't penetrate far into the make-shift cell. Some of the prisoners went back to sleep as the stygian gloom thickened. Snoring soon filled the air.

That didn't last long, though, as a brighter light filled the doorway. A couple of men carrying torches were approaching, and between them waddled the rotund figure of El Carnicero.

The torch-bearers stepped into the room. Each of them also carried a flintlock pistol in his other hand. El Carnicero stopped in the doorway and pointed at Alita.

"You, señorita, come with me," he said.

Alita flinched against Harper's side and shook her head.

"Leave her alone," Harper snapped. "Can't you see she's terrified?"

"Por que?" the Comanchero boss said as he spread his hands. "I mean her no harm. I give you my word on this, señor. I wish only to see her dance. It has been a long time since I watched such a beautiful girl dance."

"No," Alita said. "I . . . I can't—"

"Very well," El Carnicero said. Preacher knew he wasn't going to give up that easily, though, so he wasn't surprised when the Comanchero drew one of the revolvers at his waist and hooked his thumb over the Colt's hammer, drawing it back to make the trigger unfold. Alita flinched against Harper again, but El Carnicero didn't point the gun at her.

Instead he moved it from side to side so that its barrel swung from one captive to another. He said, "If you refuse to dance for me, I will shoot one of these men. Which would you like to see die? One of the old ones, perhaps? Or that one?"

Preacher found himself staring down the barrel of the Colt as El Carnicero pointed it at him.

"Yes, I should be smart and shoot this man right now. He is trouble, anybody can tell that just by looking at him. But you can save him, señorita. Simply honor my request."

Alita drew in a deep breath and said, "All right. I'll do it."

"No!" Harper exclaimed. "You can't. I won't let you—"

"I won't let this man shoot Preacher," Alita interrupted him. "Let go of me, Toby."

"No."

El Carnicero waggled the gun in his hand and said, "I can always just shoot *you*, amigo. I would prefer not to, since the señorita clearly cares for you and I would not like to cause her undue distress, but if I must . . . I believe I could put the bullet right past her pretty little ear and into your chest . . ."

Alita pushed away from Harper and pulled free from his embrace. "If you want me to dance, I'll dance!" she said.

"Ah, now you are doing the wise thing. Come along." El Carnicero lowered the Colt's hammer and slid the gun back into its holster. He crooked a finger. "You come, too, gringo. You can watch your little chiquita dance for me." He looked over at Preacher. "And you. I want to keep my eye on you, señor. You don't need to be in here plotting against me, eh?"

"Sure, I'll come along," Preacher said. "Reckon the night air's cleaner outside. Come on, Toby. Maybe it won't be too bad."

Harper didn't look like he believed that for a second. His expression was bleak as he climbed slowly to his feet. He turned and held out a hand to Alita to help her up.

Preacher stood, as well, and kept an eye on Harper to make sure the young man wasn't desperate enough to try something stupid. He was relieved when Harper didn't do anything except take Alita's hands.

Alita went out of the room first, followed by Harper and then Preacher. El Carnicero had moved aside to let them pass. Then the Comanchero stepped back into the doorway and pointed at Goose Guidry.

"You, too, scarecrow," he said. "You come with us."

"What do you want with me?" Guidry asked in a surly voice. "I sure as hell ain't gonna dance."

El Carnicero guffawed. "I do not think anyone would want to see that, *cabrón*. But come along, or I give you to Pepito. I think he would like that very much. He would not underestimate you again."

Guidry sat there and glared for a moment longer, then unfolded his lanky form from the ground and left the room, shuffling after the others as one of the torch-bearers led them out of the house.

The night air really was cleaner and more refreshing outside. A cool breeze blew from the west and carried away the lingering heat of day. Far off in that direction, lightning flickered, too distant for its accompanying thunder to be heard. There might be a rainstorm later in the night, though, if the clouds to the west held together.

Preacher saw that a long table had been set up under the brush arbor. The remains of what appeared to have been a fairly sumptuous meal were scattered across it. Sitting at one end of the table were Twisted Foot and several of his warriors, probably his subchiefs. A handful of Comancheros were clustered at the other end, no doubt El Carnicero's lieutenants. A number of jugs were in evidence, as well, and Preacher was confident these actually did hold tequila instead of water.

Torches were stuck in the ground around the brush arbor, but not close enough to create any danger of setting the structure on fire. More torches scattered light around the rest of the abandoned rancho, which was bustling with activity as Twisted Foot's Comanches and the Comancheros led by El Carnicero celebrated their imminent business deal by drinking, dancing, and carousing with the soiled doves the Mexican traders had brought with them. Music, laughter, and lustful shrieks filled the night air.

Thankfully, Preacher didn't hear the captives screaming anymore. Either their tormentors had grown bored of the grisly sport and killed them, or else those unfortunates had passed out and the torture had been postponed until they regained consciousness.

Harper draped his arm protectively around Alita's shoulders as they came out of the hacienda. She still looked frightened. El Carnicero grinned back at her and said, "You know how to dance, don't you, little one? Entertain us, and all will be well."

With a hint of her old defiance, Alita conquered her fear for a moment and declared, "I can dance."

"Good! Show us!" El Carnicero turned and bellowed, "*Attencion!* The señorita is going to dance for us! Esteban! Hernando!"

Two Comancheros with guitars broke off the tune they had been playing for a group of men gathered around them. They came over to the brush arbor as El Carnicero wrapped a meaty hand around Alita's arm and pulled her away from Harper. The young man started to react to that, but Preacher put a hand on his shoulder and muttered, "Take it easy, son."

El Carnicero led Alita around in front of the table. More men began to gather. After the Comanches had ripped her shirt open when she was captured along with the others, she had managed to tie the damaged garment together, to a certain extent, but even so, it was hardly respectable attire and she seemed all too aware of the lustful gazes directed at her. She clutched the torn shirt tighter around her but didn't succeed in covering up much more.

"Play your merriest tune," El Carnicero ordered the two men with guitars as he kicked out one of the chairs at the table so he could sit down. "And you, señorita, dance as if your life . . . no, as if the life of your blond amigo there depended upon it."

"Don't listen to him, Alita," Harper said. "You don't have to do this."

El Carnicero drew one of his pistols and placed it on the table in front of him.

"Ah, but she does, gringo," he said. "If you want to live, she does. And she had better make it good, too."

Alita took a deep breath and said, "It's all right, Toby. Really."

She swallowed hard, and as the guitarists began to play, she started moving her feet. The steps were slow and clumsy at first, but then she picked up speed. She reached down and pulled up her riding skirt slightly to give her legs more freedom. That revealed some smooth brown skin above the tops of her boots, and the sight made excited whoops erupt from the men watching her, Comancheros and Comanches alike.

Preacher glanced over at Toby Harper. The young man's jaw was set in a taut, angry line, and his eyes smoldered with fury at the degradation Alita was being forced to endure. It could have been a lot worse, Preacher knew, but he figured that wouldn't be much comfort to Harper if he pointed it out.

The guitar players were pretty good. Their fingers moved on the strings almost too fast to be seen as the music swelled up in the night. Alita's movements were faster, too, and more sure and graceful. It was hard not to get caught up in the compelling rhythm.

El Carnicero had gotten caught up, that was for sure. Grinning hugely, he slapped a hand on the table in time with the music. Some of the Comancheros began to clap and whoop. Even the fierce, solemn Comanches seemed to be enjoying themselves, other than Twisted Foot, who looked as grave as ever. But he didn't interfere and seemed willing to let everyone else have their fun.

Alita threw her head back and shook her long dark hair.

She raised her arms and clapped her hands above her head, making the swell of her breasts stand out even more against the torn shirt. At first, Preacher thought she really had gotten carried away by the music and the admiration, but then he saw how carefully controlled her expression was and knew she was just putting on an act. El Carnicero had warned her that she needed to entertain them, and she was doing her best to accomplish that.

She finished with a flourish as the musicians came to the end of the song. Standing there head down, breathing hard from her exertions, she drew every eye around her. It was too bad Captain Hays and the rest of the rangers weren't here now, Preacher thought. They would have been able to take the Comanches and Comancheros completely by surprise.

But it was too soon to hope for that, and in fact, nothing happened except a tumult of shouted approval for Alita's dance. El Carnicero lurched to his feet, picked up the Colt he had placed on the table and shoved it back into its holster, and came around the table to grab Alita's arm again.

"Come with me," he growled, and everybody there knew exactly what his intention was.

CHAPTER 32

Toby Harper paled and started to spring forward. Preacher caught his arm to hold him back. As bitter a pill as it would be to swallow, fighting back now likely would just get them killed and wouldn't do anything to help Alita.

Preacher wasn't sure he could keep his own instincts under control, though. Every fiber of his being wanted to help the girl and tackle the brutish Comanchero leader.

He didn't have to, because help came from an unlikely and unexpected source. Twisted Foot stood up, leaned his fists on the table, and growled at El Carnicero, "No."

El Carnicero glared at him in anger and disbelief and said, "You are talking to me? What is this you say to me? No? You tell El Carnicero *no*?"

"Leave her alone," Twisted Foot said. "If you take her now, she will be worth less when you trade her below the border. And you will use *that* as a reason to give me fewer rifles for her now."

El Carnicero glared at the Comanche war chief for a moment, then laughed. "You believe me to be that shrewd, amigo? You think I want this señorita because it's good *business*?"

"I care nothing for your reason," Twisted Foot snapped. "But I know what you will make of it."

"Bah!" El Carnicero shoved Alita toward Harper, roughly enough that he made her stumble. Harper stepped forward quickly to catch her and keep her from falling. "I value our friendship too much, Twisted Foot, to allow any señorita to damage it . . . no matter how pretty a piece of baggage she is."

Harper folded his arms around Alita again and held her against him. The emotional control she had displayed during the dance slipped, and she trembled a little as he held her.

El Carnicero and Twisted Foot continued to trade stares for a moment longer, then El Carnicero turned abruptly to the two musicians, waved an arm, and yelled, "Play, play! Let us have more tunes!"

The two men strummed the strings of their instruments, then broke into another sprightly melody. As they played, El Carnicero picked up one of the jugs from the table, took a swig from it, and then held it out to the war chief.

"We drink to our friendship, eh, and to all the trading we will do in the future!"

Twisted Foot took the jug, swallowed a sip of the fiery tequila, and then passed the jug along to one of his warriors. Grinning again, El Carnicero began clapping along with the music from the guitars.

At the same time, he jerked his head toward one of his men, a movement that made the silver balls dangling from his sombrero's brim sway back and forth. The man he had signaled evidently knew what that meant. Using the rifle he held, he gestured for Preacher, Alita, Harper, and Guidry to march back into the old house.

"Wait, not that one!" El Carnicero called.

He pointed to Goose Guidry.

"Hold on," Guidry said as his eyes widened. "You promised you wouldn't give me to that Pepito hombre."

"I made no such promise," El Carnicero said. "But do not worry. Pepito is asleep somewhere, recovering from his injury, and I would not disturb him. I want you to sit here and talk with me."

Guidry frowned in confusion, but one of the Comancheros poked him in the back with a rifle barrel and prodded him toward the table. Reluctantly, he went to join El Carnicero, while Preacher and the others had to go back inside the *hacienda*.

Preacher didn't like the looks of this unexpected development. Didn't like it at all.

Thunder rumbled in the distance as he went back into the house with Alita and Harper. That storm to the west was getting closer.

Laurenco and Pablo must have heard them coming. Both old-timers were on their feet and hurried forward to meet them, ignoring the nervous Comanchero guards who trained rifles on them.

"Señorita," Laurenco said anxiously. "You are all right?"

"Yes," Alita told him. "No one harmed me."

"Any more than she's already been harmed by all the rough treatment," Harper said. Anger had replaced weariness on his gaunt features. "I swear, I'll make them pay for what they've done, all of them."

"Let's concentrate on livin' through this first," Preacher said.

Styles Mallory spoke up, saying, "Wait a minute. Guidry

went out there with you. Where is he? What happened to him?"

"Don't know. El Carnicero had him stay behind when he sent the rest of us back in here. He didn't say what he had in mind."

Mallory cursed. "That fat varmint's gonna torture him, or let the redskins do it." Mallory ran his fingers through his tangled hair in exasperation. "Goose is a hotheaded, arrogant son of a gun, but he's one of us."

"So were the other men who were tortured earlier," Lupe Garza pointed out. "I agree with the gringo. The men who have done these things must pay . . . somehow."

Silence fell over the room as Preacher, Alita, and Harper sat down again, along with the two old-timers. Everybody in here wanted vengeance, but the question remained—how were they going to get it?

Once the Comancheros with the torches were gone and only the guards remained with their candle, the prisoners began to doze off again. Preacher remained awake, though, with his back propped against the wall.

Like most frontiersmen, he knew the value of sleeping whenever it was possible, even if it was only for a short time. He had the ability to fall asleep quickly and wake up instantly, fully alert. Tonight, however, some restless instinct kept him awake.

He listened as the muffled rumbles of thunder became separate booms. He saw flashes of lightning reflected through the holes in the roof.

He had studied those holes earlier, while it was still light, to see if they might represent a way out of here. None of them were large enough for a person to get through, though, not to mention the near-impossibility of reaching them. But they did allow him to tell that the storm was still approaching.

Not long after that, it began raining. Water dripped down through the openings and splattered on some of the prisoners, waking them. They sat up and cursed bitterly.

"It's not bad enough that we're in this mess," Mallory said, "but now it has to rain on us, too?"

"There's an old sayin' about how rain falls on the just and the unjust," Preacher said.

"That's from the scriptures, ain't it? Are you a real preacher now?"

"Nope, far from it. But there's no denyin' that it's true."

"No, I reckon not. The rain's sure fallin' on us."

The thunder was loud now as it pealed through the night, and lightning flickered almost continuously. The racket made it difficult to sleep. Alita and Harper sat up, and as she huddled against him, Alita said, "I hate storms."

Harper put his arm around her shoulders and said, "It'll be all right. A little thunder and lightning can't hurt us as long as we're inside."

That was probably true, Preacher mused. He had heard about fellas who had been struck by lightning, but that had happened when storms came up quickly and caught them out on the plains with nothing else around.

And in another way of looking at it, they had plenty of other worries more pressing than a little thunderstorm . . .

Such as the fact that somebody carrying a torch was approaching the cell again, staying in the areas where there was still enough of a roof that the rain didn't put the torch out. As Mallory had put it earlier, this couldn't be anything good.

Even so, Preacher wasn't expecting what he saw. The Comanchero with the blazing torch came up to the doorway and then stepped aside to let someone else past. The garish light fell on the narrow features of Goose Guidry as he came into the room. Guidry stopped after a couple of steps, and the man with the torch followed him, holding the brand high so that its glare filled the chamber.

Not only did it appear that Guidry hadn't been tortured, but he wore a sombrero now, like one of the Comancheros, and had a pair of flintlock pistols tucked behind his belt. He slouched there and grinned as he looked around the room.

This was bad, Preacher thought. Really bad.

"Goose, what the hell!" Mallory burst out after a moment, unable to contain his confusion any longer. "What's goin' on here?"

"What's goin' on is, thanks to me, some of us got a chance to get outta this alive," Guidry replied with his habitual sneer. "Come on, Styles. You, too, Lupe. You're comin' with me." He looked at the other survivors from Mallory's original group and shook his head. "Sorry, fellas. El Carnicero told me I could only pick two more to throw in with him."

"You're throwin' in with that blasted Comanchero?"

Guidry shrugged. "What can I say? He was impressed with the way I took care of big old Pepito and said I was the kind of hombre he wanted workin' with him, not against him. He's got other gringos in his bunch, you know."

"So you're gonna just let the rest us die?" one of the men demanded. "Styles, tell him to go to hell!"

Mallory drew in a deep breath and then said, "Well . . . the problem with that is I don't want to die. And if that means becomin' a Comanchero . . ."

Preacher drawled, "Y'know, Styles, somehow I never expected any more outta you than this."

Mallory scrambled to his feet and motioned for Garza to join him with Guidry. He said, "I'm sorry, Preacher, I really am, but sometimes a fella's just got to go where the river takes him."

"Sí, it is a shame," Garza said as he stood up. "But who knows, maybe we make good Comancheros, eh?"

"There's just one more thing," Guidry went on as he pulled a pistol from behind his belt. "Since El Carnicero is doin' me a favor by sparin' my life and lettin' me pick a couple of friends to come with me, I had to repay him in kind by tellin' him all about your plan to tip off those Texians, Preacher. So he's gonna wrap up the deal with Twisted Foot tonight and pull out for the border first thing in the mornin'." Guidry eared back the pistol's hammer and pointed it toward Preacher. "And he's givin' *me* the privilege of gettin' rid of you, once and for all, you son of a—"

The damaged roof crashed in, and a huge shape hurtled down at Guidry.

CHAPTER 33

The man with the torch jumped back in surprise but didn't drop the burning brand, so there was still enough light for Preacher to see Bigfoot Wallace crash down on Guidry and drive him to the ground. The pistol flew out of the rail-thin hardcase's hand.

At the same time, the two rifle-toting guards rushed into the room, drawn by the commotion. Preacher was already on his feet, having uncoiled from his sitting position on the ground like a striking rattlesnake. He didn't know how Wallace had gotten here or what was going to happen next, but his instincts told him he'd better deal with those guards.

He grabbed the barrel of the rifle held by one of them and wrenched the weapon upward, then thrust it forward into the guard's face with enough force to break bone. The man let go of the rifle and staggered backward. Preacher whirled and drove the rifle butt into the belly of the other guard.

From the corner of his eye, he saw Wallace and Guidry rolling across the ground. Guidry was trying to use his speed, as he had against Pepito, but this time he was up against an even deadlier opponent than the giant. Bigfoot Wallace was pretty big himself—although not as big as Pepito—and he was a match for Guidry's speed.

That was all Preacher had time to see, because at that moment someone tackled him from behind and knocked him to his knees.

"I have him, Styles," Lupe Garza grunted. Clearly, Garza wanted to hang on to his new position as a Comanchero.

Preacher drove his right elbow back into Garza's body, but the man was big and powerful enough that the blow didn't have much effect. Garza clamped an arm around Preacher's throat and hauled upward in an attempt to snap the mountain man's neck.

Abruptly, Garza loosened his hold and cried out in surprise, "He has guns!" He had felt the Colts under Preacher's shirt and recognized them for what they were.

That respite might not have been enough to save Preacher, but at that moment Garza screamed in pain and let go of him entirely. Preacher whipped around and saw Garza bending over and clutching at his right leg. Laurenco knelt nearby, holding a bloody knife. Preacher didn't know where the old-timer had gotten the knife, but he had used it to hamstring Garza. Laurenco called, "Preacher!" and tossed the knife to him.

Deftly, Preacher caught the handle and, in the same movement, plunged the blade into Garza's chest all the way to the hilt, then ripped it free. Garza, eyes wide with pain and shock, stumbled, pawed at the wound in his chest, and then fell with a crash and didn't move again.

With that immediate threat disposed of, Preacher had a chance to glance around. He saw that the torch lay on the ground now, still burning, although it was starting to gutter because of the water that had collected in puddles since the rain began. The Comanchero who had held it must have fled.

He wasn't the only one. Styles Mallory and the rest of his men were gone, probably figuring this might be their only chance to try to escape, even though it meant taking their chances with the Comancheros. Some of them might be able to run off into the dark, stormy night without being noticed.

That left Wallace and Guidry, whose struggle had taken them to the other side of the room. Wallace surged to his feet now, holding the still-flailing Guidry by an arm and a leg. In a prodigious feat of strength, the Texian raised Guidry above his head and then smashed him down across an upraised knee.

Preacher had thought that Pepito might snap Guidry in two like a stick. Bigfoot Wallace actually did that. The crack that came from Guidry's backbone was loud, even with the thunder booming. Guidry screamed, and then his head lolled back limply on his neck. Wallace tossed him aside like a broken doll.

Alita, Harper, Laurenco, and Pablo were all on their feet. Preacher asked Laurenco, "Where'd you get the knife?"

"I took it from the man you hit in the face with his rifle." Laurenco pointed. Both former guards were still down. Preacher grunted as he saw the dark pools spreading around their heads as blood welled from their slashed throats. Laurenco had been busy, even before hamstringing Lupe Garza.

Preacher turned to Wallace and said, "I'd ask you how you came to fall through that roof just in the nick of time, Bigfoot, but I reckon that can wait until later."

"Simple enough," Wallace said. "Cap'n Jack and the rest

of the rangers showed up a lot sooner than we expected, so I come to look for you. Dog sniffed you out, even through that wall. So I clumb up on the roof, saw what was goin' on through those holes, and jumped up and down. Only took one jump to bust through."

"The rangers are here?"

"Yeah, and they ought to be gettin' into action—"

A tremendous burst of gunfire came from outside, punctuating the crash of thunder.

Wallace grinned and concluded, "Oh, right about now."

Preacher reached behind him, under his shirt, and curled his hands around the Colts. As he pulled them out, the other four prisoners gaped at him, having had no idea he'd been armed like that the whole time.

"Sounds like a ruckus we need to get in on," Preacher said.

Wallace grinned and drew his own revolvers. "After you, amigo."

Preacher turned to Harper and gestured toward Guidry's flintlock pistols. "Take those," he told the young man. To Laurenco and Pablo, he added, "Grab those guards' rifles and pistols. Señorita, you stay back. I'd tell you to stay in here where you'll be safe, but I don't reckon you'd do it."

"I can shoot a gun, too," Alita said. "Give me one of the pistols."

Preacher shrugged. He didn't doubt that she could do what she said. As the others armed themselves, he and Wallace stepped to the doorway and looked out. The Comanches and the Comancheros might have figured out by now that something had gone wrong in here, but since they were under attack by the rangers, they had their hands too full to do anything about it.

Holding the Colts ready, thumbs looped over the

hammers, he and Wallace charged out into the night as thunder crashed and lightning clawed across the sky.

The first thing Preacher saw as they entered the courtyard in front of the house were spurts of orange muzzle flame from the top of the bluff on the other side of the creek. Some of the rangers were up there, he realized, using rifles to pick off the Comancheros and Comanches whenever they could spot them in the lightning flashes.

The rain had tapered off to an intermittent drizzle, even though the electrical storm continued unabated. Preacher turned and told Harper to fetch the torch they had left in the building. The young man ran to the cell and hurried back. The torch hadn't gone out yet, although the pitch-soaked cloth wrapped around the end of it wasn't burning as strongly as before.

Preacher thrust it up against the underside of the brush arbor's roof. For a moment, he thought it was going to be too damp to catch, but then more flames leaped to life and began to spread. The top side was a lot wetter, but as the bottom began to burn, the flames were hot enough to catch that part on fire, too.

As the arbor flared up, the hellish light from the blaze spread across the courtyard and gave the Texian sharpshooters across the creek better targets.

But it also told the Comanches and Comancheros who had taken cover behind the crumbling walls that there was a new threat for them to deal with. Some of them whirled around toward Preacher and Wallace to launch arrows and trigger shots from flintlock pistols and rifles.

Preacher and Wallace opened fire, too, and as they spread out, so did Harper, Laurenco, and Pablo. The Colts did the most damage, as shot after shot roared from their muzzles as fast as Preacher and Wallace could cock and fire. They swept the guns from side to side, mowing down the enemy.

Then the hammers clicked on empty chambers, and there was no time to reload as Comanches and Comancheros charged them. Preacher spotted Styles Mallory with El Carnicero and Twisted Foot. Clearly, Mallory had taken the Comanchero leader's offer and sworn allegiance to El Carnicero. His face twisted in hatred as he lifted a pistol.

Preacher dropped the empty Colt in his right hand and grabbed the knife he had shoved behind his belt after using it to kill Lupe Garza. His arm swept back and then forward, and the blade flashed in the firelight as it flew straight and true into Mallory's throat. Mallory stumbled and staggered, dropping the pistol so he could claw futilely at the steel buried in his throat. As he ripped the knife free, blood fountained outward from his severed veins and arteries in a dark, glistening spray. He pitched forward onto the ground, twitching a few times before he lay still.

Twisted Foot rushed forward as well, his awkward, hobbling gait not really slowing him down. He slashed at Wallace with a knife. The big Texian barely darted aside from the blade. His Colts were empty, too, so he dropped them and grappled with the Comanche war chief hand to hand.

They were evenly matched. Wallace grabbed Twisted Foot's wrist and kept him from burying the knife in him. With his other hand, Wallace groped for Twisted Foot's neck and got his fingers wrapped around it despite the Comanche's efforts to fend him off.

Then it was a contest of strength against strength, a question of whether Wallace could choke Twisted Foot to death before the war chief could break his grip and plunge the knife into him. They swayed back and forth in the leaping firelight for long moments before Twisted Foot finally began to weaken. He didn't pass out, but his eyes rolled up in their sockets.

That gave Wallace the chance to wrench the knife around while it was still in Twisted Foot's hand and ram the blade into the Comanche's belly. Twisted Foot cried out in pain as Wallace ripped the knife to the side. He no longer had the strength to resist as Wallace slammed him down on the ground and knelt on top of him.

It was a good question whether Twisted Foot died from the knife in his guts before Wallace choked him to death—not that it mattered either way.

The barrage of lead from Preacher and Wallace had scythed through the Comancheros and Comanches and left many of them dead or dying on the ground. Harper, Laurenco, and Pablo had taken a toll with their fire as well. Now Preacher heard a rumble that wasn't thunder but came from the hooves of the horses charging up to the old, abandoned *rancho*.

Jack Hays and the rest of the rangers had arrived, and armed with the deadly Colt Patersons as well, they tore through the rest of the enemy like a lethal storm. The Comanches and Comancheros couldn't stand up to that, although they battled stubbornly to the last and inflicted some damage of their own.

Howling curses in Spanish, El Carnicero plunged toward Preacher. He had the only set of revolvers among the Comancheros, and he intended to use them on the mountain man.

Before he could fire, a single shot rang out. El Carnicero's head jerked back as a red-rimmed hole appeared in his forehead. His sombrero, with the decorative silver balls swaying wildly, flew off. He stumbled forward another step, then collapsed face-down on the ground.

Preacher looked around and saw powdersmoke curling from the muzzle of the pistol Alita held level in front of her. Her face was pale but composed.

"I'm much obliged to you, señorita," he said.

"I told you I could shoot."

Preacher smiled. "You sure proved it, too."

She started to lower the pistol, then reaction caught up with her. She started to shake again, but Harper moved in quickly to embrace her. Laurenco and Pablo stood nearby in case they were needed.

Preacher felt something nudge his leg and looked down to see Dog leaning against him. The big cur's bloody muzzle revealed that he had been part of the fight, too, but now he was looking up at Preacher with a big, friendly grin on his face. Preacher laughed and scratched Dog's ears.

"I'm obliged to you, too," he said, "for helpin' Bigfoot find me."

Wallace said, "That's about the best dog anybody could ever hope for. You've got mighty good trail partners, Preacher."

The mountain man nodded in agreement with that, then turned to look toward the gate as Captain Jack Hays rode through the opening. Wallace raised a hand in greeting and called, "Over here, Cap'n!"

Hays rode up to them and dismounted. He shook hands with Wallace and then Preacher, who said, "We didn't expect to see you so soon, Cap'n."

Hays smiled and said, "That's because we didn't go all the way to Austin like I planned. The itch to follow you was just too strong. I sent the wounded on back, along with a couple of men to help them, but the rest of us turned south. Howard and Mose ran into us earlier today and led us straight here."

As if they'd heard their names, the Strickland brothers rode up and greeted Preacher, Howard being the more talkative of the two, as usual. Mose did say, "Good to see you made it," though.

While some of the rangers checked over the Comanches and Comancheros to make sure they were either dead or out of the fight, Hays turned to Alita and said, "You'd be Señorita Montez, I assume."

"Yes," she said. "Thank you, Captain. We would not have made it out of here if not for you and your men."

Hays touched a finger to the brim of his hat and said, "Ridding Texas of varmints like that is our job, ma'am." He looked at Harper. "You're the fella Preacher told us about, the one who was captured by Twisted Foot's war party?"

"That's right."

"Looks like you've had a pretty rough time of it."

Harper shrugged and tightened his arm around Alita's shoulders. "I'm all right," he said, "and better now. I just hope all this is over."

"Looks to me like it is," Hays said as he looked around the abandoned *rancho*. "Until the next threat comes along. I have a feeling it'll be a long time before Texas is truly tamed."

Bigfoot Wallace grinned at Preacher in the fading lightning from the receding storm and said, "I reckon there's some of us who'd just as soon that never really comes to pass, Cap'n."

* * *

By the next morning, the storm was long gone. The bodies of the Comanches and Comancheros had been hauled out of the courtyard, and the rangers had camped there. Once the sun was up, Preacher checked the bodies and saw that some of Mallory's men weren't there, which probably meant they had gotten away in the bloody chaos the night before.

If so, they were unarmed and on foot, a long way from anywhere. They probably wouldn't make it out, but if they did, more power to 'em, Preacher thought.

Hayes, Wallace, and Preacher went through the Comancheros' wagons and found numerous crates of rifles and pistols, kegs of powder, and bags of shot. It would have been plenty to arm Twisted Foot and his warriors, and with those guns they would have cut a bloody swath across Texas. Getting rid of that threat—at least for the time being—had been a good night's work.

"Texas owes you a debt, Preacher," Hays said. "Without you, we might not have uncovered Twisted Foot's plot and put a stop to it." He cocked his head to the side and added, "I don't suppose you'd like to keep on helping Texas and join our company?"

"We'd be mighty glad to have you," Wallace said.

Preacher said, "I've got a hunch that rangerin' with you boys would be mighty fine sport, but I'm afraid I still have a job. I'm gonna make sure Señorita Montez, Harper, and those two old-timers make it back to Santa Fe safe and sound, and then I've got to deliver Daniel Eckstrom's money to him in St. Louis."

"You found the money?" Hays asked.

"Toby knew where Twisted Foot had stashed it among his possibles," the mountain man explained. "It was all still there, since Twisted Foot hadn't traded it yet to El Carnicero for those guns, and there's sure as blazes nothin' *else* out here to spend it on."

"It's a long way to Santa Fe through some dangerous country. There are plenty of guns and horses and supplies here, so take whatever you need to be properly outfitted. We'll go part of the way with you. I wish we could escort you the whole journey, but that would take us too far out of our bailiwick."

"That's all right, Cap'n. I'm obliged to you for whatever you can do."

"There is one more thing . . ." Hays turned to Wallace and nodded.

Wallace reached into one of the wagons and brought out a belt with two attached holsters, each of which had one of the Colt Patersons in it.

"This was El Carnicero's rig," he said. "We all figure you deserve to have it, Preacher."

"We're going to give you a couple of spare Patersons, too, and some extra cylinders," Hays said.

Preacher took the gunbelt from Wallace and buckled it around his hips. He gripped the Colts and moved them up and down, testing how well they slid in the holsters.

"I'm mighty obliged for this gift," he told the two rangers. "I'll try to put these smokewagons to good use, too."

"By shootin' lowdown varmints who need shootin'?" Wallace said.

"That's right. There are plenty of 'em out there."

The big Texian clapped a hand on Preacher's shoulder and said, "From what I've seen of you, amigo, you may *never* run out of folks who need shootin'. . . or folks who need your help."

"And that would be all right with me," Preacher said as he looked toward the spot where Dog and Horse were waiting for him, eager to get back on the trail toward new adventures.

The Battle of Bandera Pass has long been an accepted part of Texas history, although in recent years some revisionist historians have begun to cast doubt on whether it really happened. There is *no* doubt, however, that the ranging companies of the Republic of Texas, armed with the new Colt Paterson revolvers and including the company led by Captain Jack Hays, fought numerous battles against the Comanches and helped make Texas safe for settlement in its early days.

Of course, Preacher wasn't actually there and never met William "Bigfoot" Wallace, another famous real-life Texan . . . but he could have been, and the two of them would've been a pair to stand aside from!

Keep reading for special excerpt....

BLOOD IN THE DUST
A HUNTER BUCHANON BLACK HILLS WESTERN

by William W. Johnstone
and J. A. Johnstone

*The greatest Western writers of the 21st century
continue the adventures of Hunter Buchanon,
a towering mountain of a man who made his name
as a Rebel tracker in the Civil War.
Now he and his coyote sidekick Bobby Lee are trying to
forge a new peaceful life in the Black Hills, Dakota.
But they'll have to fight to the death to keep it . . .*

THERE'S COYOTES IN THEM THERE HILLS.
Ex-Rebel tracker Hunter Buchanon is down on his luck.
He lost his family's ranch in a fire.
He lost his gold to a thief. And he just might lose his
fiancée—a beautiful saloon girl named Annabelle—
to a stinking-rich rival. But Hunter's not ready to give
up just yet. He's got a temporary sheriff's badge,
a long-range plan to rebuild his ranch,
and his loyal coyote Bobby Lee by his side to make
things right. Too bad it all goes wrong—
when Annabelle gets kidnapped . . .

The mayhem begins with a stagecoach robbery in the
Black Hills town of Tigerville. It won't end until
Sheriff Hunter Buchanon gets back his girl and his gold—
on a long, dusty trail of blood-soaked vengeance . . .

Look for **BLOOD IN THE DUST.** *On sale now.*

CHAPTER 1

"That coyote makes me nervous," said shotgun messenger Charley Anders.

"You mean Bobby Lee?" asked Hunter Buchanon as he handled the reins of the rocking and clattering Cheyenne & Black Hills Stage, sitting on the hard, wooden seat to Anders's left.

He spoke through the neckerchief he'd drawn up over his nose and mouth to keep out at least some of the infernal dust kicked up by the six-horse hitch.

"Yeah, yeah—Bobby Lee. He's the only coyote aboard this heap, and that there is a thing I never thought I'd hear myself utter if I lived to be a hundred years old!"

Anders slapped his thigh and roared through his own pulled-up neckerchief.

"No need to be nervous, Charley," Hunter said. "Bobby Lee ain't dangerous. In fact, he's right polite." Buchanon leaned close to the old shotgun messenger beside him and said with feigned menace, "As long as you're polite to Bobby Lee, that is."

He grinned and nudged the shotgun man with his elbow.

"If you mean by 'polite' give him a chunk of jerky every time he demands one, he can go to hell!" Anders glanced uneasily over his left shoulder at Bobby Lee sitting on the coach roof just above and between him and Buchanon. "Hell, he demands jerky all the damn time! If you don't give him some, he shows you his teeth!"

As if the fawn-gray coyote had understood the conversation, Bobby Lee lowered his head and pressed his cold snout to Anders's left ear, nudging up the man's cream sombrero.

"See there?" Anders cried. Leaning forward in his seat and regarding the coyote dubiously, the shotgun messenger said, "I ain't givin' you no more jerky, Bobby Lee, an' that's that! If I give you any more jerky, I won't have none left for my ownself an' we still got another half hour's ride into Tigerville! I gotta keep somethin' in my stomach or I get the fantods!"

Hunter chuckled as he glanced over his right shoulder at Bobby Lee pointing his long snout in the general direction of the shirt pocket in which he knew Anders kept his jerky. The coyote's triangle ears were pricked straight up.

Hunter gave the coyote a quick pat on the head. "Bobby Lee understands—don't you, Bobby Lee? He thinks you're bein' right selfish—not to mention womanish about your *fantods*—but he understands."

Hunter chuckled and turned his head forward to gaze out over the horses' bobbing heads.

As he did, Bobby Lee subtly raised his bristling lips to show the ends of his fine, white teeth to Anders.

"See there? He just did it again!" Charley cried, pointing at Bobby Lee.

When Hunter turned to the coyote he'd raised from a pup, after the little tyke's mother had been killed by hunters, Bobby Lee quickly closed his lips over his teeth. He turned to his master and fashioned a cock-headed, doe-eyed look of innocence, as though he had no idea why this cork-headed fool was slandering him so unjustly.

"Ah, hell, you're imagining things, Charley," Hunter scolded the man. "You an' your fantods an' makin' things up. You should be ashamed of yourself!"

"He did—I swear!"

A woman's sonorous, somewhat sarcastic voice cut through Anders's complaint. "Excuse me, gentlemen! Excuse me! Do you mind if I interrupt your eminently important and impressively articulate conversation?"

The plea had come from below and on Buchanon's side of the stage. He glanced over his left shoulder to see one of his and Anders's two passengers poking her head out of the coach's left-side window. Blinking against the billowing dust, Miss Laura Meyers gazed beseechingly up toward the driver's box. "I'd like to request a nature stop if you would, please?"

Hunter and Charley Anders shared a weary look. Miss Meyers, who'd boarded the stage in Cheyenne a few days ago, was from the East by way of Denver. Now, Hunter had known plenty of Eastern folks who were not royal pains in the backside. Miss Meyers was not one of them.

She was grossly ill-prepared for travel in the West. She'd not only not realized that the trip between Cheyenne and Tigerville in the Dakota Territory took a few days, she'd not realized that stagecoach travel was a far cry from the more comfortable-style coach and buggy and train travel to which she'd become accustomed back east of the Mississippi.

Here there was dust. And heat. The stench of male sweat and said male's "infernal and ubiquitous tobacco use." (Hunter didn't know what "ubiquitous" meant but he'd been able to tell by the woman's tone that it wasn't complimentary. At least, not in the way she had used it.)

Also, the trail up from Cheyenne into the Black Hills was not as comfortable as, say, a ride in an open chaise across a grassy Eastern meadow on a balmy Sunday afternoon in May. Out here, there were steep hills, narrow canyons, perilous river crossings, the heavy alkali mire along Indian Creek, and, once you were in the Hills themselves, twisting, winding trails with enough chuckholes and washouts to keep the Concord rocking on its leather thoroughbraces until you thought you must have eaten flying fish for breakfast.

Several times over the past two days, Miss Meyers had heralded the need for Hunter to stop the coach so she could bound out of it in a swirl of skirts and petticoats and hurl herself into the bushes to air her paunch.

So far, they hadn't been accosted by owlhoots. They'd even made it through the dangerous country around the Robbers' Roost Relay Station without having a single bullet hurled at them from one of the many haystack bluffs in that area. Nor an arrow, for that matter.

Indians—primarily Red Cloud's Sioux, understandably miffed by the treaty the government had broken to allow gold-seeking settlers into the Black Hills—had been a problem on nearly every run Hunter had been on in the past year. He'd started driving for the stage company after his family's ranch had been burned by a rival rancher and the man's business partner, his two brothers murdered, his father, old Angus, seriously wounded.

He wanted to say as much to the lady—a pretty one, at

that—staring up at him now from the coach's left-side window, but he knew she'd have none of it. She was a fish out of water here, and in dire straits. He could see it in her eyes. She was not only road-weary but world-weary, as well.

Though they'd left the Ten Mile Ranch Station only twenty minutes ago, after a fifteen-minute break, and would arrive in Tigerville after only another ten miles, she needed to stop.

"Hold on, ma'am—I'll pull these cayuses to a stop at the bottom of the next hill!"

She blinked in disgust and pulled her head back into the coach.

"Thank you, Mister Buchanon!" Charley Anders called with an ironic mix of mockery and chiding.

"Now, Charley," Hunter admonished his partner as the six horses pulled the coach up and over a low pass and then started down the other side, sun-dappled lodgepole pines jutting close along both sides of the trail. "She's new to these parts. I reckon you'd have a helluva time back East your ownself. Hell, even in the newly citified Denver!"

"Yeah, well, I wouldn't go back East. Not after seein' the kind of haughty folks they make back thataway!" Charley drew his neckerchief down, turned to Hunter, and grinned, showing a more-or-less complete set of tobacco-rimmed teeth ensconced in a grizzled, gray-brown beard damp with sweat. "She's hard to listen to, but she is easy on the eyes, ain't she?"

They'd gained the bottom of the hill now, and Hunter was hauling back on the ribbons. "I wouldn't know, Charley. I only look at one woman. You know that."

"Pshaw! You can't tell me you ain't admired how that

purty eastern princess fills out her natty travelin' frocks!
You wouldn't be a man if you didn't!"

"I got eyes for only one woman, Charley," Hunter insisted. Now that the mules had stopped, the dust swirling
over them as it caught up to the coach from behind, Hunter
set the brake. "You know that."

"Yeah, well, sounds to me like it's time for you to start
lookin' around for another gal. Sounds to me like you an'
Annabelle Ludlow are kaput. Through. End-of-story."
Charley narrowed one eye in cold castigation at his
younger friend. "And you got only one man to blame for
that—yourself!"

Gritting his teeth, Charley removed his dusty sombrero
and smacked it several times across Hunter's stout right
shoulder. "Gall-blamed, lame-brained, cork-headed fool!
How could you let her get away?"

Hunter had asked himself that question many times over
the past few months, but he didn't want to think about it
now. Thinking about Annabelle made him feel frustrated
as all get-out, and he had to keep his head clear. You didn't
drive a six-horse hitch through rugged terrain haunted by
desperadoes and Sioux warriors with a brain gummed up
by lovelorn goo.

He climbed down from the driver's boot and saw that
Miss Meyers was trying to open the Concord's left-side
door from inside. She was grunting with the effort, her
fine jaws set hard beneath the brim of her stylish but somewhat outlandish eastern-style velvet picture hat trimmed
with faux flowers and berries.

"I'll help you there, ma'am."

She looked at him through the window in the door—a
despondent look if he had ever seen one. She was, however, a looker. He couldn't deny that even if he had denied

noticing to Charley. He felt a sharp pang of guilt every time he looked at this woman and felt . . . well, like a man shouldn't feel when he was in love with another gal.

"It's stuck," she said, her voice toneless with exhaustion.

"I apologize." Hunter plucked a small pine stick from the crack between the door and the stagecoach wall. "A twig got stuck in it somehow, fouled the latch. I do apologize, ma'am. How you doing? Not so well, I reckon . . ."

As Hunter opened the door, she made a face and waved her gloved hand at the billowing dust and tobacco smoke. "The smoke and dust are absolutely atrocious. Not to mention the wretched smell of my unwashed fellow traveler and his who-hit-John, as he so colorfully calls the poison he consumes as though it were water!"

Hunter helped the woman out. He glanced into the carriage to see the grinning countenance of his only other passenger—the Chicago farm implement drummer, Wilfred Farley. The diminutive, craggy-faced man with one broken front tooth and clad in a cheap checked suit— which seemed the requisite uniform of all raggedy-heeled traveling salesmen everywhere—raised an unlabeled, flat, clear bottle half-filled with a milky brown liquid in salute to his destaging fellow passenger's derriere, and took a pull.

Hunter gave the man a reproving look, then turned to the woman, removing his hat and holding it over his broad chest. "Ma'am, let me apolo—"

"Will you please stop apologizing, Mister Buchanon? I'm sorry to say your apologies are beginning to ring a little hollow at this late date. My God, what a torturous contraption!" She looked at the coach's rear wheel and for a second, Hunter thought she was going to give it a kick with one of her delicate, gold-buckled, high-heeled ankle boots.

She thought about it for a couple of seconds, then satisfied herself with a chortling wail of raw anger and tipped her head back to stare up at the tall, blond-haired, blue-eyed jehu hulking before her. "And must you continue to call me ma'am?"

"Uh . . . uh . . ."

"How old are you?"

"Twenty-seven, ma'a . . . er, I mean, Miss Meyers." At least, he hoped that was the moniker she'd been looking for. If not, he might end up with a swift kick to one of his shins, and in her state of mind, even being such a light albeit curvy little thing, he didn't doubt she could do some damage.

"Now, see—I'm younger than you are. Not by much, maybe, but I am young enough that you can feel free to call me Miss. *Miss Meyers.* Not ma'am. For God's sake, don't add insult to injury, Mister Buchanon!"

"I'm sorry, Miss Meyers, it's just that you seemed older . . . somehow." *Wrong thing to say, you cork-headed fool!* Backing water frantically, Hunter said, "I just meant you *acted* older! You know—more mature! I didn't mean you *looked* older!"

He'd said those wheedling words to her slender back as, fists tightly balled at her sides, she went stomping off into the brush and rocks that littered the base of the ridge wall on the west side of the stage road.

"Don't wander too far, ma'am . . . I mean, Miss Meyers!" he called. "It's easy to get turned around out here!"

But she was already gone.

CHAPTER 2

Hunter stared after the pretty, angry woman.

Something nudged his right arm. He looked down to see Wilfred Farley offering his bottle to him, and grinning, his thin, chapped upper lip peeled back from that crooked, broken tooth.

"No, thanks. If that's the stuff you bought at the Robbers' Roost Station, it'll blind both of us."

"Pshaw!" Farley took another deep pull. "Damn good stuff, and I see just fine."

"That's how Hoyle Gullickson lost his topknot." Charley Anders was climbing heavily down from the driver's boot, his sawed-off, double-barrel shotgun hanging from a lanyard down his back.

"What?" Farley asked. "Drinkin' his own skull pop?"

"No—brewin' it." Anders stepped off the front wheel and turned to face Hunter and the pie-eyed Chicago drummer. "He sold it to the Sioux. Several went blind, and the others came back and scalped him."

Farley looked at the bottle in his hand as though it had suddenly transformed into a rattlesnake. "You don't say . . . ?"

Hunter snorted softly. He knew the story wasn't true. Hoyle Gullickson had lost his topknot when he'd been out cutting wood one winter and was set upon by four braves who'd wanted whiskey.

Gullickson had refused to sell to them because he'd already done time in the federal pen for selling his rotgut to Indians, and he wasn't about to risk returning to that wretched place. Incensed, the braves scalped him, so now he wore the awful knotted scars in a broad, grisly swath over the top of his head, making any and all around him wince whenever he removed his hat, which he loved to do just to gauge the reactions and turn stomachs.

Charley Anders, however, preferred his tall-tale version, which he related often and usually at night around some stage station's potbellied stove to wide-eyed pilgrims in his and Hunter's charge.

Hunter glared at the drummer. "I thought I told you not to smoke around that woman, Farley. And to stay halfways sober."

"Kills the time," Farley said with a shrug, raising a loosely rolled, wheat-paper quirley to his mouth and leveling a defiant stare at Buchanon. "I offered to share my panther juice with her, but she turned her nose up. That offended me. So I got the makings out and rolled a smoke."

He pointed his bottle toward where the woman had disappeared in the rocks and brush. "That pretty little bitch can go straight to hell."

"He's got a point, pard," Charley said, reaching through the stage window. "Give me a pull off that, Farley. I could use a little somethin' to cut the dust."

"I thought you said it'd blind a fella!" Farley objected sarcastically.

Anders jerked the bottle out of the drummer's hand and

swiped the lip across his grimy hickory shirt. "I been drinkin' the rotgut so long I'm immune to blindness by now." He stepped back and started to take a pull from the bottle. As he did, a rabbit poked its head out from between two shrubs roughly ten feet off the trail.

Hunter, who'd been looking around cautiously, wary of a holdup and also starting to get a little worried about the woman, had just seen the gray cottontail pull its head back into the shrubs. Bobby Lee gave a mewling yip of coyote excitement and leaped from the roof of the coach onto Charley Anders's right shoulder to the ground.

Charley jerked back with a startled grunt, dropping the bottle.

Bobby Lee plunged into the shrubs between two boulders, then shot up the ridge, hot on the heels of the streaking rabbit, the rabbit and the coyote darting around the columnar pines.

"Damn that vermin!" Charley wailed, clutching his right shoulder with his left hand. "He like to have dislocated my arm! What gall—using me as his damn stepping stool! Has he no respect?"

Hunter snorted a laugh. "That's what you get for being so tight with your jerky, Charley."

"The bottle! The bottle!" wailed Wilfred Farley, pointing at the bottle lying on the ground between Anders and Buchanon. "Good Lord, you're spillin' good whiskey!"

Hunter crouched to pick up the bottle. There was still an inch or two of rotgut remaining. Not for long.

Grinning at Farley, Hunter turned the bottle upside down. The whiskey dribbled out of the mouth, which dirt and pine needles clung. The liquid plopped hollowly onto the ground.

Farley was flabbergasted. "Good lord, man! Are you *mad*?"

"Jehu's rules, Farley." Hunter tossed the bottle high over the coach and into the trees and rocks on the other side. "No drinkin' aboard the coach."

"You're sweet on that gal!" Farley shook his head in disbelief. "You must like a gal who runs you into the ground with every look and word. Me—I got some self-respect. No purty skirt's gonna push Wilfred Farley around!"

"Speakin' of purty skirts," Anders said, staring off toward where the woman had disappeared. "What in the hell's she doin' out there—knittin' an afghan?"

Hunter glanced around, making sure no would-be highwaymen were near. He didn't like standing still here on the trail like this, making easy targets. It was always best to keep moving between relay stations, as a moving target was always harder to attack than one standing still in the middle of the trail with good cover all around for would-be attackers.

Hunter stepped forward and called, "Miss Meyers? You all right?"

No response.

"We'd best get movin', Miss Meyers!"

Hunter took another couple of steps forward, then stopped again, concern growing in him. "Miss Meyers?"

He didn't want to call too loudly and risk alerting anyone in the area to their position. He and Anders were carrying only two passengers, but aboard the stage they had ten thousand dollars in payroll money, which they were hauling to one of the many mines above Tigerville.

Hunter glanced back at Anders, scowling his frustration. Anders shrugged and shook his head.

"I best look for her," Hunter said. "Charley, stay with

the stage. Keep a sharp eye out. I don't like sitting out here like a Thanksgiving turkey on the dining room table."

"You an' me both, pard," Charley said behind Buchanon, as Hunter stepped off the trail and walked into the rocks and brush littering the base of the western ridge.

Hunter pushed through the brush, wended his way around rocks. "Miss Meyers? Time to hit the road, Miss Meyers!"

He saw a deer path carved through the brush. It rose up a low shoulder of the ridge. Hunter followed it, frowning down at the ground, noting the sharp indentations of the heels of a lady's ankle boots.

As the path turned around a large fir tree, the indentations of the lady's heels became scuffed and scraped. Amidst the scuff marks was a faint print of a man's boot.

Instantly, Buchanon's hand closed around the pearl grips of the silver-chased LeMat secured high on his right hip in a gray buckskin holster worn to the texture of doeskin. He clicked the hammer of the main, .44-caliber barrel back and, his heartbeat increasing, the skin under his shirt collar prickling, he continued following the scuffed trail.

The prints led up and over the rise then down the other side, through tree shadows and sunlight. Somewhere ahead and to Hunter's right, a squirrel was chittering angrily. That was the only sound.

Hunter continued forward for another fifty feet before he stopped suddenly.

Ahead, a man crouched between two aspens. He seemed to be moving in place, making jerking movements. He was also talking in a heated but hushed tone.

Hunter could see a second man—or part of a second man—on his knees on the other side of one of the aspens. Hunter could see only the man's boot soles and the thick forward curve of his back clad in a blue wool shirt. This man, too, was making quick jerking movements.

He seemed to be holding something down.

Hunter stepped to his right, putting the left-most aspen between himself and the crouching man. He moved slowly forward, both aspens concealing his approach from both men before him. As he moved closer to their position, muffled cries blazed into the air around him.

Muffled female cries.

Hunter stepped behind a tree. He peered around its left side. From here, he had a clearer view of the two men and of Miss Meyers on the ground between them, partly obscured by tree roots humping up out of the forest duff.

The man on the right knelt by the woman's head, leaning down, holding her head against the ground with both of his hands pressed across her mouth. Miss Meyers was kicking her legs out wildly and flailing helplessly with her arms, making her skirts flop and exposing her pantaloon- and stocking-clad legs.

Thumping sounds rose as did the crackle of pine needles and dead leaves as she thrashed so desperately, her cries muffled by one of her assailant's hands. The kneeling man laughed through his teeth as he held the woman down, his brown-mustached face swollen and red.

The other man, tall and skinny with long black sideburns and a bushy black mustache, had pulled his pants down around his boots and was opening the fly of his longhandles, grinning down at the struggling woman.

"Hold her still, Bill. Hold her still. I'll be hanged if she ain't as fine a piece o' female flesh as I—"

Leaning forward, exposing the evidence of his craven lust, he grabbed Miss Meyers's ankles and thrust them down against the ground. Leaning farther forward, he slid his hands up her legs from inside her dress, a lusty grin blooming broadly across his long, ugly face with close-set, dark eyes set deep beneath shaggy, black brows.

The man clamped her legs down with his own and reached for her swinging arms, grabbing them, stopping them as he lowered his hips toward the woman's. He stopped abruptly, turning his head sharply to see Buchanon striding toward him.

The man's eyes widened in shock. "What the . . . *hey!*"

Hunter had returned the big LeMat to its holster and picked up a stout aspen branch roughly five feet long and about as big around as one of his muscular forearms—as broad as a cedar fencepost.

It made a solid thumping, cracking sound as he smashed it with all the force in his big hands and arms against the black-haired man's forehead. The branch broke roughly a foot and a half from the end. As the would-be rapist's head snapped sharply back, his eyes rolling up in their sockets, the end of the branch dropped with the man into the deep, narrow ravine behind him.

The other man cursed and leaped to his feet, his amber eyes as round as saucers and bright with fear.

"No!" he cried as he saw the stout branch swing toward him.

He tipped his head to one side, raising his arms as if to shield his face. Buchanon grunted as he thrust the branch down through the man's open hands to slam it against the man's left ear, blood instantly spewing from the smashed appendage.

"Ohhh!" the man cried as he hit the ground.

Buchanon stepped forward, raising the club again, rage a wild stallion inside him. Only the lowest of the lowest gut wagon dog did such a thing to a woman. This man would pay dearly—and he did as Hunter, straddling the man's flailing legs, smashed the club again and again against the man's head. After the third or fourth blow from the powerful arms and shoulders of the big, blond, blue-eyed man standing over him, the man's cries faded and his flailing arms and legs lay still upon the ground.

Hunter raised the club for one more blow but stopped when the crackle of guns rose from the direction of the stagecoach. His heart shuddered. He hammered the second rapist's head once more, then kicked the still body, the dead eyes staring up at Hunter in silent castigation, into the ravine.

It landed with a thump near the other carcass.

Hunter whipped around, crouching and drawing the LeMat from its holster, facing in the direction from which guns blasted angrily and men shouted.

Another man screamed.

Yet another man bellowed, "Ah, ya lowdown dirty devils . . . !"

Hunter recognized the bellowing voice. It was followed by the twin blasts of Charley Anders's sawed-off shotgun and one more scream.

Charley's scream.

Connect with Us

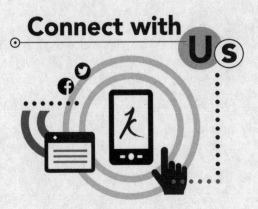

Visit us online at
KensingtonBooks.com
to read more from your favorite authors, see books
by series, view reading group guides, and more.

for sneak peeks, chances to win books and prize packs,
and to share your thoughts with other readers.

facebook.com/kensingtonpublishing
twitter.com/kensingtonbooks

Tell us what you think!

To share your thoughts, submit a review,
or sign up for our eNewsletters, please visit:
KensingtonBooks.com/TellUs.